"The author of *Wild Women and the Blues* is back with another historical fiction novel to dazzle and amaze."
—*BookRiot*

"Denny S. Bryce's page-turning novel opens with a murder that transports readers from Black Hollywood in the 1920s to an unforgettable road trip across the US during the 1960s. Bryce weaves the two timelines together in a fascinating story arc that leaves readers marveling at the connections between characters as the echoes of the past shape the present."
—Chanel Cleeton, *New York Times* bestselling author

"Hollywood scandal lovers, this one's for you."
—*BookRiot*, "11 Books to Read After *The Seven Husbands of Evelyn Hugo*"

I0637170

Kensington books by Denny S. Bryce

Wild Women and the Blues

In the Face of the Sun

The Trial of Mrs. Rhinelander

Where the False Gods Dwell

Also by Denny S. Bryce

The Other Princess: A Novel of Queen Victoria's Goddaughter

Can't We Be Friends: A Novel of Ella Fitzgerald and Marilyn Monroe (with Eliza Knight)

WHERE THE FALSE GODS DWELL

DENNY S. BRYCE

KENSINGTON
PUBLISHING CORP.
kensingtonbooks.com

ISBN: 978-1-4967-3789-2
First Trade Paperback Printing: March 2026

ISBN: 978-1-4967-3790-8 (e-book)

10 9 8 7 6 5 4 3 2 1

Printed in the United States of America

The authorized representative in the EU for product safety and compliance is eucomply OU, Parnu mnt 139b-14, Apt 123
Tallinn, Berlin 11317, hello@eucompliancepartner.com

For Aunt Hazel

PROLOGUE

———◆•◆———

I have shed a thousand tears, yet the silence in my head screams at me to hang on. Just hang on. One moment longer. Don't let go.

Debris and sand fill my nostrils and lodge between my fingers and toes. My back aches, and my body feels weak. Still, I cling to the mud-soaked earth, my arms hugging a jutting piece of limestone, preventing me from falling into the abyss.

I should have expected this—sensed the danger weeks ago, even months ago. But I am stubborn and naïve, and with a nature like mine, I don't see what lingers in front of me— plain as day, dark as night, with a tortured gaze, sweat-drenched cheeks, and large, white teeth in a dazzling smile.

Christ. I can't catch my breath. Do I even have breath?

Why didn't I see it before?

Why did it elude me for so long?

What did the old woman say?

This is where the false gods dwell. Beware, or you might miss the true God when She comes calling.

A sudden peace surrounds me, quieting my raging thoughts. I pull myself up just enough to peer over the edge and, to my surprise, the old woman is wrong.

There are no false gods here.

PART ONE

———◆·◆·◆———

THE PARTY: AUGUST 1935

CHAPTER 1

OTHELLA

State Street, Chicago, Illinois

The train from Chicago to Kenosha, Wisconsin, departs from the Northwestern Terminal at midnight. I've checked the schedule every day for the past two weeks, so I know I'm right. I also know I'll be on that train by hook or by crook.

I just wish it were easier said than done.

My old man, Perry Merriweather, lies in bed next to me. He doesn't know I plan to hightail it outta town and outta his life before the day is done. I can't be saddled with no man, no matter how handsome or what promises he makes, not when I can be something more, someone else in a new town with a new name and a different occupation. There has to be more to me than gold-digging, picking pockets, and lying.

Rolling onto my side, I glance at the alarm clock on the nightstand. It's four o'clock in the afternoon. For heaven's sake. I wanted to be long gone by now. But Perry with his pockets full of stolen goods from our very late night out only got in bed an hour ago.

I shoulda set the alarm, I think, as I ease out of bed.

"What time is it, Othella?"

Damn it. Why I keep forgetting he's a light sleeper? Then again, I usually ain't awake before him.

"Four o'clock," I reply.

He grabs the lace trim of my silk briefs. "Where you going? Why don't you stay in bed with me for a spell?" He squeezes my bottom, wanting something he ain't gonna get. There will be no last-minute roll in the hay for him. Not today—not ever again.

"Can't a gal go to the bathroom when she wakes up?"

He turns onto his side, and I swear the mattress groans. One day, he'll break those worn-out springs.

I'm halfway across the room when his heavy feet thud against the floor.

"If you ain't coming back to bed, make me some coffee," he snarls. "I got places to be."

"Give me a minute." I close the bathroom door and feel my legs buckle. Stumbling forward, I grasp both sides of the sink. How am I gonna get outta here with him up and moving about? I stare at my reflection in the bathroom mirror. Only nineteen, yet I feel like I'm forty-five. I close my eyes, take a deep breath, and urge my insides to calm down. I open my eyes. Okay. The truth is, I'm still a pretty girl with smooth brown skin and a curvy figure—and I can still get outta this house. I just have to use my wits.

Except Perry is muttering under his breath on the other side of the bathroom door, and he's about as patient as a starving raccoon.

Madness inspires madness.

That's my mother's voice in my head. She used to say that when I was a little girl and worried about something I shouldn't worry about. I wasn't sure what it meant back then, but two weeks ago, I learned how quickly sanity can slip away.

Perry and I had swindled a wealthy widow in Bronzeville. We got so caught up in the thrill of the con that we lost ourselves. Or rather, Perry lost himself, and I just followed along.

Without a fuss, the old gal handed over her pearl-handled switchblade, which I slipped into my clutch purse along with her wedding ring. So why did she refuse to unpin the diamond brooch on her lapel? Perry beat that old woman half to death and scared me silly. We'd roughed up marks before, I told myself, but those folks were younger and swung back.

That widow woman wasn't gonna hurt nobody. But as horrified as I was, I just watched.

That night, I made up my mind. I had to get outta this racket. I stashed some cash and trinkets and packed a suitcase while Perry was out drinking with his brother. Then I hid everything in the back of the closet, where he never looked.

Now, the only thing left is to get out of the apartment in one piece.

The bathroom door suddenly swings open, and there stands Perry, fully dressed, swinging my bag of cash in my face. "What the hell you doing hiding this shit from me?"

My vision blurs, and I might faint, but what good will that do? I have to think fast. Lord knows, I can't tell him the truth, but I can change the subject. Maybe make him feel guilty.

"What you so mad about?" I demand. "I just set aside a few dollars for a rainy day. You spend nearly every penny we make on clothes, liquor, and automobiles. What if you get hurt or, even worse, get caught by some coppers and thrown in jail? Where would I be then?" I snort. "Holding a bag of nothing—that's where."

"That's a bucket of bull, Othella."

I shove him aside. "It ain't no bull."

"I smell a rat," Perry hollers. "I found your goddamn suit-case packed, too." His fist slams into the wall. "You're beg-ging for a beatin' if you think you're leaving me."

My heart pounds in my chest so hard that my whole body aches. "Stop flapping your gums at me. If I were gonna leave you, I woulda been gone."

"You're a liar." He grabs me from behind and spins me around. I see his huge paw coming for my face, but I can't get outta its way. He hits me in the jaw so hard that tears spring to my eyes. "If you stopped lying, you wouldn't get hit."

Rage and pain burn through my veins. I feel my face swell, tasting blood as Perry pulls back, getting ready to pop me in the jaw again.

Christ. He is pissed as hell, but damn it, so am I.

"You're right!" I snap, and his fist halts in mid-air. "I'm a liar 'cause I am leaving you. And don't even think about hit-ting me again. I swear, I'll fight back."

"Oh you will?" Perry laughs harshly. "Then tell me, how far will you get with a broken leg or two?"

He has me, and I am half-dragged, half-carried toward the living room, my legs sweeping the floor like a broom. His long fingers wrap around my throat. I claw at his wrists, try-ing to break free, but suddenly my feet leave the ground and I'm flying through the air.

I scream, bracing for a hard landing, but the sofa softens my fall. Then, quick as a cat, Perry is on top of me, holding me down.

"You want to leave me?" he shouts, blowing his stinking morning breath in my face. "No bitch leaves me!"

"Get off me," I rasp, "before I hurt you."

A harsh laugh bursts from his wide mouth. He is gagging on laughter as if my words are a punchline he pretends to find funny. He loosens his grip in that instant, and I see my opening. I pull my knee in and, shifting my weight into the blow, drive my leg forward, striking him squarely in his private parts.

Screaming, he tumbles off me and crashes onto the coffee table, smashing it into pieces. He lies on his back, cradling his groin and cursing.

Rising as quickly as I can, I grab the handle of the Smokador, the carbon steel standing ashtray. Like me, it has some weight, and I slam it into his skull with all my might and rage.

Perry hollers, but I keep swinging, landing shot after shot until he stops moving and blood spurts from the gash in his head. His eyes flutter shut.

I drop the Smokador, dash to the bedroom closet, and grab the first outfit I can reach—one of my favorites: a blue-and-white, polka-dot, slim-waisted frock with butterfly sleeves. I dress quickly, glancing into the living room to see if Perry has stirred. I pin my long, coarse curls into a bun, then snatch up my suitcase and bag of trinkets. But it's the other bag—the most important bag—the one with my money—that I need to find.

Where did Perry toss it? I race through the apartment. It has to be here.

"Othella."

Oh, God. Is that Perry calling me, or have I imagined it?

"You g-gonna pay for t-this. You little bitch."

Shit. Any second now, he'll be on his feet and coming for me. Money or not, I've got to go.

I'm out the door a second later.

My day isn't going as planned. After leaving Perry on the living room floor, I make a stop I should've skipped—the AME Fellowship Church and Reverend Nathan. I've known him for a long time and expected something different from him, but I end up leaving there quick and head to a juke joint a few blocks away. All the while, my mother's voice is in my ear as if she's standing next to me, reciting her old-world sayings: "If you're around the insane, beware—the symptoms spread."

I grip the handle of my tweed suitcase and squeeze my clutch purse under my armpit. It's not a long walk, but I might collapse in this heat. If I do, I'll be carted off by the police and thrown in a cell with wayward women, never to be seen or heard from again.

I wonder if that's what happened to my mother—snatched off the street, with no chance to call home and check on me. But it no longer matters how or why she left—gone is gone.

Out of cigarettes, I spot a man across the street puffing on a smoke. I stroll over and ask if he can spare a couple. I think better with a cigarette in my hand. I put a sad look on my face, appearing quite desperate and girlie. He gives me a pack of cigarettes—bless him—and a handful of coins, all he can spare. He has a job, a wife, and he's a churchgoing man. The only thing bulging in his pockets is a spare undershirt. He claims he likes to change into a clean shirt before returning home to his wife.

Now, that's a nice fella. I wish there were more nice fellas in the world like him.

I step inside the juke joint and ask the owner, who I know from one of the nightclubs where I used to work, if I can use the horn to make a call. He nods, and I dial the only number I have for Tony Schaefer.

One of his goons answers.

"Can the boss spare some time for me this afternoon?"

The reply is a quick yes. The man on the other end adds that Tony mentioned me just the other night.

That might be a coincidence, bushwa, or whatever—it makes me no never mind. I couldn't care less about the particulars as long as Tony gives me enough dough to catch that midnight train to Kenosha.

I have to tread carefully around him. During Prohibition, his occupation was bootlegging, and Perry was one of his drivers. I know that asking a bootlegging mobster for help shouldn't be one of my first choices, especially if I'm trying to turn over a new leaf. But a gal must do what a gal must do. I excuse myself to the bathroom, rummage through my suitcase, and slip into a gold chiffon dress with a plunging neckline and a slit up the middle of my right thigh. It's a bold outfit and hardly fashionable, but it will attract the attention I need. When approaching a man like Tony Schaefer for a fistful of cash, a girl has to be a hot mama—or she can forget about getting out of Chicago anytime soon.

CHAPTER 2

❦

VIVIAN JEAN

Hartfield House, Bronzeville, Chicago

My home feels small, suffocatingly small—an odd notion because, to some, Hartfield House is a mansion. Yet, my modest 4,000-square-foot home lacks a butler's pantry, a morning room, a veranda, or a gazebo—unlike the estates of Marshall Field or Robert S. Abbott. The founder of the *Chicago Defender*, Abbott is one of the richest Negroes in the city, and lives just around the corner from us on 47th and Grand Boulevard. So, Hartfield House does have some of what it takes: a grand staircase, a second floor with three bedrooms and two bathrooms, a new library, and a live-in cook and housekeeper who has been with me since 1915, when she came to Chicago from Jamaica. I was ten years old.

We also have a parlor, which is where I am now.

I open the door and am greeted by a chorus of voices.

"Happy Birthday!"

My mother, Regina Thomas, sits stiff-backed and devilishly polite on the settee next to Katherine Dunham, my dear friend and soon-to-be accomplice. But my first duty is to make the rounds. After all, I am the birthday girl—or birthday woman—because today I turned thirty.

On the other side of the room, in front of the mullioned windows, are my husband's parents, Dr. Clifford Hartfield Sr. and his wife, Constance. I'm surprised to see them. They rarely come to the city. Retired and fed up with Chicago after my first husband's death, they moved to Joliet.

My first husband was their eldest son, Clifford Jr., a doctor like his father, who made me a widow on December 10, 1933. My second husband is their youngest, Tobias "Tully" Hartfield. He stands across the room. I can feel his gaze on me, and I'm tempted to walk over to him, grab him by the shoulders, and shake some sense into him. But that's something I'd never do. Like my mother, I am too damn polite for my own good. Or is it fear of confrontation that cripples us?

"Dr. and Mrs. Hartfield, I had no idea you would be able to join us."

"We wouldn't miss your thirtieth birthday celebration," Constance Hartfield states in her usual monotone. A well-preserved woman in her seventies, she always sounds rehearsed, no matter which of her sons is my husband.

"You look divine." Dr. Hartfield pulls me in for a hug. "I'm very proud of you and Tully. It has been a challenging eighteen months, and you've both been so brave. I am very glad you have each other to lean on."

I return the embrace and hang on a moment longer than I should, but despite the awkwardness of it, the sincerity of his words is so heartfelt that I am deeply touched.

Unlike his wife, Dr. Hartfield Sr. is openly affectionate, kind, and generous. I wish Tully and I could spend more time with him, but that would mean more time with his wife.

Dressed in her maid's uniform, Maxi Green stands proudly beside the brass-and-walnut buffet, with good reason. The parlor is her handiwork and looks truly magnificent. The Royal China Madeira dishes, adorned with wine-colored edges, are elegantly arranged alongside the sterling silver cutlery set, a gift from Katherine. Twin Jazz Moderne vases at each end of the long buffet hold vibrant red and pink poppies—my birthday flowers. But it is the centerpiece that outshines everything else. It showcases a two-tier black rum cake, and the aroma of rum, molasses, and deliciousness fills the room. Additionally, there are bottles of champagne in two steel ice buckets with a frosty sheen, ensuring that the bubbly is perfectly chilled. I smile lovingly at Maxi, for she is more than a maid. She has been my teacher and secret keeper for most of my life. I am tempted to hug her but refrain from doing so in front of this crowd. Instead, I give her an enthusiastic thumbs-up.

After another quick scan of the parlor, I don't see my father, Major Leonard Thomas.

"Where's Father?" I ask my mother.

"He's on the telephone in your husband's office, discussing a business matter," she replies. "He'll return as soon as he's finished. Don't worry. He'll be here when you open your birthday presents."

A pile of wrapped boxes of various shapes and sizes rests on the round table in the center of the parlor. "You didn't have to do all this."

"Of course we did, dear," my mother responds dryly. "It's your thirtieth birthday."

"Do we really have to wait for Major Thomas?" Katherine inquires. "Knowing him, he could be on the horn until midnight."

My mother's expression tightens, her typical reaction to

anyone questioning my father's desires. "We can't begin without him."

I give Katherine a knowing wince. We have another party to attend in a few hours and neither of us wants to miss it: a reception at the Abbotts' mansion, honoring Josephine Baker.

I continue my rounds—a handshake, a kiss on the cheek, a brief hug. "It's good to see you," I tell each guest, "and I hope you're well."

My husband is the last one I greet.

Leaning against the cottage piano is Tully, my handsome man with his square jaw, full lips, high cheekbones, and beautiful black eyes. He possesses an athlete's physique, which shouldn't be a surprise because he is a professional baseball player. Dressed in a short-sleeved knit shirt and high-waisted, wide-legged pants, he swigs from a glass of champagne and watches me over the thin rim.

As I draw closer, the tension between us is palpable. I wish it didn't exist. I wish I could love him without the guilt crawling down my spine or that note of accusation he keeps waving beneath my nose.

He lowers the glass—a slightly tipsy smile curves the corners of his mouth.

"Happy birthday, Vivian Jean." His baritone is emotionless, yet I crave the sound of it like a warm bath. I feel it in my chest and on my skin.

"Thank you, darling." I kiss him on the cheek, but he subtly shifts his posture, removing any chance of him returning my show of affection. "How's your leg feeling today?" I ask. It's the first thing that comes to mind, though I know it's the last thing he wants to be reminded of. He was the starting third baseman for the Chicago American Giants until a line drive shattered his kneecap in June.

"It's the same as it was an hour ago," he replies, his eyelid twitching.

"I didn't mean it like that. I just wanted you to know I took care of all that business at the bank this morning." I lower my voice. "I'm about to announce our trip."

Tully closes his eyes briefly, his jaw clenched. "What if I changed my mind?"

"About coming with me to Jamaica?" There's that feeling in my chest, like someone has reached through my rib cage to squeeze my heart. "Don't tease me. You want to get out of Chicago as much as I do." Panic sears through me. My plan won't work without him. "So don't even play around, or—" I hesitate, trying to think of something heinous to say to stop him from spouting such madness. "I'll tell your parents what happened the night Clifford died."

He steps toward me, standing so close that I can smell the champagne on his breath. "Don't talk about the night my brother died—" His lip quivers.

"Why not? I'll just show them the note he wrote, and they'll fabricate some twisted nonsense about its meaning, just like you have."

Tully shakes his head. "Don't play games with me, Vivian Jean. You don't want anyone to know about that note, any more than I do."

"It's my birthday. Shouldn't I be able to do something I wouldn't normally do?"

"And when has that ever happened?"

"The day I married you."

"Vivian Jean." Katherine suddenly appears at my side, squeezing my hand. "Maxi told me you needed to speak with me. Is this a good time?"

Did I? A glance at Tully reveals a flicker of hurt in his eyes, but thankfully, Katherine has shown up to keep us from embarrassing ourselves in front of our family and friends. But I did mention to Maxi that I wanted to speak with her.

"Yes, I did." I look away from Tully.

Katherine beams at me before asking my husband, "Is it okay if I borrow your wife for a few minutes?"

"Please, take her. She's yours." He is back to normal, distant and unaffected by anything I do or say. "Just don't take too long," he adds. "Your father might arrive at any moment."

I pucker my lips and blow him a kiss before Katherine, holding my hand, tugs me toward the exit.

The moment has come for me to confide in Katherine Dunham. Four years younger than I am, she is already an acclaimed dancer and choreographer—she founded her own dance company, Ballet Négre—and an anthropologist. A determined woman who prioritizes her ambitions, talents, and desires, she agreed weeks ago to let me (and Tully) join her Caribbean anthropology and African dance expedition. It's her party. We do as she tells us. Of course, there are things she doesn't know about my reasons for my trip to Accompong, the Maroon village in the heart of Jamaica's Cockpit Country—things no one other than Maxi knows. If I am to tell Katherine the truth, the time is now, the place is here. After following her, I wait until we're a little farther from Tully and everyone else. Then the door to the parlor suddenly bursts open, and just like that, the moment is gone.

My father strides into the room. "Vivi, all grown up at thirty. Finally, right?"

I release Katherine's hand and whisper, "We'll talk later." Then I smile at my father, overlooking the nickname he knows I detest. "Thank you, sir. So glad you could make it."

"How's everyone?" He gestures broadly around the room. The response is less than enthusiastic. "Why haven't you cut the cake yet? There's no reason to wait for me."

"Mother said we should wait," I explain.

"I said wait to open the presents," my mother defends herself.

"And only one bottle of champagne uncorked?" Major Thomas looks at Tully as if serving champagne is his duty. "Well, I'm here now. Let's get on with it."

Maxi strikes a long match to light the candles on the cake stand.

"Hold on there." My father raises his hand and gives her a tolerant squint, one he often casts her way. "Vivi doesn't need to blow out the candles. She's too old for such nonsense. Let's open the presents."

I lower my gaze. "Sure, if you say so, sir."

"Major Thomas." It's Katherine's voice. "How about we toast the birthday girl before she opens her gifts?"

My father grunts, never liking it when a woman contradicts him. Katherine takes a breath, preparing to deliver the toast, but my father won't have it.

"I'll give the toast," he says. "Pass me a glass of champagne."

Maxi places a glass of champagne in my father's hand.

"All right, let's do this then," he says.

Before my father begins, Maxi barely gets the champagne flutes into everyone else's hands.

"To my daughter, a young woman who deserves all the kindness that comes her way. Happy birthday."

My fake smile at his remarks, I trust, isn't as obvious as it feels. The others in the parlor seem just as uneasy with the brevity of the toast as I am.

"I guess I'll open my presents now." I walk over to the round table in the center of the parlor, intent on grabbing the nearest gift, when my father stops me.

"Open this one first," he orders, placing a small, narrow box in my hand.

I take the box. "Of course, sir." It isn't wrapped. All I have to do is open the lid. It's a pocket watch.

My hands tremble. My grandfather, who was enslaved for most of his life, "inherited" the pocket watch from his father, the master of the plantation where he was born. The significance of the gift leaves me utterly baffled. My father's usual gifts typically include clothing or candy, a scarf, a sweater, a new coat, or a box of Frango mints from Marshall Field's.

He takes the pocket watch on the necklace from me and, moving behind me, fastens the clasp around my neck. "I put it on a gold chain so you can wear it as a necklace."

I lift the pocket watch, grasping it delicately, and finally say, "Thank you. It's beautiful, Father." I consider hugging him. An embrace seems right, but I can't recall the last time we shared more than a handshake. I hold back. I haven't told him about the trust fund, let alone Jamaica. Perhaps this is the perfect time to share my news. After all, he's in such a good mood that he might not be upset.

"May I have everyone's attention?" I do a short spin, and when all eyes are on me, I say, "I have an announcement."

The parlor fills with a collective gasp and then falls silent. I feel like I'm in a theater as the curtain rises and the audience quiets in anticipation. This is the reaction I expect after I say what I have to say, not beforehand. Even my father looks stunned.

Tully is the exception. The look of what the hell in his eyes helps me realize my mistake. "No. No. No. That's not the announcement. I'm not with child. I'm so sorry."

How could anyone think I'd mention another pregnancy so casually, given everything Tully and I have been through?

"If that's not the news, what is?" my father asks sharply.

I don't look at him. I just dive in. "Tully and I are leaving at midnight on the 20th Century Limited for Grand Central Station. Then, on Thursday, we'll board the SS *Talamanca* for Jamaica." I then turn to Katherine. "We're joining the Dunham expedition to the Caribbean to conduct fieldwork on African dance in the Maroon village of Accompong."

"That's outrageous." The alarm in my father's voice feels like a slap. "You aren't qualified to assist her. Moreover, how can you afford it?"

"My trust fund," I reply, striving to maintain a calm tone.

"You're not the administrator of that fund—your late husband and my federal loan are the trustees."

"Before he died, he put the trust fund in my name."

"Jesus Christ," my father mutters. "That makes no sense."

Tully clears his throat and steps forward. "You can check all you want, sir. It's Vivian Jean's money to do with as she chooses. And everything for Jamaica has been arranged—our travel plans, and accommodations in Accompong."

I appreciate Tully's vocal support, but I can tell it's primarily to egg on my father, who he enjoys provoking.

"Are you telling me the transfer wasn't handled through the Bronzeville Federal Savings and Loan?" my father grumbles, referring to his company, which originally managed the trust fund. "And you knew about this?" My father glares at Tully. "And didn't think to inform me?"

Tully smirks. "Vivian Jean is perfectly capable of handling her own affairs."

"Christ almighty," my father scoffs. "So, you received access to your trust fund this morning and already made arrangements for your trip? How did you move so fast? You had to have help."

Katherine raises a delicate hand. "I helped."

"Of course you did," my father sneers at Katherine.

"Leonard, it appears your concerns are unnecessary," Dr. Hartfield interjects, his higher-pitched tone distinctive among the other male voices. "The best choice here is to wish them well."

The major grits his teeth at Dr. Hartfield's words and immediately dismisses them. "Who assisted you with the arrangements?" he fires at me, but then turns to Maxi. "Or do I need to ask?"

Maxi holds her head high but doesn't make eye contact with him.

"And you're leaving tonight," the major mumbles.

"Yes, sir," Katherine replies in an unrestrained tone. "She and Tully begin our journey this evening after Mr. Abbott's reception."

"Maybe we should continue this conversation another time," Dr. Hartfield makes a second attempt to quell the tension.

My father walks over to where my mother is seated and extends his hand, which she quickly takes. "We're leaving."

I stare in disbelief, while also feeling a sense of satisfaction. With his departure, I can set aside my worries. It is done. My father knows everything about my plans—well, almost. He doesn't know my secret. Only Maxi knows my true intentions once I reach Accompong and the sacred silk cotton tree. "Father, please don't behave this way. I thought you were coming to Robert Abbott's reception."

My mother doesn't appear rattled by my exchange with Father or his rudeness—which isn't a surprise. It's something I am used to.

"It's the Palmer House Hotel, Vivi," she says, using the deplorable nickname. "I love that hotel, and your father arranged for us to have a suite."

I sometimes wonder if there's anything my mother truly cares about besides hotels, fashion, and her women's groups—that and, of course, not contradicting the major.

"Don't worry, Katherine," Father adds. "I won't miss this evening's celebration. Besides, I must spend time with my daughter before she heads to Jamaica."

Major Thomas tucks his wife's hand into the crook of his arm as they leave the parlor, and I let out a long sigh.

"How about we all have another drink?" Tully says, alleviating the awkwardness in the room. He pops the cork of another bottle of champagne. "What do you say, everyone?" He holds the uncorked bottle high in the air.

I lift an empty glass. "I'd love another champagne."

CHAPTER 3

─ ◆ ─

ZINZI

Kingston Harbour, Kingston, Jamaica

On a sweltering August day that has melted into a steamy night, I stand outside the Harbour Street storefront, listening to the excited voices beyond the door, and a thrill runs through me.

They have a pop, a zing, a pulse of anticipation—like the rhythm of change that every Jamaican worker needs. Some call it hope. Others call it a dream. I call it the labor union.

I arrive at the entrance of the storage room. Inside, it feels like a party. Rows of folding chairs are set up in the center, while long tables hold pitchers of water, slices of melon, and a few pots of strong coffee, the aroma so intense that it stings my nose. A podium, similar to those used by ministers, stands at the front, and a paper sign pinned to the wall reads LABOR UNION MEETING.

This evening, I will give a speech, or, as I prefer to call it, a talk. Speech sounds too formal, and only leaders like Allan Coombs give speeches. I keep records, collect names on sign-up sheets, and write and distribute pamphlets. I am no Allan Coombs.

It doesn't take long for the rows of chairs to fill up. Those without seats find places to stand or lean against the wall. I move among them, smiling, offering sincere nods, and reaching out for outstretched hands. Admittedly, I avoid those with too much grief in their eyes—those who have lost a loved one to sugarcane, bananas, machetes, boiling pans, or burning stalks of cane. I understand those feelings all too well. I, too, have lost loved ones to the sugarcane fields. That pain lives beneath my skin.

I quicken my pace and take the seat saved for me in the front row. It doesn't take long for the voices to go silent, but only for a moment. A name is whispered and repeated, gaining momentum until it becomes a chant: "Allan Coombs! Allan Coombs!"

He is the reason I joined the movement. The power of his words, the timbre of his voice, and the passion he openly displays—no hiding his emotions, no shielding his soul—he shares his heart, his mind, everything he has to offer—all to confront the injustices faced by workers on sugar plantations, banana plantations, in rum factories, at the docks, wherever Jamaican workers are mistreated.

Allan steps up to the podium. He begins his typically magnetic oration by advocating for an end to low wages and the absence of workers' rights.

"Did you hear what I said?" He cups his ear. "I asked if you heard me." His booming voice reverberates through the storage room, and the response is deafening.

"That's right!" He pumps his fist in the air. "That's how we will achieve our goals—together. A union!"

The thunderous applause feels like an earthquake. Allan surveys the room, his chin jutting forward with pride.

The crowd erupts, shouting, "Union! Union!" The room is in a frenzy, but Allan watches with a wide smile. He lets the ovation continue for several minutes before finally raising a hand and signaling for silence.

"Thank you. Thank you, everyone. There's more to be said, and a young woman you all know is here to share her story. Please welcome Miss Zinzi Green."

Why did I think I could speak in the same space as Allan Coombs? Walking to the podium, I keep my eyes on the floor. It feels better not to look up.

"You've never been shy before, Zinzi," Allan whispers so only I can hear. "Speak from the heart. That's who you are and what we need from you."

I grip the podium and slowly lift my gaze. All eyes are on me, yet Allan's words help ease my fear. "This truth I've shared before, but never with so many at once," I say with a trembling smile. It's the largest gathering the movement has attracted to a meeting.

"My family hails from the Maroon village of Accompong. Our ancestors were Mandinka from West Africa, warriors who fought against enslavement. My father inherited that warrior spirit. When our land failed to produce enough to fill the bellies of his wife and eleven children, he left home to work on a sugar plantation, believing he could earn more money there than farming could provide. His wife and children would tend to the land while he was away.

"At the sugar plantation, he volunteered for the dangerous job of the pan man, stirring sugarcane in large iron pans over an open flame until it melted into a molten liquid. His body, arms, hands, and legs were exposed to the unimaginable and the unbearable, but he endured as long as possible.

"My father died in late August, thin, weak, burned, and scarred." I pause, holding back the fact that three years later, Marvin, the man I was meant to marry, died while working under the same perilous conditions at the same sugar plantation as my father. I still wasn't ready to share that story, not even for the sake of the labor movement. I look at Allan for a moment, who nods, encouraging me to continue.

"Workers must unite for everyone to benefit. Our country

needs jobs, but we deserve employers who respect and care for their employees—"

A commotion in the back of the room captures attention. A man in a light-colored suit with a tall, lean silhouette yells, "The constables are coming. Disperse. Disperse. Now!"

He forces his way to the front of the room. "They're here to arrest everyone," he informs Allan.

"Are you certain?" the labor union leader inquires. "They're arriving now?"

"Yes. Someone alerted the authorities," the stranger replies. "The constable and his men are on their way." He shouts again, "Trust me. Leave now. The cops are almost here."

For a moment, people are frozen in fear and distrust. I don't recognize this man any more than anyone else in this room. But then Allan steps up to the podium. "Don't just stand there. Run!"

Chairs are overturned. Water pitchers spill. Coffee cups are tossed aside. A small stampede charges toward the store's exits—cries of shock and fear blend with angry shouts. Suddenly, strong fingers grip my forearm and pull me toward the storeroom exit.

We move quickly. The stranger knows his way through the harbor, darting in and out of alleys and side streets. We race through the docks for several minutes. He doesn't let go of me until we stop a block from where we started. From our position, I can see the storefront. A half-dozen constables surround it. We would have been arrested if we hadn't left when we did. I might have spent the night or longer in jail, instead of the wooden shack in Trench Town where I live.

"You can let go," I say.

He releases me. "I didn't hurt you, did I? I just wanted to make sure you got away safely."

"It's fine," I reply, raising my voice above the sounds of banjos, hand drums, and rhumba boxes. We stop in front of a tavern where a folk band is playing.

"We had to move quickly. I apologize if I was too harsh." I observe him for a moment and quickly identify him as a man who spends his days lounging on the veranda, sipping martinis, or playing golf. His clothing validates my assumptions: a cotton shirt from Paris, tailored trousers by Frederick Scholte, and Italian shoes by Ferragamo. He resembles a wealthy British, American, or European tourist.

"You've never worked on a plantation. Why warn a group of labor union supporters about the police? Why bother?"

A smirk plays on his lips, as if he can read my mind. "You pass judgment quickly."

"I ask questions because I value answers," I reply.

His body tenses. "Then ask me another question."

Judging by the jut of his chin and the crease between his eyebrows, he thinks I won't. Well, I'll take that challenge. "What made you take such a risk?"

"Why do you assume I've never worked on a plantation?"

"Because you're white."

"Take a closer look."

I do as he suggests. His skin is lightly tanned, his hair wavy and blond, and his eyes are green. But there's more to him than I had noticed.

"Are you mulatto?"

"I'm colored. My mother was mulatto, the daughter of a Jamaican woman and a British officer."

I shrug. There are lots of mixed-race people like him in Jamaica. "You could pass."

"I wouldn't want to."

"So, you've stirred a pot of boiling sugar and swung a machete in a sugarcane field?"

"Yes, I've done that and more."

"I don't trust you, even if you did save me and the others from a night in the hoosegow." I extend my hand. "The name is Zinzi. Zinzi Green."

"I'm not lying but believing me is up to you." He exhales before adding, "My name is Byron Tynesdale."

My hand falls back to my side just as he reaches for it. "Tynesdale?"

"Yes, of the Tynesdale Estate," he replies. "One of the labor movement's most fervent opponents."

My breath catches. "I know your plantation well." I try not to show too much emotion. It's the same sugarcane field where my father and my fiancé were worked to death. "I wish I could say it's a pleasure to meet you."

"Believe me." He sighs deeply. "I wish you could, too."

Myrtle Bank Hotel, Kingston

Twenty minutes later, I'm not sure I can take another step. "We're not being followed, now, are we?" I place my hand on my chest. "I need to catch my breath."

Byron Tynesdale and I have traveled quite a distance, initially moving in a huge circle, but now we've made our way further along Harbour Street.

"Do you mind if we don't stay here?" Byron says, his gaze darting. Still watching out for danger, I suspect. "There's a place just around the corner. Can you make it that far?"

The vile taste in my throat spreads. "I'm going to be sick."

"It's okay if you are." He offers me his arm, which, although tempted, I don't take.

"I imagine it's the adrenaline," he says, taking my rebuff in stride. "Our bodies produce it when we're stressed or in danger, and it can make you feel unsteady."

"Are you a doctor?" I ask sarcastically.

"I was a cook in a hospital cafeteria in New York City."

"Oh." He's trying to lighten the mood with a joke, but the pain in my stomach worsens with each step. I look up as a shooting star streaks across the night sky. Following its path, I hope it will take my aching belly with it as it fades from view.

"We're here," he says.

"I can't go in there."

"Why not?" he asks.

We stop in front of a crescent-shaped driveway on Harbour Street, where uniformed doormen greet a line of cars as guests enter the Myrtle Bank Hotel.

"The United Fruit Company owns this hotel. You know who they are, right?"

"I do. They are the largest distributors of bananas in the Caribbean."

"The working conditions at their facilities are as horrific as those on the sugar plantation you own." I don't hold back. "Banana factories are no better than sugar plantations."

His dark brows knit together. "Let me be clear—I don't own the Tynesdale sugar plantation." Abruptly, he points toward the hotel entrance. "I rent a room here—Suite 357. If you'd like, you can go upstairs until you feel better." He reaches into his pocket, pulls out a key, and extends it to me.

I want to throw it at him. "No, thank you. All I need is to get home."

"Look, I'm not trying to be rude, but you don't look well. I'm not sure you'll make it home," he says. "I'll wait for you downstairs—at the bar. Then, I'll drive you home, or if you prefer, we can have a late supper—whatever you'd like."

As much as I want to escape, the nausea in my stomach feels like it has a mind of its own and deserves some privacy. "You've already done enough for one night." I wish I felt well enough to leave.

"I could never do enough," he says, his tone heavy with apology.

What does he mean? He could never do enough of what? He can do any number of things, such as burning down the

Tynesdale sugarcane fields, and not just a seasonal burning of the sugarcane stalks. No, he can have the whole estate burned to the ground—also one of my recurring dreams.

I have plenty of ideas I'd share for making him useful if it weren't for my stomach. I take the key from his hand. "Room 357. I'll be right back."

"Take as long as you need."

CHAPTER 4

———✦———

OTHELLA

Savoy Ballroom, Chicago

Tony Schaefer doesn't have an office. He holds his meetings—at least the ones he's had with Perry and me—at the Savoy Ballroom on 47th and South Parkway, near the Regal Theater. An entertainment "it" neighborhood for Negroes, the Savoy has as many white couples showing up on its dance floor as colored. Not that I mind. The more the merrier. The dance hall is my favorite place in the whole wide world.

Everything about the Savoy is top-notch: the colorful lighting, the beautiful red leather lounges, and that new dance floor—so smooth you can glide across it. There are also two wall-length bars, one at each end of the remarkably long dance floor, staffed by the best bartenders in the city. The waiters, too, are dapper, in bright white dress shirts and large red bow ties as they serve the lounges and box seats.

The highlight is the music. Two bands alternate on one stage every night, so the music never stops. One hour, I swing to Benny Goodman and his orchestra. The next hour, I shake my hips to Chick Webb and his band. All night long, the most jumpin' jazz and the hottest music play on a brightly lit stage against a blue-sky backdrop. When I leave Chicago, I'll miss the city's nightlife the most—the nightclubs, the juke joints, the Savoy Ballroom, and all the dancing.

I am a swell dancer, too. Folks think I've been dancing since I was a kid. That's how good I was right off the bat.

Swing. Lindy Hop (or jitterbug). Shimmy. Foxtrot. Just name it. And Perry is an excellent partner. Such a strong boy! He can fling me between his legs, over his head, and around his waist as easy as pie. And I ain't no pint-size filly. Pleasantly round in all the right places and extra busty, I have a healthy figure that has helped me draw (and keep) the attention of some roughly woven men, both colored and white. But Perry wins the prize for handling me on the dance floor, and sometimes in the bedroom, too.

My heart races in my chest. "Lord have mercy," I say out loud. Could it be that I am gonna miss Perry Merriweather? Have I lost my mind? I can still feel the weight of his big body on my chest, my fear, as he slammed me into the sofa and wrapped his fingers around my throat. I lean against a wall and close my eyes. I'll miss many things about Chicago, but Perry Merriweather better not be one of 'em.

"Excuse me, miss. You can come right in." The maître d's voice is a rope, pulling me back to my senses.

"Thank you," I reply as I walk by, briefly noticing that he didn't charge me the thirty-cent admission fee. Tony must've left word—that's a good sign.

As I stroll past the lounges and tables, I take everything in, committing it all to memory. This might be my last visit to the Savoy.

A row of young, doe-eyed cuties sits at the hostess station in one of the lounges, ripe for the picking. They are various shades of beautiful, all flashing come-and-get-me smiles. Silk-covered legs crossed at the ankles and skirts hiked up to mid-calf reveal just enough leg to tease but not enough to sig-

nal for a copper. I was one of them before I met Perry, searching for a dance partner and whatever else I could get from a
man. I flash a broad smile at the girls as I walk by.

I arrive at his box and am surprised to find it empty. Not
that I expected Tony to be waiting for me, but I thought some
of his pals would be around. I stroll casually to the front and
wrap my fingers around the railing. The music is loud and
the band is swinging hard and fast. The dance floor is hop-
pin'. My hips sway, my fingers snap, and my head moves
from side to side. The band's rhythm is so hot that the whole
building feels like it's bouncing on springs. The music takes
hold of me, and I forget the troubles this day has brought me
until the crowd parts before me like the Red Sea. In the center of the swirl are Tony Schaefer and his goons coming toward me.

For a white man, he certainly is quite a nice slice of beef.
Some men can change the quality of a room with a handshake or a tip of the hat, while others fade away like wilting
flowers, their backbones melting like ice on a hot day. But
Tony shouts his power. Everyone knows he is one of them—
a mobster, a hooligan, a tall drink of trouble.

"Hey there, doll." Tony leans over the railing and kisses
me while his bodyguards form a protective circle around him.

"Hey there yourself," I reply, fluttering my eyelashes. "It's
been too long."

He flashes a charming, toothy grin. "Likewise, sugar. Likewise."

Decked out in a double-breasted beige suit and Oxford
shoes, his hair slicked back with pomade, he is aces no matter what he wears. "You look delicious."

I shimmy around the gate to join him outside the box. "I
need to be close so you can hear me over the music."

"That's right, baby girl. I want to hear every word you
have to say," he says, his gaze fixed on my cleavage. "You
look like a ripe, juicy tomato."

"Oh, I don't know how to react when you say things like that."

"Try to think of something."

I laugh. "Thank you for the compliment, and for really seeing me. I don't want to take up too much of your time, so I'll get right to it, if that's okay?"

"Sure, sugar. Just tell me what you need."

"I'd like to borrow some cash, a loan against Perry and my next payday."

He frowns. "I'm surprised. I pay y'all enough. From what I hear, you two are quite the team and make a decent haul with your cons. So why you asking me for more money?"

"Perry left town two days ago and cleared out our stash. I kinda get why, though. He was mighty worried about his mama. She's sickly, and he took off to Joliet lickety-split when he got the call. That's where his family lives—in Joliet." I talk a mile a minute. A lie sounds better when it spills out of your mouth.

Tony's right eye squints. He doesn't believe my story, but I keep at it.

"I called Perry yesterday and asked him to wire me some cash. I don't think anyone got my message. With so much happening—his mother so sick, maybe dying in the hospital—nobody's paying attention."

Tony pulls me closer, not too gently. "You've always struck me as a judicious girl," he says, minus the flirty tone he had just a moment ago.

"What does *judicious* mean?"

"Don't worry about it," he says dismissively, his attention shifting elsewhere.

The music has changed. It's no longer jazz or swing but a number called, "The Peanut Vendor." My mother used to do a dance she called the rhumba.

"They're playing my song," Tony says. "Let's dance."

"I can't rhumba," I lie, not wanting my last dance at the Savoy to be in Tony Schaefer's arms.

He senses my hesitation—and I don't think he likes it. "Goddamn it, Othella. Do you think I don't know you're telling a bald-faced lie?" He grips me tightly, his hand around the back of my neck. "I said we're gonna rhumba."

He spins me onto the dance floor, and I stumble into his arms. He says it's the same, but it isn't the same dance my mother did in our kitchenette. Still, I follow his lead and hate every second.

"Could you please loosen your grip on me? You're hurting me."

He chuckles. "I don't care."

"I can't talk if you're holding me like that."

"Then shake your head if you're gonna stop lying to me."

I lock eyes with him. "Okay. You got me. I need some dough to leave town and hoped you'd help me out 'cause you like me and I've done you a favor or two before."

"That wasn't a favor." He touches my cheek, his thumb sliding over my lower lip. "That was a good time. And you're right, I do like you, Othella, and I'll help you. Give you all the cash you need to get out of town, but first, you gotta do a job for me."

My heart races. "I can't. You don't get it. I gotta leave tonight."

He shakes his head, smiling all the while. "Nah. You ain't going anywhere until you lift something for me."

"I can't."

His hand tightens around my neck. "Give me a good reason why you can't."

"Perry is out of town. Remember?" My veins feel like they're about to burst. "I don't have a partner."

"You're the queen of the fingersmiths, aren't you?"

"No one calls me that," I reply.

"I do, and I'm the only one who matters."

"I don't need the dough bad enough to do a job solo," I lie again.

"Yes, you do need it that badly," Tony says, loosening his grip on my neck. "You need it worse than you know."

"How's that?"

"The coppers are looking for you, honey. Or they will be by morning, and they'll throw you in jail if Perry's brother doesn't find you first."

"What are you talking about? Why would Jerry Merriweather be looking for me? And why would the police want me? They've got nothing that proves I did anything."

"You killed your boyfriend and the cops want to arrest you. Meanwhile, Perry's brother, Jerry, just wants to bash your head in."

I'm sure I didn't hear him right. "What are you talking about?"

"A neighbor heard y'all arguing this afternoon, saw you run out of the apartment, and called the cops. They found his body on the living room floor."

I step back. "Perry ain't dead. He can't be. I didn't hit him hard enough. And he talked to me right before I left." I start shaking so hard I think I'll fall. "He wasn't dead, I swear to you. When I left that apartment, Perry was alive!"

"Calm down—no need for histrionics." Tony leads me from the dance floor to his box. "When he was found, Perry lay dead on his living room floor, a gash in his head that was the size of a baseball. The Smokador you used to kill him was covered in blood."

The pounding in my chest is unbearable. "I didn't kill him."

"Doesn't matter what you say. Nobody will believe you, especially not Jerry. But that's where I come in. I'll keep him off your back, and the coppers, too. Most of 'em in that neighborhood work for me. How do you think I found out so quickly that Perry was dead and the police were looking for you?"

Tony lights a cigarette. "So, you're gonna do this job for me, and I'll pay you and protect you until you're safely out of town. Deal?"

Fuck. Is Tony telling me the truth about Perry? Is he really dead? I swear, he was alive when I left the apartment. But if the cops have my name on a ticket, it doesn't matter whether I killed him or not. They'll arrest me if they find me, and I can't go to jail. I'd be no good in jail. Christ. But if the cops don't catch me, what about Perry's twin, Jerry?

"Okay. I'll do it."

"Good girl," Tony replies.

"So, what do you want me to steal?"

"Nothing big, just a pocket watch from an old man."

We move to a quieter part of the Savoy, a room in the back, so Tony can give me the rundown on the party I'm about to crash. It's at Robert Abbott's mansion—he owns the *Chicago Defender*. He and his wife are hosting a reception for their guests, Count and Countess di Abbatino—or Josephine Baker. The famous showgirl and amazing dancer, she is someone I'd love to meet. But I know I won't get within ten feet of her. What if I acted a fool and drew all sorts of attention? That wouldn't be good for a gal trying to steal a watch.

"How can a colored man make that much cabbage without having served time?" he says. "Some damn newspaper for colored folks shouldn't earn him that much money—especially during the Depression. I bet he's running a scam. Ain't no way he's wealthy and legit." Tony has a bunch of Negroes he either works with or goes to bed with, but funny how he hates a colored man who makes more money than him.

He says almost the same thing about the mark, the only part of his rant I commit to memory—the bits and pieces I need to do my job.

The man is Major Leonard Thomas, and Tony's object of desire is a priceless pocket watch—soon to be in my clutches. It will be a simple grab and go. Lickety-split and I'll be on my way to the midnight train, just like that.

Finally finished, I head to the ladies' room to change into a gown one of Tony's goons fetched for me. I touch up my makeup—rouge, raspberry-red lipstick, and mascara—and tame my unruly eyebrows. But there's nothin' to be done about the dress. It's a pale blue gown with drop sleeves and a pink bow around the waist—they call it the sweetheart look—and something I'd never wear voluntarily.

As I put the final touches on my hairdo—a neat bun at the nape of my neck, my long bangs swept to the side and pinned behind my right ear—I keep thinking about what Tony told me about Perry. What if Tony lied just to get me to steal this pocket watch? What if Perry isn't dead? On the other hand, does it even matter? I know I heard him call after me. He was alive when I left. I'm still leaving town. It's all aces once I deliver the watch, and Tony pays me my money. But can I leave Chicago without knowing for sure if Perry is dead? Shouldn't I check with someone other than him, just in case Schaefer is a big fat liar?

Another glance in the mirror. I look as good as I'm gonna look for the job I have to do. I just wish I could stop thinking about what Tony told me about Perry. Did I kill him? I don't rightly know. I wish I could find out for sure. But I can't ask Tony. I'll have to get the truth from somebody else.

CHAPTER 5

VIVIAN JEAN

Hartfield House, Bronzeville, Chicago

The birthday celebration ends shortly after my parents' departure. I bid farewell to our guests and promise Katherine that I'll be ready for the Abbotts' reception in an hour. I still haven't had a chance to talk to her, but I will make time during our ride over to the party.

"We can all go together," Katherine says, winking at Tully as we escort her to the foyer. "Send a car for me. I hate driving at night." She gracefully exits the house, and I watch from the vestibule window as she enters her automobile, parked in our circular drive. She waves just before lowering herself into the driver's seat, knowing I'll be watching enviously. I can't drive a car. Teaching me how wasn't a priority for my father or my first husband, and after Clifford's accident, I lost interest in learning. Though Tully promised to teach me—but that was before.

"I'll wear my pink silk gown to the reception—and the gift from the major." I waltz into our bedroom ahead of Tully. "The jeweler did a splendid job, don't you think?" I touch the pocket watch nervously. No matter how we might have acted toward the end of the party, the tension between us weighs heaviest when Tully and I are alone.

He walks past me and dumps the gifts he's carrying onto our canopied bed.

"You should've talked to him before this afternoon." He immediately beelines for the small table beside the dresser where he keeps his bottle of Jack Daniel's and a tumbler. "We could've avoided that little show."

"It's water under the bridge," I say, and Tully grunts as if he's been punched in the gut. My poor choice of words triggered his reaction.

Clifford died when his car crashed into the Clark Street Drawbridge and he drowned in the Chicago River. The accident occurred on the evening of December 10, the same day he transferred the trust fund and the same date written on the note that has caused Tully and me so much pain, sorrow, and discord.

This note, lost for months, was discovered by a carpenter four weeks ago under a file cabinet in Clifford's office, now the new library of Hartfield House.

December 10, 1933
I know what you've done. For all these years, you have been nothing but a liar—a fraud.
And I know who you don't love and who you truly love.
It's wrong, and you will come to regret it.
Clifford

The note was too cryptic to take seriously, I told Tully. There's no way to know to whom Clifford was writing or what he was writing about. "You keep insisting that the note, the trust fund, and the car accident are connected, but it's a tragic coincidence," I argued. Except Tully doesn't believe in coincidences.

"Water under the bridge, huh?" Tully growls, pulling me out of my memories. "Like the note Clifford wrote?"

"Don't do that, Tully. Please don't change the subject. I made a mistake. I wasn't thinking when I said it."

"I'm not changing, I'm trying to finish a conversation you don't want to have."

"Because it's ridiculous. Clifford didn't write that note about us. He had no reason to. We weren't having an affair."

"I know that, but what if he thought we were?"

"What if nothing?" I shout. "Clifford never questioned my loyalty, and if he hadn't died, you and I would never have married." I cover my mouth. "I'm sorry. That didn't come out the way I meant it."

"You said it exactly as you meant it. I am fully aware that I married a woman who doesn't love me."

"Oh my God. How can you say that? After all we've been through. You know I love you, but you're using that damn note to tear us apart, and I don't understand why."

"I need another drink."

"You've had enough, Tully."

"I'm a grown man, Vivi. I can drink as much as I want, whenever I want.

"Don't call me Vivi. I don't like it."

"Don't get your feathers ruffled, honey." He holds up the bottle of Jack Daniel's. "You sure you don't want one?"

"Tully, don't do this."

"Do what?" he replies flippantly. "Get angry when we aren't being honest with each other, Vivi?"

"Damn it, Tully. Stop calling me that!"

"No need to get hysterical, my love."

"I am not fucking hysterical." I begin taking off my dress. "If you keep that up," I point at his glass, "you'll be boiled as an owl at the reception."

"I'm already boiled."

With a groan of frustration, I slip out of my dress, nearly ripping a seam. Then, freeing my silk stockings from the garters, I roll them down as if they're made of razor blades. "Sarcasm is not attractive on you, dear."

"Lies aren't attractive on you." Tully steps away from his makeshift bar toward me. "You're too scared to admit you believe me about the note."

There is a strangeness in his voice, a warning. He'll say something awful if I don't stop him.

"Let's not fight tonight. Not before we leave for Jamaica," I plead. "I can't stand listening to you say the same cruel things over and over." I stab at my chest with my fingertip. "Here, in my heart, in my soul, it hurts so badly I could die from some of the things you imply. Clifford didn't kill himself."

"How can you be so sure?" Tully cries.

"Shut up!" I grab a bottle of perfume and brace to throw it at Tully, but I don't want to hit him. I don't want to hurt him, and I wish he didn't want to hurt me. My arm falls limp. "The note isn't about us. I don't know who it's about, but I'm going to figure it out, and when I do, you'll have to swallow your lies, because there's no reason for them." I charge forward and grab his shoulders. "You need to stop this."

He gently grips my wrists. "Let go."

The walls move in on me, surrounding me, dangerously close. They know I am losing control. And I can't allow that. Not before I receive forgiveness at the sacred silk cotton tree. I lower my arms and step back.

The anger washes out of me, leaving Tully and me in an uncomfortable silence.

It lasts an endless, heart-sickening moment, and then Tully strides toward the door with long, quick steps. "I'll see you on the midnight train."

I flinch. "You're not coming to the reception?"

He halts and pivots, retracing his path until he reaches my side. Gently touching my face, he caresses my cheek. I lean into him, and he kisses me softly on the lips, a lingering kiss that ends too soon. "You'll have a better time without me."

"Tully, please. Katherine will be disappointed."

He looks at me as if I were a rare, mysterious beauty, but I am none of those things. When his lips brush against mine once more, I tremble. "I do love you, Vivian Jean. It's just that I hate how much I love you."

Then he's gone, leaving me staring blankly at the spot in the bedroom where he stood just a moment ago. I feel the pressure of his hands on my face, smell the whiskey on his breath, and feel the warmth of his lips on my mouth.

What had Tully's father said? Tully and I are survivors. Can we survive this?

Terrible things happen.

Things that rip your heart apart and smash your bones. Horrible things that sneak around a corner or rise from under the bed and slam the door in your face. You pray you'll be ready for those sorrows—but can you truly prepare for every heartbreak?

I sink to the floor, feeling my chest ache and gasping for air, fighting back the tears I can't stop. I bury my face in the folds of my pink gown and weep.

Maxi finds me on the floor, a sobbing mess, and immediately begins to piece me back together. Working swiftly and silently, she helps me stand, leads me to the bathroom, and guides me onto the vanity stool, where I collapse, still weeping.

She douses my face with cold water. "Stop crying," she says sternly. "You've shed enough tears."

But have I? It isn't what Tully said that disturbs me. It's the look in his eyes, the coldness of his stare, and the finality of that kiss.

"What if Jamaica is a fool's errand, Maxi? What if there's nothing that can save Tully and me? No miracles, no spirits, no sacred silk cotton tree?"

It's the truth: The real reason I must journey to Jamaica's Cockpit Country, the real reason I must join Katherine's expedition, the real reason I have persuaded my husband to join me on this journey is Clifford. I must talk to him. His ghost will forgive me. The duppies, the ancestors of the sacred silk cotton tree, will help me talk to him.

Turning slightly, I catch sight of the crumpled pink fabric in a pile on the bedroom floor. "I ruined my evening gown."

"Don't worry about that dress," Maxi replies as she picks it up from the floor. "You have others." She takes the gown into my walk-in closet and comes out with a mint-green sheer chiffon dress. "This one looks great on you, and the neckline will showcase your father's gift perfectly."

I had forgotten about the dress, its gorgeous puff sleeves and matching green rose corsage. "I wish you'd come with us to Jamaica."

"I told you, I'll never return to the Cockpit or Accompong."

Maxi has told me this before—numerous times—but she rarely shares more than a few words about the reason. I know it involves Obeah, a healing practice from her village that is rooted in African tradition but also illegal in Jamaica, as I learned from Katherine.

I glance in the mirror. My eyes are puffy and my hair is a mess. "God. Should I even bother?"

"Bother to go to Jamaica or to the reception, or both?"

I am tempted to respond *both*, but before I can, Maxi is brushing my hair, and none too gently.

"It doesn't matter what you say. You're doing both. So, let's wash your face again, fix your hair, and put on this dress. Your silk slip will look lovely beneath the sheer chiffon."

"If you insist."

"I insist. Now, let's get you into this gown. The car has already left to pick up Miss Dunham. They'll be here any moment."

CHAPTER 6

ZINZI

Myrtle Bank Hotel, Kingston

I step into Byron Tynesdale's hotel suite, my stomach pro-
testing with every step. Hurrying to the first closed door, I
pray it's the bathroom—and I'm right. After several long
minutes bent over the toilet bowl, I finally feel better and
offer a silent thank-you to Byron Tynesdale.

Standing unsteadily, I splash water on my face and rinse
my mouth. I grab a hand towel and dry my face while taking
in my surroundings.

The sea-blue bathtub's gorgeous tiled archway and the
penny-round-tile flooring of the bathroom captivate me. The
blue color confirms my love for bathrooms and baths, which
I attribute to the Cockpit. As a child, I dreamed of the rare
river or stream, often seeking them out to indulge in fantasies
of becoming a mermaid. But not just any mermaid—River
Mumma, the magnificent goddess my father described, who
sat on the rocks by the riverbanks, combing her long black
hair.

Momma Jayden, an elder in the Maroon village where I

was raised, told me about her. My mother was upset when she found out I knew the story. She had a less romantic view of the goddess: "If you look at River Mumma for too long or dare to touch her, she will put you in a trance, drag you out of the mountains, and drown you in the Black River." My mother aimed to scare me with her superstitions and rituals, and would've succeeded if my father hadn't taught me how to swim. He didn't mind that I loved mermaids.

I reluctantly step out of the bathroom to look around. Byron's suite is similar to those at the Constant Spring Hotel. The décor features an abundance of rattan, wicker, and bamboo, as well as carved mahogany furniture, lamps with tulip-shaped shades and fringe, two large ceiling fans, painted vases filled with freshly cut gardenias, and green plants in clay pots. French doors open to a balcony that offers a stunning view: the sea with its rolling waves, tranquil palm trees swaying in the gentle night breeze, all bathed in moonlight. I could stay on the balcony all night, but I should leave.

Walking through the dining room, I notice a typewriter on the table with a sheet of paper in the carriage. It appears to be a list, and I pause to read what is typed.

The very next second, I sit at the table, lift the typewriter carriage, take out the sheet of paper and read from the top. In less than a minute, I lean back in my chair, pondering the detailed recipe for gallons of rum I am reading. It's not that I know rum recipes by heart, but what Jamaican isn't familiar with rum? My mother makes rum. Everyone in the Cockpit has a jug of rum or wine they've concocted. And every large sugarcane plantation has a rum operation.

But why would the son of the owner of one of Jamaica's largest rum distilleries type up a rum recipe? What if someone finds it, like a maid or a labor union activist, and assumes it belongs to his family? It could end up in the hands of a union-friendly newspaper or one of his competitors, and overnight destroy his family business. Did he forget it was here? Did he want me to find it?

"Damn." The rum industry is ruthless. Forget the newspapers. That recipe could be sold to the highest bidder and finance a revolution—or a labor union movement.

I carefully return the paper to the typewriter and hurry out of his suite, locking the door behind me.

When I reach the hotel lobby, I'm out of breath, but I feel like myself again. I search for Byron, wanting to get the key into his hands and out of mine, but the place is packed with too many people and too many vases of gardenias.

I finally spot him, partially hidden behind a tall potted palm. He's not alone either. The other man bears a striking resemblance to him, though he is taller and a bit heavier. Judging by the width of his shoulders and the girth of his middle, he has occupied his body a few more decades than Byron. They aren't having a friendly conversation. The older man's jaw snaps like gunfire, and the pith helmet he holds looks on the verge of being torn in two. I take a deep breath and approach them.

"Hello, Byron." I extend my hand—not for a handshake, but to show the room key. "Thanks for letting me take a moment to freshen up."

Byron's expression shifts rapidly from anger to surprise. I almost giggle and nearly miss the subtle smile on his lips.

He takes the key with a steady hand. "Thank you, Zinzi." He turns to the older man. "I'd like to introduce you to my father, Bernard Christian Tynesdale."

It takes every fiber of my being not to spit in his face, but I know better than to follow my instincts. Notwithstanding, Bernard Christian Tynesdale—with that ridiculous middle name—has the audacity to glare at me as if he is superior.

"Zinzi?" The old man raises an eyebrow. "Byron didn't mention your last name."

"Green, sir. My name is Zinzi Green."

"May I ask how you two young people know each other?"

Byron steps in as I struggle to find a response that doesn't overflow with profanity.

"Honestly, Father, no, you can't," Byron replies. "Or rather, you can, but I won't respond. It's up to Miss Green to tell you if she wants to."

Both men look at me. "I met Byron at a labor union meeting earlier tonight."

Bernard Christian Tynesdale's expression is blank, as if I hadn't said a word. "So, Byron, you won't be coming home with me tonight?"

"I'm surprised you came all this way so late, Father, knowing that I have no intention of returning home tonight or anytime soon."

The flush of red creeping up the elder Tynesdale's neck above his collar makes him look like he's on fire. He puts on his hat and tips the brim in my direction. "If we meet again, Miss Green, it will be my pleasure." He scowls at Byron, pivots on his back leg, turns sharply like a soldier, and marches out of the lobby.

"Thank you for your discretion," Byron says with a playful tone.

"Should I have lied about where we met?"

"No, not at all. You have no obligation to play cat and mouse on my behalf with my father."

"You're right, unless it was your father's idea to send you to a labor union meeting."

"So, are you calling me a spy?" Byron chuckles. "I'd be

the last person on earth my father would choose to attend a labor union meeting."

"You're an ideal candidate for the job."

"He has many more dependable people on his payroll who are far better at deceit than I am." He glances around the lobby as if he suddenly remembers where he is. "Would you like to join me for dinner? If you feel better, and if you're hungry. I'm starving. The restaurant here is fantastic. After dinner, I'll arrange a car to take you home."

His name is still Tynesdale, but I've never been invited to have a meal in the dining room of a fine hotel—not that I've particularly longed for it. "Okay, I'll join you. But only because I noticed the rum recipe on your typewriter—and I'd like to ask you about it."

He smirks at me. "I'd love to answer any of your questions."

The restaurant on the veranda offers a view of the beach and the ocean, with palm trees swaying in a warm breeze and soft moonlight.

A rushed waiter leads us to our seats, places the menus on the table, and stands by as we look them over. I order Jamaican rice and peas with grilled snapper, while Byron chooses a steak, a potato, and a whiskey neat. I nearly ask him why he didn't pick rum, but I'll hold my questions until after we've eaten.

Dinner with Byron begins with a flurry of polite, nearly inconsequential conversation. We talk about the summer heat, beaches, whether I prefer fish or beef, and if I've ever visited England. He rambles about his extensive travels, having been educated in British boarding schools and attended Oxford University. He spent summers in Paris, winter holidays in Germany, and a semester in New York City, where he took anthropology classes at Columbia University.

"That was how I spent my youth until my mother fell ill, and that brought me back home."

"To the Tynesdale Estate."

"Yes. But I left again," he says. "Ten years ago, when my mother died."

He was twenty-two at the time and headed straight for America, spending time in cities like Detroit, Chicago, and New York. After that, he worked on the Panama Canal and even picked sugarcane in Cuba. He also returned to Britain for a while, enrolled in university, and took courses in English literature and anthropology.

"You never thought to settle down?" I ask.

Byron takes a sip of his drink. "I always knew I'd return to Jamaica someday."

"The Tynesdale Estate is one of the largest rum businesses on the island."

He glances at me over the rim of his glass. "Yes, it is."

"How did you know about the cops' raid on our meeting tonight? And why did you warn us?"

"Do you think I have a hidden agenda for what I did?" He presses his tongue against his cheek. "I do, but it's not sinister. If my name wasn't Tynesdale, would you question my motives as stringently?"

"Yes, I would. I make it a habit not to trust anyone I don't know."

He rubs the lower half of his face as if peeling off the last remnants of a mask. "That's what Allan told me. He also said you're an excellent judge of character and that I needed to meet you—before he'd consider having someone with my last name join the labor movement. Of course, I didn't plan for it to be tonight, but after the close call with the constables, I figured, why not tonight?"

I'm sure I look confused. "Why would Allan ask you to

speak with me?" I say this almost to myself because, as the words come out of my mouth, I also feel proud. Allan trusts me.

Byron leans back in his chair. "He believes in your instincts, especially regarding new people. I want to join the movement, and Allan is a smart, cautious man. He is someone I've known and respected for quite a while. Of course, he will ultimately decide if I am worthy, but if you say no, I'm out before I'm in. I don't want that to happen. So, I'm trying to impress you with the truth about who I am and who I aspire to become."

"Who do you aspire to be?"

"One of the first plantation owners to support and implement a labor union for workers."

"That's a nice speech, but it'll take more than nice speeches to convince me you're not your father's spy. Besides, I thought you had nothing to do with your family business."

"It will be my business one day."

"And you aren't in cahoots with the constable?" I ask in a mocking tone.

"This is not a joke to me, Zinzi."

"It's not a joke to me either," I reply. "You were the one who said you wanted to share. I am simply encouraging you."

He places the empty glass on the table.

"Touché." He takes his napkin, wipes the corners of his mouth, and clears his throat.

"My mother died a decade ago, and I blamed my father. He never struck her or did anything to harm her physically, but he married her and ignored her. I hated him for that. So I left Jamaica, never intending to return." He adjusts his shoulders, and his eyes cloud over.

"Sorry," he says after a moment. "She and I were very close."

"My condolences for your loss."

"And for yours."

"How do you know about my losses?" I ask, offended, but then I remember. "Oh, that's right." He heard some of my story at the union meeting. "Thank you."

"You see, my mother was mulatto. My father was a womanizer, but despite that, she fell in love with him and gave birth to a blond-haired, green-eyed son." He points at himself. "When he married her, she had to live as white in his world. Some of her family—my family—worked as field laborers on his sugar plantation. I can't understand why she loved him." He exhales loudly. "Anyway, when she died, I didn't handle it well. So, I left." He gestures toward the waiter passing by.

"Another whiskey, sir?" the waiter asks.

"Coffee, please." He turns to me. "Will you join me for a cup?"

"Sure, why not?" I reply, adding to the waiter, "With extra milk and sugar, please."

He has shared far more than I expected, and the information about Allan and Byron's pasts intrigues and unsettles me. I know nothing about Allan's connection to a plantation owner's son. At the very least, I owe Byron the courtesy of joining him for coffee.

"So, you want to join the movement because of your mother?" It's a cynical question, and he flinches. But I don't apologize. "Why did you come back to Jamaica?"

"I'm an only child. My father wants me to take over the business."

"And he'll be okay with you starting a union for your workers?"

"My father is very ill."

My anger at his family's plantation leaves me momentarily without words, but I recover enough to be polite. "I'm sorry."

"Thank you." He bows his head slightly. "There is much about my father that I detest, but I would not wish him to suffer from an illness."

"I understand."

"The more I learn about the labor union, the more I want to make changes when Tynesdale Estate is under my management."

"That's quite a bold statement."

"You don't believe me?"

I gaze at him for a long moment. "I'm not sure."

"I need you to believe me." His voice is almost a plea.

"There's something you should know. Sugar plantations are the villains in my story—the devils in my Bible. The plantation workers who matter most to me are already lost, and my grief is unending. So, while I may smile, make small talk, and ask intrusive questions, the thought of the owner's son from Tynesdale Estate joining the movement repulses me.

"You don't get it. I dream of burning your father's plantation to the ground." I slam my fist on the table but the sharp pain I feel is mostly in my heart, not my hand. "Look, this is more than I planned for one evening. I need to call it a night."

"I understand," he says. "Maybe after you talk to Allan, we can meet again tomorrow and have dinner at a reasonable hour."

I frown noting how he didn't react to my dream of destroying his family plantation. "Tomorrow? What's the rush?"

"Ten years—it's taken me to figure out what I want, and now that I know, I'm eager to get started."

"What if I tell Allan you're a no-go?"

"I'd still like to have dinner." He smiles.

I don't react to his obvious attempt at flirting. He didn't react to my threat of arson. I'd never consider such a thing. "As I mentioned, I'll talk to Allan and be in touch."

An hour later, I lie in my narrow bed in my shabby home in Trench Town, exhaustion pulling me toward sleep. But first, I jot down a few thoughts in the journal by my bedside. Not that I'll forget anything about Byron Tynesdale. I just need to see it in writing. *Meet Allan after work and share my first impression of the man who showed up yesterday to save us.*

CHAPTER 7

———⋅◆⋅———

VIVIAN JEAN

Grand Boulevard, Bronzeville, Chicago

"Where's Tully?" Katherine asks as soon as I poke my head into the limo.

"Not coming." I slide into the back seat beside her.

The driver closes the door just as I settle in and brace for the interrogation. Katherine won't be satisfied with my brief answer. I need time to collect myself after my collapse at Hartfield House. "You look beautiful. That dress is incredibly flattering on you."

The limo turns onto Grand Boulevard, heading toward Mr. Abbott's home, while Katherine straightens the lavender lace sleeve of her white satin gown.

"Oh, this old thing?"

"Quit pretending. You bought it at Marshall Field's last weekend."

"Oh, right. I almost forgot we went shopping together." Katherine shrugs. "But seriously, that was quite a show you and your father put on. We never had a chance to talk."

I call out to the driver, "Let's circle the block a few times.

We don't want to arrive exactly on time." I gesture to Katherine, saying, "Let's talk now."

"Of course. As long as we're not too delayed."

"I just wanted to thank you. Tully and I are very excited about the expedition, and personally, I truly appreciate your allowing us to join you."

"You're welcome, but I don't need the company. I was ready to make the trip solo, but you're only coming with me to Accompong. Correct?"

Her abrupt tone isn't meant to be dismissive, but over the years, I've learned some things about Katherine Dunham. She is outspoken, independent, and sometimes rude, even to her friends. I believe that when it comes to her work, friendships are almost the last thing on her mind. It's her genius that makes her intolerant. So, I've developed a thick skin and learned to take her impatience in stride.

"Yes, that's correct," I reply. "My focus is on the Maroon people and Accompong."

"Just making sure you know I won't need you or your husband in Haiti, Martinique, or Trinidad."

These are the islands she plans to explore after Jamaica, and I am not interested in them. But even if I were, her bluntness would not insult me. Katherine is accustomed to running her own show. At least she and I agree on the importance of the Maroon people. In the 1700s, the Maroons, descendants of enslaved people who escaped, fought for their freedom throughout the Caribbean. In Jamaica, after winning their war, they negotiated a series of treaties with the British and maintained political autonomy long after the abolition of slavery. Now, they have their own government, land rights, and justice systems deep in Jamaica's Cockpit Country.

Katherine looks out the car window. "Accompong wouldn't be part of my itinerary without Melville Herskovits. He suggested I study the Maroon people. Their culture is as connected to African culture as any in the Caribbean, but their numbers are dwindling."

"I've been reading journals and articles by some of Herskovits's colleagues," I say, "including Dr. Jean Price-Mars, the Haitian anthropologist."

"That's great to hear." She furrows her brow. "Honestly, I was surprised when you asked to join my expedition a few weeks ago. You've been away from anthropology, dance, and the university for quite a while. Since—"

"I married Clifford in '32."

"I remember. I was at the wedding."

"Yes, you were."

"I'm sure Maxi had a lot to do with your renewed interest in Accompong."

We circle the block again. The lights from the Abbott mansion glow in the night sky. It's still blasphemously hot. I roll down the window, hoping for a breeze, but I'm also killing time, making up my mind whether to tell Katherine the secret I'm keeping about why my trip to Accompong is about more than the Maroon people.

"Yes," I say. "Maxi was raised in the Cockpit and calls Accompong a living archive of African culture, religion, and traditions."

"And she told you about all the myths and folklore, too."

"From the rolling calves to duppies to the power of the silk cotton tree."

"You could even be an asset," Katherine says. "But what about Tully?"

I chuckle, hoping she's joking, even if it doesn't seem like it. "Yes, I might well be, but come on, you know, Tully is an excellent camera operator and skilled in using recording devices."

"You two seemed rather prickly toward each other at the party. And now he's not coming to this reception—is there something you want to tell me?"

"No. Nothing. His leg was bothering him, and he wanted to rest before tonight's train ride," I reply, touching her elbow. "I swear. You can count on us to behave."

"I trust you understand why I'm asking," Katherine states.

"I do."

"I'm not so sure you do. I want to create choreography that does more than regurgitate the history of dance from the viewpoint of Russian ballerinas or choreographers like Ruth Page or Martha Graham. Their works embody their cultures. But what about the American Negro? How do we represent our African roots? How can I choreograph without honoring our ancestors and our dances? I want my art to reflect who I am as a Negro woman. I want families of color to see their heritage on stage. I don't wish to be the dark-skinned girl only choreographing the dances that white women teach me."

The emotion in her voice reminds me of the thrill of watching her dance on stage.

Katherine continues, "I want to give Negro dancers on the concert stage an authentic vocabulary born of their own heritage. What if my choreography could give Negro audiences a chance to see their ancestors alive again in motion?"

I get what she's after. "Then you intend to go beyond mere observation."

"Exactly," Katherine replies with a smile. "I plan to immerse myself in the Maroon community, not only to document their dances, drum ceremonies, and songs, but also to become a part of the culture.

"I've even created my own notation system to detail the footwork and gestures of the dances, enabling me to capture what traditional ballet notation misses. Our field notes will connect each step and chant, revealing the spiritual heartbeat of Maroon life and linking it back to the silk cotton tree ceremony."

"The silk cotton tree." I can't hide my excitement at hearing those words. I learned about it from Maxi, who told me about the tree's power and the duppies, the ghosts of the dead, that inhabit it.

"So you know about the silk cotton tree?" Katherine smirks. "Maxi told you, right?"

I nod.

"That's good." Katherine shifts her posture. "But you swear you and Tully are okay? I apologize for pushing the point."

"It's okay if you're still peeved at me about Ballet Négre."

"Hard to forget. You missed my dance company's World's Fair performance." Her tone is light, but it holds an edge.

"You haven't forgiven me, have you?" I don't wait for her answer. "My not performing with Ballet Négre was Clifford's decision. He didn't want his bride traipsing on stage half-dressed in front of strangers."

"Aww. Husbands."

I can't protest the implication of just a few words. Instead, I turn the tables. "Speaking of husbands . . ."

"Don't you dare—" Katherine giggles.

"I can't help it," I respond. "And where's your husband? Is Jordis joining us tonight or heading off to Jamaica?"

"He's at the post office," Katherine replies. "So he won't be joining us tonight—or in Jamaica for that matter."

"Remind me again, why did you marry him?"

"As if you're unaware—he's one of the most handsome men alive. I felt compelled to marry him, even if I should have asked more questions. Marriage is challenging, especially when you're balancing film and choreography projects while forming Negro dance companies and ensembles." She takes a deep breath. "Sometimes, a woman's ambition clashes with her husband's idea of marriage."

My thoughts race. I don't have Katherine's drive. Ambition has nothing to do with my conflict with Tully. It's his fear and my guilt that stand between us. I look out the window, realizing I hadn't noticed the car had come to a stop. We're already in a line of limos, waiting to be dropped off in front of the entrance. The limo pulls up in front of the Abbotts' house.

"What if we agree not to discuss husbands tonight?" Katherine proposes. "We're here to celebrate."

"I completely agree."

The limo driver opens the door and I step out ahead of Katherine. The moment I do, we're swarmed by reporters and cameramen, but *us* feels incorrect. They are snapping photos of Katherine Dunham, but I'm not bitter. The limelight belongs to her, so I leave her to it and walk into the Abbotts' home alone, where the reception is already in full swing.

A grim-faced butler hands me a glass of champagne before I enter the grand ballroom. One hundred guests are packed into a shimmery, candlelit room where chandeliers add dazzle and sparkle. A wall-length buffet includes fancy hors d'oeuvres, champagne, and eye-catching decorations. Tall Egyptian vases and bouquets of colorful fresh flowers adorn the space while a quartet plays George Gershwin's "Summertime."

I am drawn to a rectangular alcove where the Abbotts have arranged an exhibition of various works of art.

The first piece I spot is a sculpture of a Negro woman by Augusta Savage, and then a bust named *Gamin* of a Black boy in a cap, also created by her. I adore her work and have seen these pieces displayed in several museums I've visited, but this exhibit feels more intimate, perhaps because it's in a home rather than a museum. There is also the photography of James Van Der Zee and the paintings of Archibald Motley, Palmer Hayden, and Hale Woodruff. I could spend the rest of the evening in this alcove.

Eventually, I turn a corner and come face-to-face with Ruth Page, the director of the Chicago Opera Company ballet, and Ludmila Speranzeva, the Russian ballet teacher who taught Dunham and, for a short while, me. The two dancers are courteous, offering me perfunctory kisses on the cheek and a brief hug. Ludmila Speranzeva's greeting feels as if it also includes a measuring tape.

"You are quite slender," the former prima ballerina remarks. "Are you practicing your barre routine at home? Not eating too much bread or cake, I trust."

How considerate of her to mention my weaknesses, from when I took daily classes from her before I married Clifford. Her words bring back the same insecurity and self-consciousness I felt then.

"Yes, I hardly eat cake or bread, and I practice every day, Mademoiselle." I use the French honorific that Ludmila insists upon from her students.

"I haven't seen you in class for a while," Miss Page remarks. "What have you been up to?"

"I returned to school and have been working on my thesis."

"That sounds impressive," says Mademoiselle Speranzeva.

"It just so happens that I'm traveling to Jamaica with Katherine." As soon as the words leave my lips, I wish I hadn't said them.

"Really?" Mademoiselle Speranzeva sounds dubious.

"Are you working for Katherine?" Ruth Page asks straightforwardly.

"Our expeditions are entirely independent. Katherine is studying African dance in Caribbean culture—"

"Yes, we know," Miss Page interrupts.

"Of course," I reply. "I will focus on the history of the Maroon people by recorded interviews of their oral storytellers."

The two women exchange glances, their eyebrows raised.

"How interesting," Miss Page says in an unconvincing tone. "When did you make this decision? Katherine hadn't mentioned you'd be joining her."

"My joining her expedition happened rather suddenly."

"It would have to be very recently," the Russian ballet teacher states.

The conversation follows the familiar pattern that always occurs when I'm around them. A rush of inadequacy washes over me, and I hate that I can't seem to shake this feeling.

I wave at an imaginary friend across the room. "Oh, excuse me. I'm being summoned." With a smile, I hurry off, hoping to avoid running into either of them again that evening.

The friend I mention seeing is actually Katherine. She is standing at the buffet table, holding a glass of champagne in each hand.

"Are you ready for this?" she asks, handing me a glass.

"How did you manage to escape the photographers so quickly?" I respond, impressed.

"How did you manage to run into Ruth and Mademoiselle?" Katherine shoots back.

"Oh, you saw that? It was no trouble. They were delightful." I gently pick up a shrimp-filled deviled egg from the tray on the buffet.

"The reporters aren't here for me," she adds nonchalantly. "Did you know Mary McLeod Bethune was here?"

"No, she's not. She's in New York City."

"Then it must be someone wealthy, like Edith Rockefeller McCormick."

"She died three years ago."

Katherine squints at me. "So, do you know the whereabouts of every famous woman in Chicago?"

"No, just those two. But if you don't recall, Mr. Abbott and his wife are hosting this reception primarily for the Count and Countess di Abbatino."

"I thought it was for Josephine Baker?"

"She got married? I didn't realize she was a countess now."

"Well, she's not, and ha-ha. You don't know everything. I don't think she's even married." Katherine raises her glass of champagne, toasting to several people as they pass. "What a wonderful reception! Don't you agree? Here's to our hostess, Mrs. Abbott!"

This behavior is unusual for Katherine—she is bold and attention-grabbing on stage but more reserved, much like me, at social gatherings.

"How many glasses of champagne have you had?" I ask.

"Since your birthday celebration?" Katherine counts on the fingers of her right hand. "More than two." She smiles.

"Do you need some coffee?"

"No, I'm fine. Just a bit lightheaded, and honestly, it feels fantastic. This evening will be less stressful if I'm a little tipsy." Katherine stops a waiter and sets her flute on the tray. He offers her another glass, but she declines. "No, thank you. My friend says I need coffee and something more substantial than rum cake in my stomach."

"I could use a sandwich. Though the shrimp-filled deviled eggs are delicious."

Katherine and I spend the next fifteen minutes filling our tummies, grabbing every hors d'oeuvre within reach. We might have stayed at the buffet all night and had a grand time if we hadn't been rudely interrupted by Katherine's husband, Jordis, who showed up uninvited and in a foul mood.

CHAPTER 8

OTHELLA

Robert S. Abbott's Mansion, Chicago

The Lincoln turns onto Grand Boulevard, just a block from Robert S. Abbott's mansion. I tap the driver on the shoulder—he's one of Tony's boys. I tell him to stop and let me out. "I'll walk from here."

"You sure, doll?"

"I'm sure," I reply quickly. What would people think if I stepped out of a Lincoln that looks more like a hearse than an automobile, with one of Schaefer's goons as my chauffeur?

I go to slam the door shut but hold back because my brain is working. After I steal the pocket watch, I'll need a ride back to the Savoy. I tap on the driver's window. "Pick me up on this corner in an hour."

"That's all the time you need?"

"That'll be plenty."

As I stroll toward the Abbott residence, it sinks in that I'm about to hobnob with some of the wealthiest Negroes in Chicago—shoot, in the world. I've conned plenty of fat cats, primarily men, both colored and white, but the thought of testing my skills in this grand old house thrills and rattles me at once. It's a big night.

A line of well-dressed people exits their Bentleys and Cadillac limousines, accompanied by properly uniformed chauffeurs. They parade up a wide walkway and vanish into the house. I blend in with a group toward the end of the line, and within minutes, I find myself in a spacious ballroom filled with people. I can smell the money and the jewels—necklaces, brooches, diamond rings, and silver lapel pins. They sparkle in the candlelight, gleaming as brightly as the chandeliers. My fingertips tingle with excitement. Perry and I could make a fortune at this party. But he's not here, and I need to stay focused, keep my fingers nimble, and find my mark quickly. Tonight, I'm a Single O.

An army of waiters glides gracefully through the room, carrying large silver trays filled with champagne and hors d'oeuvres. I hate champagne—just give me a gin and tonic or a Coca-Cola. Those tiny hors d'oeuvre sandwiches seem pointless. I prefer a hearty Italian beef, Chicago style.

I stop a waiter to grab a glass of champagne. Moving from group to group, I pretend to recognize this person or that. People at these parties rarely question an it's-been-so-long greeting from someone they don't know. That would be impolite.

After a few moments, I spot my mark, and he looks just like Tony described. He's in his sixties, with a mustache, a goatee, and salt-and-pepper hair, and is sporting those peculiar nose glasses.

I approach him as a young man in a tuxedo blocks my way.

"May I assist you, miss?"

"Excuse me?" I reply, slightly too forcefully, temporarily forgetting my façade as a delicate young socialite.

"I apologize for being so forward, miss, but you're quite lovely, and I've admired you since you arrived. You seem to know everyone, and I know just about everyone, so I thought

I'd introduce myself. I'm Robbie Barnes," he states in what I imagine is his usual long-winded manner, accompanied by a deeply dimpled smile.

"I'm a student at the University of Chicago, majoring in botany, specifically plant ecology and tropical botany."

What the hell is he talking about, and how can I get him to leave? I can't lose sight of Major Thomas. I mustn't miss my chance.

"It's a pleasure to meet you, Mr. Barnes," I say hastily. "I'm Othella Montgomery."

His expression brightens, as if I've just given him a piece of the sky by sharing my name. "Oh my, Miss Montgomery, it's such an honor to meet you. I'm delighted to make your acquaintance—please call me Robbie."

Why does he speak like that? Like some smarty-pants college student. Am I supposed to be impressed? "The pleasure is mine, Robbie," I mimic his tone. If he can talk that way, so can I. He then starts quizzing me about my favorite flowers and plants. My blank expression doesn't deter him, either. He continues chatting while I keep glancing over his shoulder to keep tabs on Major Thomas.

It dawns on me that he's not gonna leave me be. I need to think. There has to be a way to escape without causing a scene. I take a long look at him. He's not unattractive. He has decent height and a strong jawline. Despite his tendency to ramble, what else is there about him? He claims to know everyone and that everyone knows him.

"Robbie." I put a lilt in my voice. "Could you do me a favor?"

"I'm sorry, I've been talking too much."

"No, that's not it."

"Good," he replies softly. "What do you need?"

"That gentleman over there, next to the stone statue. He's the center of attention in his group. I'd really love an introduction."

"That statue is the work of Augusta Savage," Robbie says, as if I need to know that before he gets to the important part of my request.

"Augusta Savage, right. Got it. Now, how about that introduction?" I almost point but manage to lower my hand just in time. It would be too bold a gesture and wouldn't suit the girl I'm supposed to be. I touch his elbow. "You mentioned you knew everyone."

"Oh, oh, yes. I do."

"You did say that, didn't you?" I bat my eyelashes and glance up at him.

"Of course I know him." Robbie puffs out his chest. "That's Major Leonard Thomas. He heads the scholarship program that's putting me through college."

"I already know his name," I let slip, but I might as well keep going. "He owns the Bronzeville Federal Savings and Loan, the only colored-owned financial institution in Chicago since Mr. Binga's bank went belly up after the stock market crashed." I recite every word Tony said about him from memory. "But I've never met him."

"Then, of course, I'll introduce you."

Robbie holds my hand, keeping me close as he pushes through the group of men. He stops in the center of the circle.

"Major Thomas, it's a pleasure to see you here," he says.

My mark doesn't flinch at the interruption. Instead, he welcomes Robbie with open arms. "Mr. Barnes, how are you?" They shake hands vigorously. "And who's this young lady?"

"Sir, this is a young woman I'd like to introduce you to." Robbie grins. "Frankly, she insisted that I introduce you."

Major Thomas frowns. "Insisted? And why is it so critical for her to meet me?" His direct, slightly gruff manner might rattle some, but not me.

"Doesn't everyone want to meet you, sir?" His circle of associates, admirers, and friends—or whatever these men are to him—burst into laughter.

"She already knows who I am, Robbie," the major replies. "So why don't you pick up where you left off and tell me this young lady's name?"

"Yes, sir. This is Othella Montgomery, a friend who hopes to join me at the university." Robbie, the geek, has skillfully told a lie. I could almost hug him for catching me by surprise.

"Major Thomas, I'm thrilled to meet you."

He looks at me with skepticism. "Why did you want to meet me?" His bluntness is unexpected, but I can handle it.

"I'm very interested in the scholarship program your Building and Loan offers."

As he ponders a response, the major adjusts his suit jacket, tucking his thumbs into his waistcoat pockets. That's when I notice the diamond-encrusted pocket watch I'm supposed to steal is missing. Instead, he's wearing a Rolex Oyster wrist-watch. Although likely a decade old and worth taking, it's not why I'm here.

Where is the damn pocket watch?

My chest feels tight, my stomach is in knots, and my head aches as if it's being crushed between two doors. Did I really make this trip for biscuits?

While I suffer, Major Thomas talks about botany and asks me silly questions about my "area of study." I stammer out some of the nonsense Robbie mentioned about tropical plants and ecology. But nothing can soothe my growing panic.

I need that pocket watch.

A striking young woman steps into the group and approaches Major Thomas. Tall and slender, she resembles a reed, with cheekbones so sharp they could be carved with a scalpel. There is something else about her that leaves me slack-jawed. When I figure it out, I feel as if I've been trampled by a motorcar. It's her eyes: dark brown, deep-set, slightly sad, and eager to be elsewhere. They remind me of Perry.

I also love her dress, a stunning mint-green chiffon gown with a cloth rose corsage. I can't help but imagine how incredible I would look in that dress. Perry once said that when I wore that shade of green, I brought springtime into his life.

The woman apologizes for the interruption and leans in to whisper in Major Thomas's ear.

"I'm sorry, but my daughter, Vivian Jean, needs my help." Major Thomas and his daughter walk off side by side, and I thank God. Her interruption is a blessing. The watch I need to steal is dangling from Miss Vivian Jean's neck on a gold chain. I know the style and am familiar with the clasp. I also have a keen sense of the watch's weight. Stealing it will require skill—lifting a pocket watch hanging from a gold chain around a woman's neck is slightly trickier than taking it from a man's vest pocket—but doesn't Tony call me the queen of the fingersmiths?

Tonight, I'll just have to prove him right.

Using an excuse about needing to visit the powder room, I ditch Robbie Barnes, telling him to wait for me by the gazebo in the garden. I have no idea if there is a garden or a gazebo, but he is as happy as a clam at the prospect of a rendezvous with me. As he rushes off in one direction, I head toward the direction taken by Major Thomas and his daughter.

I stay behind them at a respectful distance, passing the Augusta Savage statue and the small stage with the quartet until they arrive at the buffet and greet another woman, pretty like her but different. This woman is as beautiful as Josephine Baker, with the same long neck, graceful arms, and a tilt of her head that reminds me of the chorus girls at the Dreamland Café or the Plantation Café—back before the stock market crash. My mother used to sneak me into those nightclubs when I was a little girl, when Prohibition, bootleggers, and jazz were the only currency that mattered to her.

Whatever Vivian Jean told her father involves this woman, who looks like a dancer.

They huddle together, I guess to comfort her, but she is not in tears. She's just angry. I don't even bother eavesdropping. I'm plotting my next move on the watch.

If handled correctly, I anticipate an easy grab and go. I just need to be patient and wait for the right moment and a distraction.

I move closer, unable not to overhear snippets of their conversation about husbands or boyfriends, boat rides, and the sea. The two women are planning to travel to New York later that night, but one of their boyfriends or husbands has unexpectedly shown up at the reception, and he isn't welcome. It's a lovers' spat. I smile, thinking it's refreshing to know that wealthy women have man trouble, too. The major reassures her not to worry. He'll take care of it.

That's my cue. I pivot as the major walks away, causing him to bump into me. He apologizes, just as I expected, but now I'm close enough to nudge his daughter's elbow. Vivian Jean spills her champagne away from her body and onto the other woman's dress. Apologies fall from her lips as she and the woman are drawn to the spilled champagne on the dancer's white satin gown. Major Thomas is long outta sight by now. And while the two women attend to the mishap's damage, my nimble fingers work their magic.

A few hectic minutes pass. "Don't worry," Vivian Jean finally assures the woman. "No damage has been done."

She smiles at me, and I smile back, patting her arm with one hand. With my other hand, I unfasten the necklace clasp, and within those brief seconds, the pocket watch on its gold chain is mine.

"Still, I'm sorry," I repeat, positioning myself within the group.

Vivian Jean introduces me to Katherine Dunham, the woman with her, who is a dancer (so I was right). She mentions a boat leaving New York for Kingston on Thursday, just two days away. I miss a chunk of the conversation, thinking about the pocket watch on its gold chain safely hidden in my brassiere. My ample breasts are the perfect hiding place for stolen goods. That's what I'm counting on.

The only thing left for me is to hightail it to one of the exits I scoped out. First, though, I scan the room for new marks. Feeling lucky, I might as well go for some easy sleight-of-hand jobs—wallets and money clips—just in case Tony shortchanges me.

I walk away from the two women without them noticing. I decide to make a move on a sparkly brooch worn by a girl far too young to appreciate it, but I don't get very far. I'm suddenly grabbed around the waist from behind. My first thought is, *oh no, it's that boy, Robbie Barnes.* But whoever has me is strong and hurting me. A sharp ache cuts across my midsection. This isn't Robbie Barnes, but I know who it is. Nobody smells like olive-oil-scented soap quite like Perry's brother, Jerry—nobody in Chicago.

Jerry spins me around so we're face-to-face but not eye to eye. He's a foot taller than I am. That doesn't mean I can't get away. I might if I start a brawl or at least a scuffle. Then when others notice, I'll run, which might jostle the pocket watch loose. The cops will show up and arrest me because Tony says they have me pegged for killing Perry. If that happens, it'll be Jerry, who runs off, free as a bird.

My imagination is quick, but that means I'll be better off talking my way out of this.

"Why are you here? I didn't kill him, Jerry. I hit him in the head, but he was alive when I left the apartment. Talk to Tony Schaefer—there was a witness. I betcha that witness killed Perry."

"Tony said you'd say that."

"You talked to Tony?"

"I had a chat with him," he replies.

"He didn't tell you where to find me, did he?"

"Naw. I saw you at the Savoy and followed you here." His fingers dig into my skin and I gasp.

"You're hurting me."

"Too bad. I bet that fucking gash you gave Perry hurt, too."

"Someone should wash your mouth out with soap." I need to stall, even if I'm just talking nonsense. I need time to come up with a plan on how to escape. "What's that greasy soap you like called? Palmolive? You should eat it, too. Might help with your bad breath."

"Is that supposed to hurt my feelings?" He pulls me close, and I wonder why no one notices what he's doing to me. Maybe it's because there's music, and we could be dancing.

"You don't have feelings. You're a thug. All you got is a nasty mouth and two fists. And no brains."

"Your tongue is gonna get my boot in your face. You'll be as good as dead with that pretty face ruined."

I'm scared. Truly afraid. Suddenly, I regret sending Robbie Barnes to the garden. He'd rush to my rescue. Or is that just what I want to believe? That someone, somewhere, cares enough to risk themselves to save me.

I try to yank away from Jerry, but suddenly his enormous fist comes at me, and all I can do is close my eyes.

"Excuse me, young lady, are you okay?"

Is someone here to help me? My eyes flutter open. Oh God. It's Vivian Jean and Katherine.

"Young man, what's happening here?" Katherine says loudly, attracting the attention of nearby guests.

"None of your business, lady," Jerry growls as he lowers his fist.

"How dare you talk to me like that?" Katherine responds defiantly.

Jerry shoves me aside, and I fall to one knee, hoping to attract the attention of bystanders while he bolts through the crowd toward the nearest exit. The last thing I need is for Jerry to be caught. He'll expose who I really am—and I can't have that.

Vivian Jean helps me stand. "Child, are you all right?" she asks again.

"Honestly, I don't know," I reply, speaking the truth for a change.

A crowd gathers around us, everyone staring and whispering. Vivian Jean wraps a protective arm around my shoulders. "Are you sure he didn't hurt you?" she asks.

"He was a pickpocket, ma'am, and he tried to take my brooch—" The lie slips smoothly from my lips. "Thank you for saving me."

I hug Vivian Jean, careful not to squeeze too tightly. I don't want to dislodge the item hidden in my brassiere.

CHAPTER 9

———◆———

ZINZI

Allan Coombs's Office, King Street, Kingston

The next day, after my shift at the Constant Spring Hotel, I make the forty-five-minute trip to Allan's office on King Street.

"Glad you could make it," he says. "Want a cup of coffee?"

"I would love one."

He's the only person I know who makes my coffee just the way I like it—with more cream than coffee and several generous teaspoons of sugar. Three years ago, when I met him, I was nervous and popping candies in my mouth, filling the room with the scent of peppermint. He asked me if I wanted a cup of coffee. We were discussing the labor movement, but without a second thought, even though the movement was the most significant thing I'd ever considered doing, I blurted out, "Never mind. I can make my own."

"You have quite the sweet tooth," he remarked. "Are you positive you want to go into battle against sugarcane?"

"There is little connection between the two," I said, then continued. "I might crave homemade tamarind balls, coconut drops, store-bought peppermint candy, and rock cakes, but what happens on sugarcane plantations is an atrocity. I will fight plantation owners even if I never have another drop of sugar." I shared all this while pouring a third spoonful of sugar into my cup.

Allan and I have gotten along quite well since that first day.

He hands me a cup of coffee and sits behind his desk, surrounded by a stack of papers, pamphlets, and a ledger that he opens, closes, and opens again. "Molasses is a by-product of sugar." He taps the ledger. "And the main ingredient in rum. I never thought about that connection until I moved to Jamaica."

Allan was born in London, but his military family moved to Kingston after the Great War. He traveled back and forth between the island and Britain until his father died in 1928. After that, he decided to try working on a sugar plantation, but he only lasted a few months. "When I worked at the Tynesdale Estate, Byron was out of the country, and even if he was home, there's a considerable distance between the plantation house, the sugarcane fields, and the processing plants. But you already know that."

Allan and I had discussed our individual sugar plantation stories early on in my involvement with the union activist. "Byron says he wants a labor union at Tynesdale Estate."

"His father, like all large plantation owners, is against unions."

"He says his father is very ill."

"I've heard that, too," Allan replies. He closes his ledger. "For the labor union to succeed, we need lawyers, government officials, and a few sugar plantation owners wouldn't hurt." Allan exhales. "We could use a Byron Tynesdale."

I shrug, but I'm unsure what to say.

"Did you know I met Byron at a boarding school in London?"

"You went to boarding school?" I say, surprised.

"No, my mother worked in the school kitchen and my father was a soldier," Allan explains. "Byron's mother was alive back then. She visited him often, but I never met his father. Despite our different backgrounds, we became mates of a sort. He occasionally wrote to me about his adventures. We were both back in Jamaica when his mother passed away, but after her death, our paths didn't cross—until recently."

"Is that when he asked about joining the movement?" I glance at the posters on the wall. "Can one person really make that much of a difference?"

"The right man might tip the scales once or twice," he says, sipping his coffee. "Besides the obvious, what else bothers you about him, Zinzi?"

My mind flashes to the recipe on his typewriter. "He wants more than just to bring the labor union to Tynesdale Estate."

"Like what?"

"I'm not sure. Perhaps he's seeking vengeance and his father is the target."

"Well, we need to find out, then, don't we?" Allan thumbs through a few pages of his ledger. "How about you invite him to join us for the Victoria Park rally?"

"That's an important rally. Are you sure?"

"If he doesn't work out, we can move on. No point in wasting time. We'll find another dissatisfied heir to a kingdom to join our cause," Allan says with a cryptic smile.

I sigh.

"Talk to him about the rally, okay? When will you see him again?"

I gulp down the rest of my cold, sugary coffee. "We're having dinner this evening."

Edna's Diner, Jubilee Square, Kingston

Edna's Diner is a small, family-owned spot near Jubilee Square and one of my favorite places to eat. Fishermen, sponge divers, factory workers, hotel employees, and market hawkers agree, and grub on a tin of good food, a cup of wine or rum, along with friendly service and conversation.

When Byron picked me up at the Constant Spring Hotel, I made it clear: We are dining at a place of my choice, not at one of his fancy tourist spots. "Plantation workers don't respect a man who looks and sounds more like a Londoner than a Jamaican. You'll have to prove that you know your way around sugarcane fields, not just inside a plantation owner's mansion."

Byron and I now sit on simple wooden benches at a long, narrow table, just a slab of wood placed over a stack of bricks. Henry, the diner's cook, stands at a flat iron surface heated by a blazing firepit below, grilling meats, fish, okra, and pots of rice, along with callaloo, a leafy green vegetable. Byron closely eyeballs the plate of food placed before him.

"Have you been away so long that Jamaican food feels unfamiliar?" I chuckle.

He takes a bite of jerk pork. "This is really good."

"It always is," I reply. "Don't you trust me?"

"I never doubted you."

"I doubt you. Considering your family's businesses, I have every reason to question your commitment to the labor union movement."

He doesn't flinch at my serious tone. "That's why I'm here," he says. "To change your mind."

"You think you can?"

"Just tell me what I have to do and I'll do it," he says, planting his elbows on the table too quickly, almost tipping it over.

"Careful. The table isn't made of concrete."

"Yeah, right."

"We should have some rum, what do you say?"

"All right." He exhales and tells the cook's helper, "Rum. Two glasses."

Two cups of rum appear on the table shortly after, served from a large clay jug.

While I sip my drink, I realize there's no better moment to pose another question to Byron. "What was that recipe you had on your typewriter at the hotel?"

He laughs. "I was trying to recall the family rum recipe."

"Do you remember it?"

"I've only seen it once, on my sixteenth birthday. Now, it's locked away in the vault in my father's office."

"You could steal it and sabotage your father's rum business," I reply sarcastically.

"Certainly, if my goal was to harm my father, taking the rum recipe would be the way to do it. But you're mistaken about the rum recipe. I'm not looking to destroy Tynesdale Estate or its operations—I genuinely want it to thrive under my leadership."

"You're saying all the right things, but it might not matter if sugarcane continues to lose ground to the United Fruit Company's banana empires in twenty years."

"You keep up with Jamaica's economy?"

"Why wouldn't I? Allan keeps us informed, and I read newspapers and listen to the radio," I say proudly. "Besides, there's much more to this island than what the upper class chooses to tell us."

He raises his glass. "Touché." His jaw tightens. "We've talked about me. Now tell me about you."

"Abrupt change of subject."

"Just expanding the conversation to include more about you, Zinzi."

"There's not much more to tell," I say soberly. "You heard some of my remarks if you were paying attention."

"I was," he replies. "But I'd still like to know more."

I shrug. "As I mentioned, there isn't much to tell. I grew up in Cockpit Country, Accompong, and briefly worked at your father's plantation before moving to Kingston a decade ago. In the city, I led a quiet life, making ends meet by working in harbour shops, cleaning floors, and taking out the trash. I also studied and improved my reading, writing, and math skills. For over five years, I have worked as a maid at Constant Spring Hotel." I exhale. "That's about all there is."

"How long ago did you join the movement?"

"Five years ago."

"And in those five years, you've become one of Allan Coombs's most trusted union organizers."

"He trusts all the people he invites to join him in this mission."

"He does?"

"Yes, he does."

"What about me? Have you given me a thumbs-up?"

"As a matter of fact, Allan would like you to join us at a rally we're holding tomorrow in Victoria Park. Will that work with your schedule? It will take the entire day."

His face lights up. "Yes, of course I'm available."

"I didn't do anything. It was Allan's decision. I'm only the messenger."

"Whatever you say. I'm excited to get started."

Byron's boyish enthusiasm is somewhat contagious, and I smile, but then I become serious. "We have a lot to prepare in advance. From writing and printing pamphlets and flyers to organizing volunteers, we expect a large crowd and potential trouble with the police. We must keep our enthusiastic supporters calm and focused. While we can't control the constables, we can do our best to keep the workers out of harm's way."

He raises his arms overhead, fists clenched like a victor in a sporting event. "Thank you, Zinzi."

"Once again, this is Allan's idea, not mine."

"Well, thank you, Allan."

We've finished our dinner, and I stand with my hands in my pockets, pulling out money to pay for our meal.

"Let me," Byron insists, as I suspected he would.

"Thank you, and oh, no suits tomorrow. Find a pair of overalls and a Panama hat to keep the sun from turning your pale skin scarlet. And wear comfortable shoes. We have a lot of pamphlets to hand out."

"Your wish is my command."

Allan Coombs's Office, King Street, Kingston

On rally day, there's always a lot to do, and we begin before dawn. Fortunately, Victoria Park, where the rally will take place, is only fifteen minutes from Allan's office. As I turn onto King Street, beneath the beam of the streetlamp, I see Byron waiting outside with a few other volunteers. I'm impressed—not only is he early but he also followed my suggestion to wear dungarees, a simple shirt, and a Panama hat—and the look suits him well. As I come closer, I see he is holding a Thermos and a grease-stained brown paper bag that smells fantastic. I left my apartment in the middle of the night without breakfast, and with such a long day ahead, my stomach is growling. I hope he brought enough for me.

"Good morning, everyone," I greet the four volunteers with Byron and introduce him without mentioning his last name. I don't want to spend half my morning explaining how—and why—a man named Tynesdale is joining us on rally day. Their frown lines are already deep because he looks like a white man.

I unlock the office door. As the group enters, I direct them to their various workstations, reminding them of their tasks—from coordinating speechmakers to mobilizing workers and distributing materials. Given the remaining jobs, more volunteers will arrive as the morning goes on, but my mission for the morning is to train Byron.

He is the last to enter the main room. "I brought you breakfast," he says. "Cooked ackee, fruit, saltfish, and bammy."

That's exactly what I thought I smelled. I take the bag from his hand. "Follow me. We'll be working in here," I say. "This is the pressroom." I open a heavy door, keeping a close eye on Byron's reaction. When I see his eyes widen and the shock on his face, I feel a sense of satisfaction.

The pressroom is enormous, stretching nearly a full block, and the front door of the office on King Street offers no hint of its true size. Rows of long tables, three letterpress machines, and rolls of paper on racks line the far wall. "This is where we print the pamphlets, and we arrange them on these tables so volunteers can quickly refill their carriers," I explain.

I direct Byron to the pile of newsboy bags with wide shoulder straps and deep gussets. These bags are ideal for carrying pamphlets, newspapers, and other materials required for a rally or demonstration. "I brought my knapsack," he says.

"That's mainly for storing your items," I respond. "Are you familiar with using a letterpress machine?"

He grimaces. "Sorry, I'm not. But I'm eager to learn."

"No need," I smile, pleased with his answer. "I was just curious. We have people who are skilled with the letterpress. It won't be part of your assignment for today, which I wanted to discuss with you in private."

"Oh, okay," he replies slowly.

"Have a seat." I walk over to one of the tables, sit in a folding chair, and open the bag I took from Byron.

He sits, and as he settles in, I enjoy a forkful of ackee and saltfish and a few bites of bammy. It isn't as tasty as my mother's, particularly the dumplings, but I shouldn't criticize a free plate of food.

"You're hungry." He smiles.

"Yeah, I forgot to grab something to eat," I grunt, then realize I had forgotten my manners. "Thank you. I appreciate the food."

"You're welcome."

I swallow another mouthful and wipe my fingers on the paper bag. "This rally focuses on the issues affecting agricultural workers—right up your alley, Byron, because it includes workers from sugar and banana plantations. It's another reason we're heading to Victoria Park. Easy access for workers, and late August is the perfect time to spread the word.

"Our rally will begin with speeches from the main stage, and we expect a large crowd—a huge crowd. But this isn't a nightclub in New York City with microphones. We do what we refer to as call-and-response. People farthest from the stage and in the middle of the crowd won't hear what's being said without it."

Byron nods. "That makes sense."

"We don't want the crowd to stampede the stage out of frustration. Volunteers will hand out pamphlets, but not everyone will read them. So, you have a strong voice and good lungs, right?"

"I do." He puffs out his chest playfully.

"Seriously, we can't afford any mishaps. There has been an increase in arrests throughout the Caribbean—riots at a sugar estate in Trinidad and a sugar strike in Saint Kitts this January. Protests broke out in May along Jamaica's northern coast. Some describe the riots in Oracabessa among banana workers as a show of unity within the labor union. People have been hurt. People have died. We don't want a riot here. No injuries or fatalities. That's why your other role, besides call-and-response, is to keep an eye out for troublemakers."

Byron looks puzzled. "Who am I keeping safe from whom?"

"Both sides. The call-and-response volunteers are positioned to spot and prevent trouble, whether it comes from the police or demonstrators. And as I'm sure you know, plantation owners hire professional troublemakers to attend our rallies to stir up chaos. With how you look, you might be able to keep the coppers in line."

Byron doesn't seem especially pleased with my words. Nonetheless, he says, "I agree."

"One more thing," I begin. "Is there any chance someone might recognize you today? Owners and plantation managers sometimes attend these rallies."

"I imagine there might be, but I thought that was part of my job, to be noticed."

"Yeah, but I just wanted to be sure you knew that your name could end up on a list, and your participation could get back to your father."

"If that were a problem for me, I wouldn't be here." Byron reaches across the table and grabs a piece of bammy I haven't touched yet.

"Okay, then." I eat another forkful of food, chew, and swallow. "We have some pamphlets to distribute and a stage to set up. We're working in teams, and you'll be with me today."

CHAPTER 10

———◆◆◆———

VIVIAN JEAN

Robert S. Abbott's Mansion, Grand Boulevard, Chicago

A man in the crowd takes command. "What happened here? Are you women injured?" He addresses his questions to me, as if I were the one who was assaulted.

"This is the young girl who was attacked," I clarify. "The man fled in that direction." I gesture toward an exit.

"What did he look like? Have you seen him before?"

"Can you give us a moment to catch our breath?" I reply sharply. The girl is trembling like a leaf in a storm, and I'm not far behind. But I need to be of help. "He was big, broad, and tall." It's a feeble description, but the best I can offer. "He looked like a bull in a tuxedo."

I turn to the girl and ask, "What's your name, dear?"

"Othella. Othella Montgomery."

"Were you named after Shakespeare's tragedy?" Katherine asks.

"Yes," the girl replies shakily.

"Of course you were. I imagine you've been asked that same question a thousand times. I'm sorry," Katherine says nervously. She might be almost as traumatized as I am.

"Are you sure you're not hurt?" I check Othella's arms for bruises but don't find any. "I'm sorry I took so long to speak up." I squeeze her hand. "I shouldn't have waited."

"N-not your fault, ma'am," the girl stammers, her head down, her lips trembling.

It's no surprise she seems self-conscious and shaky. Too many curious onlookers surround us. We need room to breathe. I turn to the man in charge and say, "Othella mentioned he was a pickpocket, a thief, and he tried to steal—"

"My brooch," the girl cuts in. "He attempted to steal my aunt's brooch."

The room buzzes with tension. Those nearby check their purses, wallets, and money clips. Questions arise from different voices, and the crowd's anxiety washes over me like a wave.

I want to be somewhere else, anywhere but here.

"Let's get out of this chaos. We need some fresh air." Katherine's words are my lifeline.

"Let's go outside," she insists, leading the way. I still hold Othella's hand as I follow her toward the Abbotts' garden.

Tall gas lamps atop wrought-iron balusters illuminate a stone path near a surprising patch of night-blooming jasmine. We stroll by hollyhocks, foxgloves, delphiniums, carnations, and columbines until we arrive at a three-tiered bronze fountain with a swan base spraying a cool mist.

Katherine directs us to a nearby iron bench. "Is there anyone we should call for you, Othella? Your parents?"

"I'm an orphan, ma'am," Othella responds sweetly.

"I'm sorry," Katherine and I say in unison.

"I live with Reverend Nathan and his wife at the AMC Fellowship Church on State Street."

"I haven't heard of that church," I say.

"There are a thousand churches on State Street in Chicago, and you've only heard of the one you attend every other Sunday."

"Yes, Katherine." I smile. "That is true."

"The 24th Street church is run by Reverend Nathan and his wife, Miss Lucille," Othella explains. "They manage an orphanage in the church basement. I have lived there since I was ten, when my momma passed away. She was a wonderful mother. Her name was Ella. Born in Jamaica, she came to this country in 1915. She always talked about returning to the island one day and bringing me to meet my relatives."

"That's the same year Maxi, my maid, arrived in Chicago," I tell Othella.

"Maybe, they knew each other." Othella smiles.

"I doubt it. Maxi doesn't know anyone outside of my family and our friends. At least I've never met them."

"Did you know that Vivian Jean and I are heading to Jamaica tomorrow?" Katherine says.

"Oh, ma'am. Can I come with you? I have excellent penmanship, keep excellent records, and I can cook, too," she adds breathlessly.

"That sounds delightful, but our trip to Kingston is already booked," Katherine responds.

Out of nowhere, a young man approaches, calling Othella's name. "My goodness. Where have you been?" He kneels in front of her. "I heard about a girl being attacked and prayed it wasn't you. But it was you. Are you okay? You look okay, but my God, how awful."

It takes him a moment to notice Katherine and me.

"I didn't mean to interrupt, ladies. Mrs. Hartfield, Mrs. Dunham, my name is Robbie Barnes. I'm an undergraduate student at the University of Chicago, working to become an anthropologist, like you. My particular interest is ecology and tropical plants."

"I take it this young man is a friend of yours?" Katherine asks.

"He introduced me to Mrs. Hartfield's father."

"Oh, right, my father," I respond. "So, you're both acquainted with Major Thomas?"

Robbie chimes in. "He offered me a scholarship to the University of Chicago through the Bronzeville Federal Savings and Loan. Othella just met him, and she's interested in a scholarship, too."

"In that case, we should find my father—maybe I can help get your application in front of him and his committee."

"Oh, ma'am. Thank you, but that's okay. I don't want to impose."

"It's the least I can do."

"Honestly, it's fine."

"Well, while you two debate Vivian Jean's offer—" Katherine stands up from the bench. "Let's head back to the party. I want to enjoy more of the reception before we have to leave. We don't want to miss our train."

As we head back into the ballroom, I take a moment to speak with Katherine. "Are you okay?" Her estranged husband, Jordis, had stomped into the party, trying to cause a scene. Katherine managed to remain mostly unaffected by his blustering, but I couldn't shake my concern for her. She's a determined woman who often forges ahead without seeking help, even when she deserves it. I truly admire her independence, but sometimes accepting a helping hand is wise, even for a woman like Katherine, who believes herself capable of tackling any challenge on her own.

"I'm okay, Vivian Jean. Your father loved playing the hero, and after the day you both had, I'm pleased to have given him that chance."

I smile. "Cut the sarcasm."

"Is it sarcasm? Your father was like a knight in shining armor who came to my rescue."

"I don't understand why you sought him out—truthfully, we could have managed Jordis ourselves. He was tipsy."

"We're practically in ball gowns. Why must we deal with such unruly behavior ourselves?"

Katherine surrenders with a raise of her hand. "If you say so."

In the ballroom, it takes a second for my eyes to adjust to the candlelight and electric chandeliers after the soft glow of gas lamps. I carefully place one foot in front of the other when suddenly, Katherine grabs my arm and points shakily at my chest.

"What are you doing?"

"Vivian Jean!" she exclaims, horror in her eyes, "Where's your necklace, the pocket watch, your father's gift?"

I reach up, expecting to grasp the gold chain and, if not that, the pocket watch itself, but there's nothing to hold on to. "Oh my God! I've lost it—it's gone!"

"Where were you when you last had it, Vivian Jean?" Katherine asks.

"Here. I've had it since we've been here." I stare at her blankly, frozen, unable to think or move. I glance around Mr. Abbott's grand ballroom and groan. "It could be anywhere. How could I lose it? I'm such a careless fool."

"Is this what you're looking for?" a voice interjects.

I shriek. It's Othella, and she's holding my pocket watch.

"I started searching for it as soon as Miss Katherine said it was missing. It was on the floor by the buffet table over there." Othella glances at Katherine and Robbie, who stand with their mouths open in surprise. "I bet the man who tried to steal my brooch took it from you and probably dropped it when he ran. I warned you he was a pickpocket."

"My goodness, Othella, you're a lifesaver." I embrace her.

"I'm just relieved I found it," Othella replies.

"I'm glad that thief wasted his trip to Hyde Park tonight," Robbie enthusiastically adds.

"I'm just happy to have the pocket watch back." I put my

arm around Othella for another hug of gratitude. "Let's celebrate Othella's discovery with champagne, everyone."

"Sounds lovely," Katherine agrees.

"Can I join, too?" asks Robbie eagerly.

"Of course," I reply.

Othella leans on my shoulder and says, "I love champagne."

We share a glass of champagne and a few hors d'oeuvres before Katherine and I exchange a meaningful glance. "It's time for us to leave," I say.

"But not before one final toast." Katherine raises her glass. "I apologize for cutting the celebration short, but we have a train to catch."

I notice the sadness in Othella's eyes. "Othella, may I give you a ride home?" I ask.

She shakes her head firmly.

"If you're staying, can I rely on Robbie to get you home safely?"

Mr. Barnes steps up confidently, grinning. "It would be my pleasure to act as Miss Montgomery's escort tonight," he responds.

Othella's eyes reflect disappointment.

I had thought she liked him. Youth is a paradox. Often full of joy and life, their feelings move like the wind and just as quickly fall into despair with as little prompting as a finger prick. I tell Othella, "Swear you'll keep in touch." I pull out my purse and give her my calling card.

"This is the phone number for Hartfield House. While I'm in Jamaica, you call this number and ask for my maid, Maxi, if you need anything. Call. Okay. We'll be gone for at least a month or two," I continue. "But Maxi will be here and knows how to reach me."

Othella replies, "Okay."

"I mean it, dear. Promise me you will keep in touch."

"I promise," she responds. "I will."

Katherine and I make our way to the Abbotts' to thank them for a fantastic evening. We even spend a few moments with Josephine Baker and her husband, the Count.

It takes a few more minutes than planned, but eventually, Katherine and I find ourselves in the foyer, waiting for my driver to pull up.

"Can I give you a lift home, Vivi?"

I turn to the sound of my father's voice.

"I'd like to spend a few minutes with my daughter before she leaves for Jamaica," he says.

I hug Katherine, promise to be at the train station on time, and take my father's arm.

Grand Boulevard, Bronzeville, Chicago

Sitting beside Major Thomas in the limo, I stare straight ahead with my heart racing. "I was looking for you earlier this evening," I say, "I wanted to talk about what happened before."

I'll begin with a quiet apology, but that takes confidence, so I just blurt out, "I should have told you sooner about the trust fund."

Major Thomas looks at me sideways. "Yes, Vivian Jean, you should have. I'm disappointed you chose to keep it from me." He pats my knee. "But it's all water under the bridge."

The use of inappropriate idioms must run in the family. It's the same phrase that upset Tully when I said it, distasteful because of Clifford's death. But the major lacks that level of insight or sensitivity.

He's gone back to watching the scenery, content in the silence between us. But I'm in a confessional frame of mind.

"Father, there is something else."

He turns slowly, smiling warmly. "Yes, go on."

"There was a pickpocket at the party, and they took my pocket watch, but it was found by a young girl named Othella Montgomery." I pull the pocket watch from my clutch bag. "It might've been lost if not for her."

"I met Miss Montgomery, but it must've been before the incident. But I didn't hear any grumbling about a thief," he says, extending his hand. "Give it to me. I'll have a new gold chain made. Next time you wear it, steer clear of con artists and pickpockets."

Given his reaction to my apology about the trust fund and now this, I'm surprised. "You're very understanding, Father."

"Don't worry, sweetheart. You have bigger fish to fry with this rushed trip to Jamaica."

"When Tully and I return, we'll all have dinner together, even Mother. Maybe we can arrange a family vacation."

"Speaking of which . . ." He stuffs the watch into his vest pocket and takes my hand. "I made a few phone calls this afternoon and hired one of the Bronzeville Federal Savings and Loan scholarship students to join your expedition as your assistant. There's another young lady I met at the Abbotts' who my student wants to bring along. She'll be helpful, too. I believe you met them both, Robbie Barnes and Othella Montgomery."

I crank down the passenger door window. A blast of hot air strikes me in the face. "Mr. Barnes and Othella Montgomery," I whisper their names.

"I trust you and Tully," he begins, "but this way, you'll have help that won't cost you anything. I've covered their expenses."

Unbelievable. My father has hired two kids to spy on me. They will send daily telegrams detailing my every action, word, deed, and failure. How dare he? I am thirty years old. I don't need his kind of help. I can't have them reporting back to him what I'm really going to Jamaica to do. I swallow and say, "Thank you, Father."

"Now, don't be too enthusiastic until you hear the rest of the surprise." He smirks, sarcasm oozing from his lips. "I can't spend the next month worrying about my only child living in Cockpit Country. So, I plan on paying you a visit."

"What?" I must have misunderstood him. "Plan to visit me where?"

"In Jamaica, naturally."

I can't breathe.

PART TWO

———— ◆ ————

THE BOAT, THE TRAIN, AND THE BEAST: SEPTEMBER 1935

CHAPTER 11

———◆———

OTHELLA

The Savoy Ballroom, Chicago

As Robbie and I prepare to leave the Abbotts' house for the LaSalle Street Train Station, I think about the past few hours and how much has changed. Many lies have been told and doubt still lingers inside me, but I learned a few things.

When Tony told me about Perry, and how I was suspected of killing him, I couldn't just take his word for it. Now, could I? Too many voices in my head kept telling me one thing: Perry spoke to me before I left the apartment. He was alive. But what if he wasn't? I had to be sure. So, while I was still at the Savoy, I made a call. After changing my clothes, I slipped into an empty back room with a telephone and dialed the Deering Street Police Station.

A smart move for a gal in my profession is to make friends with members of the Chicago Police Department. The telephone conversation went like this:

"Officer Bowers, here."

"Richie, do you know who's calling you? You recognize my voice?"

"Yeah, I do, and you shouldn't be calling me unless it's to give yourself up."

My stomach dropped. "So, it's true? The cops are looking for me?"

"You betcha. You killed your old man. Most of the cops in the 4th Ward are after you."

"I didn't kill nobody. We had one of those fights we always have. Nothing serious. A few punches were thrown, and I hit him with an ashtray to keep him off me." My throat felt like dust. "Is he really dead?"

"As a doorknob." Someone shouted at Richie to hurry up. "I gotta go." Then he spoke so quietly I could barely hear him. "My advice to you, girl, is to get lost—and stay lost."

"Sure, I'll do that. Thanks for the advice. Just one thing. Why did the police decide it was me so fast? They ain't lookin' for nobody else?"

"A witness ratted you out, kid." There was more shouting in the background, but Richie, thank the Lord, didn't hang up. "They heard the fight, saw you run out of the apartment like the devil was chasing you, and then they went inside and found Perry dead on the floor."

"We got nosy neighbors, but none that nosy. Who's this witness?"

"I ain't telling you that. I'm being nice to you 'cause up till now, you ain't done nothing but steal shit. The most harm you ever caused was breaking a few men's hearts and wallets—but murder is different, Othella."

"I swear he was alive when I left. Or at least I thought he was."

But the line was dead. Richie had hung up, and I wasn't talking to nobody but myself.

The shock I felt in that moment is probably why I forgot about my suitcase until now.

Major Thomas offered to pay my way to Jamaica as an assistant to Robbie Barnes. What else could I say but yes? Robbie explained that we'd help Katherine Dunham and the major's daughter with some anthropological fieldwork. Whatever that was.

But who am I to care, as long as it gets me outta Chicago? And on a midnight train to boot?

Just one more thing to do: get the suitcase I left at the Savoy Ballroom. I tell Robbie Barnes he'll have to pick up my suitcase but I can't go in with him to the Savoy. He looks at me kinda funny. "I know it's an odd request," I say, eyelids fluttering. And that's enough for him to agree to do it. In fact, he's so excited about our mutual travel plans that he'd agree to most anything I ask. He surprises me, though, and handles the task without a hitch. Perhaps, I'm judging him too quick. Who would've thought someone like Robbie Barnes could be slick?

Robbie and I arrive at LaSalle Street Station with time to spare.

It is enormous. Thousands of people crowd the main waiting room, with its high ceilings and long black benches, which remind me of the AME Fellowship Church, a thought I don't welcome. It's almost as hot as the church, too. Even at almost midnight, Chicago can't escape the sweltering heat.

Once inside, I head to the Negro women's restroom to change out of my fancy gown and into my traveling outfit. First off, I tie my hair back in a ponytail. Then I put on a navy-blue jumper with large rose buttons, a rose-colored blouse, a matching belt, and Oxford shoes. Because I never know what role I might play, I pack as much as possible.

When I return to the main waiting room, I follow Robbie's instructions. Clutching my ticket, I present it to the ticket agent before entering the concourse lobby. From there, I make my way to the last row of pews closest to LaSalle Street.

Robbie is waiting. "Our train departs from Track 10."

"This is a fancy train, isn't it?"

"Red carpet service all the way, but we have regular tickets, not the expensive ones."

He leads me to the boarding area, where we find two seats on a bench near the back of the crowded room. "You look different, like a schoolgirl," he says shyly.

"Should I take that as a compliment?" I raise an eyebrow. "And look at you with your brown slacks, white shirt, no tie, cloth jacket, and newsboy cap. I'd say we both look like schoolchildren."

"I look my age," Robbie replies seriously. "I'm nineteen. How old are you?"

"Nineteen, too."

"When I first saw you, I thought you were older."

"Now, is that a nice thing to say to a girl?"

He looks stricken, and I laugh. "Just more mature. Not old."

Before I can jab him some more, a sound like a siren wails through the room, and I nearly jump out of my skin.

"The train is boarding," Robbie says. "We've got to go."

We grab our luggage and head onto the platform with a bunch of other Negroes. Moments later, we are seated next to each other on a hard bench in the last car of the train, the colored car.

It's smoky, noisy, and filled with the smell of food: fresh biscuits, stew, chicken, rice, and pies. I even catch a whiff of booze.

"How long is the trip to New York?" I ask Robbie.

"This is the fastest train around. It takes only seventeen hours, not counting delays. That's three hours faster than it was last year."

I shrug, not caring so much about how fast it goes, as long as it hurries up and pulls outta the station.

My heart swells with joy as the train departs at midnight—right on time. Relief washes over me like fresh rain. I am safe. I am leaving Chicago. And no one will know where to find me.

Not Tony Schaefer, not Jerry Merriweather, and not the

cops. My whole body relaxes as if I've just sunk into a warm bath filled with rose water and jasmine.

A lady sitting across from Robbie and me opens a grease-stained paper bag and pulls out a tin that smells like chicken, rice, fried onions, and cornbread.

"Did you bring anything for us to eat?"

Robbie looks at me with a distressed expression. "Sorry, I didn't bring anything except my luggage and a few supplies in my knapsack. Major Thomas arranged to transport the crate of supplies we'll need and—"

Raising my hand, I stop him. "Just say, *I didn't bring any food.*" I groan. "Are there dining cars on this train? I heard the 20th Century Limited served some good food in the dining cars."

"It's pretty pricey," Robbie grimly explains. "Major Thomas didn't give me much pocket change. We'll have to wait and eat in New York."

"I'll starve to death by then." Agitated, I study my surroundings. I might be able to scrounge up enough money using my queen-of-the-fingersmiths skills to buy some food. But I shouldn't even be thinking about stealing. What about my fresh start? I tap Robbie on the knee. "I thought Mrs. Hartfield and Miss Katherine would be on this train with us. If they're on board, they might treat us to dinner."

"I saw them when I went to find a redcap. They have a berth in a sleeping car, but we won't be able to see them until we arrive at Grand Central Station."

My disappointment knows no bounds. "Well, that's just peachy."

"You didn't expect them to be back here with us, did you?" he says.

"I didn't know what to expect. You're the one who's probably made this trip a dozen times."

"I'm not as much of a man of the world as you might think."

"Then this trip will be an adventure for both of us," I try not to sound as unhappy or hungry as I feel.

Without a promise of nourishment, I accept my fate: sleeping while hungry. After a while, the train's rocking numbs my empty stomach and I feel drowsy. I tuck my legs beneath me until I'm comfortable, fold my arms across my chest, and rest my head on Robbie's shoulder. The next thing I know, the train is jerking to a stop, and I wake up with my head in Robbie's lap. I sit up straight, rubbing the sleep from my eyes. "Where are we? What time is it?"

"About five o'clock, but we haven't gotten too far. We're picking up passengers in Toledo, Ohio." He pulls back the curtains and looks out the window.

"Sorry for falling asleep on you," I say.

"I didn't mind." He removes his cap and squeezes it in his hands. "I have a confession to make. I hope you can forgive me, but tonight wasn't the first time I've seen you."

I start to sift through my collection of lies. "Oh, really? Where was that?"

"Dancing at the Savoy Ballroom."

This could mean nothing or everything, depending on whether I was out on a night on the town or working. "I love to dance. I used to go to the Savoy a lot. Do you dance? Do you like jazz? With your education, background, and upbringing, a young man like you would have been a regular at the Savoy."

He swallows nervously. "I also saw you at that black-and-tan on 55th and State, the Club DeLisa."

"Oh, yeah. I went there a few times." Now that's different. The DeLisa brothers owned that spot. They also ran the gambling hall in the basement. If Robbie had seen me there, he would know more about me than was safe. "You decided to keep that a secret, huh?" I moisten my lips. "You didn't tell Major Thomas or his daughter, Miss Vivian Jean, or Katherine Dunham, did you?"

Robbie looks alarmed. "Oh no, I would never do that."

"I'm not sure I can trust you. I'd feel better if you shared a secret about yourself. That way, we'd be even."

"I don't have any secrets."

"Oh, yes, you do," I insist. "You stayed quiet about seeing me at the Club DeLisa, which means you were inside the Club DeLisa, and in the basement, 'cause downstairs was the only place I hung out." Sweetly wrinkling my nose, I continue, "And if you don't tell me the truth, I might have to confess to Major Thomas that you're making him foot the bill for a woman who is nothing more than a floozy." I fold my arms over my chest. "I bet he wouldn't like that at all."

"You'd be surprised."

"What? I don't believe I heard you correctly."

"You promise to keep a secret?"

"So you do have secrets?" I smile and quickly cross my heart. "Sure, I promise. Come on, Robbie. Spill it."

"I ran numbers out of the Club DeLisa for a spell. That's why I was inside that basement gambling hall pretty regularly. You know they had a policy gambling wheel, too."

"Now we're cooking," I say gleefully. "Yeah, I know that wheel. I never ran numbers. I knew a few big-time operators but made better money doing other things. You aren't the straw man I thought you were. Who'd you work for?"

"I can't tell you who I worked for unless we make a pact."

I gaze at him suspiciously. "What kind of pact?"

Robbie makes a fist, holding it too close to my face, but raises only his pinky finger. "From now on, we'll keep each other's secrets. No matter what. Pinky swear."

I look at him and then at his finger and wonder what in the hell he is goin' on about. "I don't understand what you mean."

"Pinky swear—it's the best kind of swear. It means that whoever breaks the promise must swallow a thousand needles. So we have to trust each other completely, never share our secrets with anyone else, and never lie to each other. It also means we're best friends."

"What?" I am so confused. "Are you making this whole thing up?"

"No, ma'am."

I stare him in the eye, searching for a dent in his armor. But I need him to keep his mouth shut about the Club DeLisa and me. Neither can I allow him to mention his trip to the Savoy Ballroom for my suitcase. So, I guess I'm doing this thing with him. He interlocks his little finger with mine.

"Okay," I say slowly. "Pinky swear—we're friends. It's official."

Robbie's grin is enormous. "Best friends who keep each other's secrets and never lie to each other."

"Yeah, yeah. Now tell me, who'd you run numbers for?"

He chuckles. "A few years back, right after the stock market crashed, a group of colored businessmen from Bronzeville started a small enterprise to raise capital—that's how they put it, and, well—"

"Stop stonewalling me. Who was it?"

"Major Thomas was one of the businessmen but was also in the rum-running business back in the day."

"Wow. That might explain why Tony Schaefer wants to teach him a lesson." The puzzle pieces are coming together. "How old were you?"

"Ten or eleven years old, but I saw you there a couple of years ago." Robbie puts his cap on his head. "Who's Tony Schaefer? And what lesson?"

Damn. Why did I let that slip outta my mouth? "Just a guy I used to know with some history with Major Thomas."

Grand Central Station, New York City

The attendant calls out, "Final stop, Grand Central Station, New York City."

Robbie and I cry in unison, "Thank God."

All night long, the bumpy train ride fluctuated between annoying cold and scorching heat without rhyme or reason. But now, all is forgotten and forgiven. We are in New York City.

Exiting the train is chaotic. Crowds surge, nearly knocking me over as I lug my heavy tweed suitcase and clutch my purse under my arm. I glance sympathetically at Robbie, who is far more burdened than I am. I can't fathom how he manages to stay upright with everything he's carrying. Bags are strapped to his back, stacked on his head, wedged under his arms, and clutched in each hand—every part of his body where something can be held or balanced is in use.

"Where did all this stuff come from?" I ask. "I don't recall you bringing that much aboard."

"I had a redcap help me bring them on board in Chicago, but there aren't any around here. They must all be helping the first-class passengers."

"Where are we meeting the Hartfields and Katherine Dunham?" I am distracted by his balancing act. "Hand me some of that stuff. I want to get to our meeting place now."

"All right, all right," Robbie replies.

Pushing through the train station with our luggage, knapsack, and other belongings, we finally arrive at the baggage claim after what feels like forever.

"We're supposed to meet them here," Robbie states.

"Well, I don't see them. You should search around and find them. I'll stay here and guard our things," I suggest.

Robbie comes back a few minutes later. "I can't find them anywhere."

"Are you serious? Were any of them even on this train?" Robbie doesn't respond. A redcap taps him on the shoulder and gives him an envelope. He tears it open, reads it, glances at me, and winces. It's bad news.

"What does that note say?" I let go of the suitcase handle

and let the knapsack slide off my shoulder. "Tell me what it says."

He clenches his jaw. "We missed them. They've already taken a yellow cab to Harlem. We'll meet them at the YMCA."

Without uttering a word, I lift the straps of the knapsack onto my shoulders, pick up my suitcase, tuck my purse under my arm, and take hold of another bag with my free hand. "We better get going if I'm ever gonna see Vivian Jean Hartfield and Katherine Dunham before we board the ship tomorrow," I say. "Where can we catch a cab?"

With a grimace, Robbie finishes loading the other bags. "We don't."

"So, we aren't taking a cab?" I shake my head.

"We're taking the subway."

"I've never been on a subway."

"Follow me. It'll be fun."

CHAPTER 12

ZINZI

Victoria Park, Labor Movement Rally, Kingston

The sun blinds me. I lift my hand to shield my eyes but can't see what's happening. I can only hear the shouting, the crack of police batons striking flesh and breaking bones, and the cries of agony and pain. I must get to my feet. Crouching on the ground like a frightened child isn't the woman I believe myself to be, and this isn't my first rally to go poorly. Though this one went haywire fast.

I rise unsteadily. Victoria Park is in chaos. People are crawling, running, and stumbling into one another. The metallic scent of blood fills the air, and my right leg throbs with pain. But I can't bring myself to look at it. I'm too scared.

"Help me," a voice calls out. I glance at a girl lying on the ground with blood on her face, clutching her stomach. I drop to my knees beside her. "Can you sit up? You can't stay here. You'll get stepped on if you don't get up."

The girl's gaze darts wildly between horror and fear. She's panicking and holding her breath. "You're going to pass out." I felt this way once before, when Byron and I escaped the meeting a few days ago.

Byron.

I have no idea where he is, but I can't worry about him right now.

I help the girl to her feet. "Follow me." She doesn't respond. She can't seem to focus. "Look at me!" Finally, I have her attention. "We can't stay here," I say. "We'll be trampled."

I wrap my fingers around her wrist, a slender, bony joint. Limping on my injured leg, I lead her to the back of the riser, a barrier that separates us from the crowd.

"I need you to stay here until things calm down," I tell the girl. "I have to go find someone—"

She grabs my hand. "No, no, stay, stay."

"I promise I won't leave you." I scan the park, searching for a way to escape.

People are scattering in every direction. Constables are chasing them, and union busters are attacking workers at random. Venturing into the heart of the mayhem isn't safe, but I can't abandon the girl. We'll just have to wait until things settle down.

On my tiptoes, I peek above the risers and search for Allan—and Byron. But it's futile—too many people are darting in and out of the park. A sharp pain shoots through my leg, as if someone is hammering nails into my calf. There's a gash in the fleshy part of my lower leg muscle, but I convince myself it looks worse than it feels, so I push it out of my mind.

After a while, I know we can't remain hidden much longer. "The best way for us to get out is through the market," I tell the girl. "We'll blend into the crowd heading that way."

We avoid Church Street and the police station across from Victoria Park and instead head to West Queen Street. There's a small shop whose owner is sympathetic to the labor movement. She's helped injured organizers before.

"You'll be fine," I assure the girl. "I know a place where we can get patched up."

Sometime later, I leave the girl with the store owner at Sarah's Spice Shop, where Sarah also bandages my wound, but I need to keep moving. I veer away from Victoria Park toward the harbour. If they aren't in jail, that's where I'll find Allan, Byron, and the others, safe and sound on King Street. Or so I pray.

Allan Coombs's Office, King Street, Kingston

In the stillness of darkness, I return to where my day began. It must be after midnight as I hobble onto King Street, my leg wrapped in a poultice of bitter melon and castor oil that gives off a foul smell, reminiscent of rotten fruit. Thankfully, the horrible odor distracts me from the pain in my leg.

As I turn the corner, I sigh with relief when I see him. Byron sits on the curb outside Allan's office, puffing on a cigarette. I hobble closer. His drenched shirt and the bruises on his face and forearms are ugly souvenirs from his first rally. But at least he's alive.

"Is Allan here?" I try not to stare too long at the black-and-blue blotches on Byron's face and throat.

"He and the others left about an hour ago. I told him I'd wait for you." His voice is emotionless as he glares into the darkness, his pinpoint gaze challenging anyone lurking—a leftover rioter, a for-hire constable, anyone—to show themselves. His anger rolls off him like sweat. If I hadn't had my fill of violence at Victoria Park, I could find plenty in Byron's eyes.

"We were worried about you until one of the volunteers spotted you in Kingston Market helping injured workers." He glances at my leg. "Which, I see, included you."

The office is dark, with no kerosene lamps flickering in the windows. I need to find out how the other organizers are doing. "How many of us have checked in?"

Byron takes a long drag from his cigarette. "Only a few

volunteers were jailed. The police mostly arrested the workers, but many in the crowd were specifically there to cause trouble."

"I wish I could say I'm surprised, but it escalated quickly. I swear it was the most life-threatening situation I've ever faced." I sit down next to him on the curb.

"It was a good time," he replies sarcastically, as he continues to search for something in the dark.

"Yeah, fun," I mimic his tone. "One of the least problematic rallies in labor movement history."

"I guess you're right. No one was killed." With his knees drawn up and his elbows resting, Byron blows cigarette rings into the night. His short-sleeved shirt shows forearms marked with scratches and a gash, possibly from a knife.

Does he need to go to the hospital? "Are you okay?"

"I'm fine," he replies.

I tilt my head to the side. "I'm not sure you are." I hesitate, trying to choose my words carefully. "Today wasn't unusual. It escalated quickly, but there has been trouble at all our rallies lately. I should have been clearer this morning. I'm sorry if it caught you off guard." I pause, hoping for a reaction, but the night holds him tightly in its grip. "Thank you for waiting for me, but maybe we should go to the hospital. My leg, your arm, your face, and wherever else you've been hurt could all use some professional care."

"Come on, Zinzi," he says. "I'm fine, just a bit angry. I returned to Jamaica to work with the labor movement to change how sugar plantations operate, starting with my family's plantation. I thought I could be a catalyst to help other owners embrace the union."

"You trying to be a hero?" I notice another bruise on his jaw, about the size of a small Otaheite apple. "You found out today that it's not so easy."

"You're right. It's not. But I learned more than just that today." He drops the cigarette butt and reaches into his pocket to pull out a pack of Lucky Strike. "Would you like a smoke?" he asks.

"What else happened at the rally?"

"It seems that the constables were informed that the son of Bernard Christian Tynesdale would be participating in the rally, and my father's instructions were to teach me a lesson. So he hired troublemakers and more constables than usual to disrupt the rally. Consequently, not only did I get my ass kicked but I also sparked a riot."

"What happened today was not your fault," I say. "Rallies sometimes escalate into a brawl. Besides, you only agreed to get involved last night, and you were here this morning at five o'clock. How could your father have organized such a plan overnight?"

Byron grunts. "He hired a private detective."

I lean back. "He did?"

"This fellow has been watching me since I returned to Kingston. I believe my father already knew who you were when I introduced you at the Myrtle Bank Hotel."

"How did you learn about this private detective?"

"One of the constables, a guy I've known since childhood—the same one who tipped me off about the raid the other day, told me after he stopped a group of his fellow officers from beating me to death."

"Your father *is* ill if he'd put his plantation above your life."

He looks at me with a sadness that I can feel in my chest. "It turns out he'll do whatever he believes is necessary to protect his business interests."

"I'm sorry, Byron, but why did you think any of this would be easy?"

"I'm a fool. I thought my father, facing death, would hand the reins over to me without too much fuss or, at the very least, listen to my ideas. Of course I expected a debate, but I always thought he'd come around." Byron chuckles. "I left Jamaica a decade ago, and the man I knew then wouldn't win a prize for father or husband of the year, but I still didn't believe he was evil. Or maybe I just can't see evil." His voice cracks. "My father has been corrupted by money, success, and everything that comes with it."

"I'm sorry he disappointed you."

"Sad and silly, huh?" He looks shaken. "A grown man who stubbornly believes he can convince his father that together they can make a difference for Jamaican workers and the sugar industry."

"He may not be able to, but you can."

"That's not the difference I meant."

"Working with Allan will help create change."

"Will it?"

"The movement is much more than just a rally or a difficult day," I explain. "We are committed to the labor union as long as it takes to achieve success. One day, regardless of the industry, workers across Jamaica will be treated fairly, earn just wages, and have safe working conditions."

"I'm too angry to feel hopeful," Byron says with a bitter chuckle. "I want to confront my father and make him face the pain and suffering he's inflicting on the men, women, and children who work for him." He inhales more cigarette smoke. "I want to hurt him the way he's hurt others."

"Let's channel that anger to support the movement."

"You're a crusader, Zinzi, and a reasonable woman, but I may not share your belief in the humanity of mankind, and its ability to change minds."

I tense up. "I wouldn't put it that way."

"You already did." He chuckles. "But I'm a fool, and you shouldn't believe anything I say."

"Hey, come on. Stop being so hard on yourself. You've taken enough hits for one day. Let's get out of here."

"And go where? The hospital? No, thanks."

"All right, no hospital. But we're in Kingston, Jamaica. This city never sleeps."

"That's New York City or London. Jamaica is different." He stands up, offers his hand, and helps me to my feet. "I want my father to get his head out of the clouds and do what's right. That means hitting him where it hurts—his bank account."

"Byron, you're too upset to make decisions now."

"I feel like I've been under his control my whole life. I don't want to feel this way anymore."

"What way?"

"Powerless," he growls. "I thought I knew what my father was capable of, but now I have no doubt. At the rally, I did something I've been too much of a coward to do for a long time: I defied him. I publicly declared my support for the labor union movement. And he had his goons beat me—gave me a spanking for daring to disagree with him. I'm a grown man: bruised and swollen. But I refuse to back down."

"So, you'll join the movement and become one of our most passionate supporters. That's what truly matters. Not revenge."

"That's rich, coming from the woman who dreams of burning the Tynesdale Estate to the ground."

I shrug, as he tells no lie. "Okay, you've caught me. But do you know what form this revenge might take?"

"Yes, I do," he replies. "I'm going to steal the family rum recipe and publish it in the *Jamaica Gleaner*."

I suddenly become aware of the heat and how few stars are left in the sky. "You don't want to do that. You're not that reckless."

"You don't know me. We met two days ago."

I take a deep breath. "If you're sincere and have made this choice," I say, "what do you expect from me?"

"What do I expect?" Suddenly, Byron is close enough to rest his hand lightly on my shoulder. "That you will help me steal it."

CHAPTER 13

VIVIAN JEAN

Harlem, New York City

A sleepless night on board the 20th Century Limited, alone in a berth while my husband snores loudly below, isn't the ideal way to spend a seventeen-hour train ride. Although I didn't expect a basket full of moonbeams and lollipops, a little conversation and a pleasantry or two would have been welcome. I had planned to tell Tully what my father had said, but I never had the chance—not even upon our arrival in New York. Once there, we quickly trekked across town to the Harlem YMCA—the only place in the city that had rooms to rent to visiting Negroes. As soon as we entered our room, Tully dashed out to catch up with his friends from the New York Black Yankees. I was upset, hurt, and angry, but Harlem has a way of lifting my spirits.

Katherine and I are scheduled to meet some of her artist friends for dinner this evening, but I need to get out and insist she join me. I drag her toward the exit, but she ushers me into the lounge, wanting a cup of coffee before we leave.

"I'm exhausted." She sits beside me in a chair in the YMCA's ladies' lounge. However, the tension in her angular jaw suggests that something other than weariness is on her mind.

"I am tired, too," I say. "But it's barely three o'clock, and if we stay in our rooms until it's time for dinner, we'll fall asleep, and after dinner, we'll be up all night. And I want to be alert for the first day of our cruise, and besides, I need to do some shopping."

"Shopping for what? I thought Maxi had it all organized."

"She has. She did. I just want to do some of it myself, and she gave me a shopping list." I reach into my handbag and remove a sheet of paper with Maxi's handwriting.

Katherine frowns. "How much of this trip is Maxi's idea?"

"Why would you ask that? You know I want to go to Jamaica to study the Maroon people and bring their history into academia."

"That sounds like an appropriate reason. But I only care about academia as a means to explore African culture and dance. I want to do more than study it. I want to experience the Maroon people and their traditions, rituals, and beliefs. . . ." She pauses, and a sternness comes over her. "Including Obeah. I know Maxi has talked to you about Obeah."

A woman peeks into the lounge, delaying my response. I immediately think of Maxi's cautionary tale about how talking publicly about Obeah can be dangerous. The Brits made the practice illegal in 1898. Obeah men and women in her village had to hide their identities. If discovered, the punishment was imprisonment or seventy-five lashes.

"Yes, Maxi often mentioned it to me." I wait for the woman to depart. "But I also learned about Obeah with you when I attended the University of Chicago."

"But did you really? Our professors treated it like superstition or a spectacle."

"That wasn't the case with all our professors."

"Other than Professor Herskovits, no one else actually gave a lecture on the significance of Obeah."

Melville Herskovits, a highly regarded anthropologist, is one of Katherine's mentors, but we'd end up sitting in this lounge for hours if we began discussing his teachings. "Let's not get into that conversation now. We'll have time on the ship to discuss it in more detail. Remember, I want to go shopping before dinner."

"I remember, but I'm stalling. I invited our newest protégé to meet us."

She isn't speaking about Robbie Barnes. Tully invited him to meet the Black Yankees. "Othella?"

"Your father caught me off guard by adding two extra assistants to the expedition," Katherine confesses. "I won't have time for them. They'll be your responsibility, and I'll have my hands full getting acquainted with the locals. I plan to stay in Accompong for a month, not a whole year."

"I am sorry about my father. He has a way of getting in the way."

"Or getting his way. Honestly, they both seem nice enough, but that's not the point."

I feel compelled to add, "Robbie Barnes is an up-and-coming scientist. His work in tropical botany is supposedly stellar."

"We'll see about that, or I should say *you'll see* about that. I don't want them near me."

"Then why'd you invite Othella to join us—"

"Miss Katherine." Othella rushes into the lounge, out of breath. "I've been waiting for you in the lobby."

"Oh, sorry, dear," Katherine says. "Vivian Jean pulled me into the lounge and I forgot to mention I invited you to join us."

I give Katherine a side eye. "It's wonderful to see you," I say to Othella. "So, you're going to join us for shopping and dinner."

"I am?"

"Yes, you are," Katherine chimes in. "We're having dinner with my friend Edna Guy, who dances with the New Negro Art Theater Dance Group. She's elevating the Negro in modern dance in the style of Ruth St. Denis. We're supposed to meet them at the Harlem Lafayette Theatre before dinner."

Othella appears excited as Katherine rambles on about dance and dancers.

"We'll chat, enjoy some wine, and feast on a platter of fried catfish."

"That sounds divine." Othella's smile beams with happiness.

"Let's start our shopping spree at Ray's Department Store." Katherine stands. "It sells the right gear for our expedition."

Rising to my feet, I glance at Maxi's list. "Right, we need shoes, thick socks, and hiking boots."

"It's located on 125th Street, but we can enter from around the corner on Eighth Avenue."

Othella frowns. "What's the matter?"

"Major Thomas has only given us a small budget for personal items, and Robbie, who keeps track of our funds, is quite stingy."

"Stingy, huh? Well, don't worry." I place my hand on her shoulder. "I've got plenty of cash, so this shopping spree is on me."

"Oh my, ma'am, I really need some new clothes because I only have this dress, one other, my Oxfords, two pairs of pumps, and two ball gowns. I don't know how long they'd last in the jungle."

The walk to Ray's is quick, and as soon as the three of us step inside, the shopping frenzy begins.

"We need wide-brimmed hats for sun protection," Katherine explains after walking around the store for almost an hour. "A pith helmet or a broad-brimmed straw hat would work, too. If we can't find them here, we'll surely be able to pick them up at the market in Kingston."

"We'll also want lightweight, long-sleeved blouses, cotton calf-length skirts, and riding pants," I mention.

"That's a good start, but I don't need a list. It feels like I've been preparing for this expedition for years." Katherine smiles. "There's plenty of rocky terrain that requires sturdy hiking shoes with thick soles and cotton socks to help reduce the risk of blisters or insect bites."

"What kind of insects?" Othella asks. "Like cockroaches, flies, or mosquitoes?"

"Mr. Barnes should be able to specify the types of insects we're likely to encounter in Jamaica. But Maxi mentioned doctor flies or horseflies.

"Because they're as big as horses?"

"Honestly, Othella, I don't know. You should ask Mr. Barnes. He's our bug expert."

Othella trots behind us. "I thought he liked plants."

"If you like plants, you've got to know a thing or two about bugs." I continue reading. "We'll need lightweight field coats with deep pockets for storage, a few cotton scarves, and several pairs of gloves." I hold up a bag of thick wool socks. "This is the last item on the list."

"But what will we do with everything you bought?" Othella asks.

"I've already made arrangements," Katherine replies. "The store manager will load our things into a steamer trunk for delivery directly to the dock in the morning."

I sigh. "That sounds great. Now, can we go meet Edna Guy and get something to eat? I'm starving."

CHAPTER 14

———— ◆ ————

OTHELLA

The SS Talamanca, *Bush Terminal Harbor, Brooklyn, Pier 3*

I'm stacking up new friends like poker chips.

The night before, between the fried catfish and my second beer, I decided to tell Vivian Jean and Katherine Dunham the truth about me once we board the cruise ship. After I settle into my cabin, I'll meet them on the Promenade Deck, where Katherine asked everyone to gather, and there, I'll confess. Not everything. The stuff about Perry, I'll keep that to myself just in case I did kill him, even accidentally. That might be too much for ladies like them to stomach.

I'll just share how chaotic my life has been and how I plan to fix it. Katherine and Vivian Jean will be impressed and love me even more.

"The Dunham Expedition is like a dance group," Katherine said at Smalls Paradise the night before, "We work side by side and sway to the same rhythms. From the moment we sail out of Bush Terminal Harbor for Jamaica, we are a family, but I'm the mother hen. The woman in charge. Understand?"

She said this after her second glass of wine, but her eyes

were bright and her words sounded genuine. I was so thrilled I could hear my heart pounding in my chest. And she didn't stop there. What she said next changed everything. "I won't hear any more Miss This, Miss That, or Miss Ma'am from you, Othella Montgomery. From now on, it's Katherine and Vivian Jean."

That made me so happy.

If I can call them by their first names, I should be able to confess the parts of my past that don't sound that bad. It will seal the deal on the shift in our relationship. And from then on, these women will treat me as an equal, as a friend.

I pause to think about that for a moment. Perhaps the only story I should tell is about my mother. That evening Ella Montgomery left our kitchenette to buy a pint of whiskey and never returned. No note. No goodbye. She simply vanished. I searched for her every day for a week, alongside the cop who came to our kitchenette to tell me she was gone. That was when I first met Officer Richie. He delivered the sad news to my ten-year-old self. The police suspected that one of my mother's tricks, whom she called boyfriends, had dumped her in the Chicago River. Officer Richie promised to find the man who killed her, but after a while, he either gave up or forgot.

Luggage handlers follow Robbie and me as we ascend the steep ramp of the gangway to board the steamship. Lost in thought, I reflect on a past I'm ready to leave behind. This is my fresh start, the next chapter of my life. I glance up at the enormous hull of the SS *Talamanca*.

"Come on, Othella. Don't look so down," Robbie says. "This is just as I told you it would be. We're not here as tourists."

"What do you mean?"

"You look worried."

"I'm not worried," I say. "Why do you keep staring at me?"

"I'm responsible for you."

I ignore whatever he means by that. "How much do we have to do before we meet the Hartfields and Miss Katherine on the Promenade Deck?" I ask. "I haven't been introduced to Mr. Hartfield, and I told you what she said. She wanted us to be—"

"Together," Robbie interrupts. "I know, I know, but first, I need to make sure these porters deliver everything to the right places."

Robbie has spent the morning directing the handlers on what to do with this box, that crate, and this streamer trunk as if he were a general in an army. My rambling, bumbling friend has turned into a bossy son of a gun. Equally annoying, he has also become an expert seafaring man.

"Welcome aboard the SS *Talamanca*," Robbie announces a bit too loudly as we walk the gangway. "Did you know it's one of six sister ships in the United Fruit Company's Great White Fleet? They were the fastest steamships ever built," he continues. "Oh, and this terminal is one of the few piers in New York where Negroes can board."

Uninterested in these details, I shrug. My mind still grapples with whether I should share my truths with Katherine and Vivian Jean.

Robbie and I walk through the winding corridor and ascend a flight of stairs to reach the Saloon Deck. Each stateroom contains one upper and one lower berth, along with a couch. The rooms are small, and when I bounce on my cot, I discover the mattress is paper-thin. The women's and men's bathrooms are located across the hallway. Our staterooms are next door to each other but not directly connected.

I struggle to mask my disappointment that my stateroom isn't larger or more glamorous. At least there's a small porthole to gaze out at the sea, but the room's size starkly contrasts with my expectations.

Thirty minutes later, I finish stowing my belongings and meet Robbie at the bottom of another flight of stairs. "Can we go to the Promenade Deck now?"

"You've been talking all morning about this meeting on the Promenade Deck. Why are you so anxious?"

"I haven't met Mr. Hartfield yet." I climb the stairs. "And after last night, Katherine, Vivian Jean, and I have become friends. We shopped at Ray's Department Store and had dinner with one of Katherine's dancer friends, and I was just one of the girls. Not an assistant or servant or anything like that."

"So, that's where you sneaked off to last night." Robbie pauses, his hand resting on the railing. "If you're such close friends, does she know your secret? Does she know mine?" There was a hitch in his voice.

"I wasn't sneaking," I say defensively. "And why do you sound jealous?"

He walks ahead of me on the stairs. "Because I am. Do you know what I did last night? I read a three-hundred-page book: *Tropical Forestry in the Caribbean.*"

"That's not true. You went to meet the New York Black Yankees with Mr. Hartfield."

"Oh." He laughs. "You found out about that?"

"I told you I've made friends with Katherine and Vivian Jean. They told me everything."

"But I'm not lying. Remember our agreement. I simply left out the part about the Black Yankees. I did read that book as well. I want to be prepared for our arrival in Accompong. Major Thomas covers our expenses so I can write a paper on plants and help his daughter and her friend Katherine have a fruitful expedition."

"It sounds like an exciting book," I say mockingly.

"It was," he replies. "What excuse did you give to convince her to take you shopping?"

"I blamed you and the major for being stingy with personal items, like my clothes for the Katherine Dunham Anthropology and African Dance Expedition."

"The what?"

"That's our name."

"We'll have to include that on the papers we write. We'll need to put the title on every page."

"We write?" I ask incredulously.

"Don't worry. I'll tell you more in Jamaica."

We pause for a moment to catch our breath when we reach the Cabin Deck. "One more flight to go," Robbie says.

On the Promenade Deck, I immediately start searching for the Hartfields and Katherine. I quickly spot them: two elegantly dressed women and a tall, handsome man standing slightly apart. Leaning against the railing, he seems more interested in the sea than in the women beside him.

I hurry ahead of Robbie, rushing toward the Hartfields and Katherine, waving and calling, "Vivian Jean. Katherine." I stop in front of them, grinning widely. They greet me with bright, shining smiles. Even Mr. Hartfield looks cheerful, but that isn't easy to judge because this is our first meeting.

"Tully, this is the young lady I mentioned. Thanks to the major, she'll be part of the expedition, but let me introduce you properly," Vivian Jean says, stepping aside to give me and her husband the spotlight. "Tully, I'd like you to meet Othella Montgomery."

I suppress the urge to curtsy, an unnecessary and inappropriate gesture, but these three seem as regal as any count or countess I've ever seen.

"And dear, you've already met Robbie Barnes," Vivian Jean says. "He joined you last night with the Black Yankees."

"Sir," Robbie replies. "Thank you for that invitation. I had a grand time."

"You're welcome."

A casual conversation starts about the staterooms—the

Hartfields' and Katherine's are nicer than mine or Robbie's—and the activities the group could enjoy over the next four or five days. From shuffleboard to Mah-Jongg and writing letters to playing chess—Robbie and Tully find out they both enjoy that game—it all sounds terribly dull to me. I expected a jazz quartet, dancing every night, and a bar with gin and tonics.

Everything that everyone else is so excited about just sounds tedious to me.

Standing on the deck of the ship, I am mesmerized by my surroundings. The water. The sky. The wind in my face. I think about where I was just a few days before—in a bed next to a man who I might have hurt so badly that he died. Sadness and guilt stir in my chest, and I close my eyes, wishing for the nightmare to end. When I open them, something at the stern of the ship catches my attention.

A large crowd of passengers has gathered, and although the searing midday sun beats down, one figure stands out above the rest. What I see is unthinkable, unbelievable. I nearly chuckle at the absurdity of my imagination, but my laughter is fleeting. As I gain a clearer view, my heart pounds against my chest like a hammer.

It can't be. It mustn't be.

My joy has turned into despair, and the fear threatens to choke me. My fresh start has leapt overboard and flails in the sea, choking on salty water.

A desperate sound escapes my throat. Robbie quickly comes to my side, whispering, "What's wrong?"

"Nothing," I reply. "I'm just seeing things. Or maybe I'm seasick." I grip the railing but continue staring toward the stern, and my knees weaken.

"You look distressed, Othella," Katherine says. "Is something wrong? Are you okay?"

I wrestle with fear, especially because I don't trust what I see. The thrill of escaping my past has dwindled to the size of a crumb from stale bread. Jerry Merriweather stands above the crowd. How did he get on board?

"He's here. The man who attacked me at the Abbotts' mansion."

"I don't think so, Othella. How could he be?" Vivian Jean squints in the direction I'm pointing.

"He followed us. I'm sure it's him."

Robbie leans forward. "I think I see who you mean, the big guy."

Tears well up in my eyes. "You really see him?"

Robbie nods and turns to the others. "It's been a tough morning. I believe she's worn out." He gently squeezes my arm.

"Don't worry," Vivian Jean says. "Tully will talk to the captain to find out about any last-minute passenger reservations besides the four of us."

"I hate to make a fuss," I say.

"It's no trouble," Tully replies. "I'll talk to the captain and ask him to check the manifest to set your minds at ease."

CHAPTER 15

———— ◆ ————

ZINZI

Trench Town, Kingston

Thoughts of my mother and her beliefs come to me. The rituals, the herbs, and the secrets she keeps in the cloth pouch in the basket by the hearth. I never know when I will feel the pull of her words. They are simply with me—a figure at my side, looming over me like her mysterious Rolling Calf, the fearsome creature that appears on the hillside, in the sugarcane fields, and near the silk cotton tree, a demonic, rolling ball of fire. The curse of the Rolling Calf brings calamity and torment to anyone who crosses its path. Byron's idea of stealing and publishing his family's rum recipe might not strike some as demonic, but I am desperately uneasy at the thought of it. And for him to ask me to help only intensifies my concern.

The walk from King Street to Trench Town we make in silence. I am hopeful he has calmed enough to forget what he said, but I don't want to leave him alone. "Byron, let's grab a drink."

He looks down, his eyes drifting past my face to my injured leg. "Are you sure?"

"I wouldn't have brought it up if I weren't."

With a thankful sigh, I see the tension ease from his shoulders. "All right, I could use a whiskey."

"Great. I know a place, mostly locals, and it's open all night."

He chuckles. "You always know the best spots for real Jamaicans."

I pay his teasing tone no mind, for I'm just glad to hear it.

A mile from King Street, Trench Town is my neighborhood. Overcrowded and marked by poverty at every turn, it is home to Jamaica's working class—the so-called less fortunate—compared to plantation owners, government officials, and the mixed-race wealthy. It is also the liveliest and most fun-loving community in Kingston. Despite broken hearts and empty wallets, it remains vibrant, sweaty, and electric. The rhythms of mento and jazz fill the air beneath gas lamps and moonlight.

In my neighborhood, laughter and love strengthens the bonds of community. They don't tear them apart.

Trench Town is famous for its all-night lawn parties, rum shops, mento bands, and endless dancing and singing. The festivities never stop.

Byron and I arrive at a backyard lawn party and are instantly swept up in the excitement.

"Let's make a pact." I pass Byron a cup of Jamaican white rum while I hold on to my ginger beer. "If you even hint at stealing the recipe or look at a jug of rum, you'll have two choices."

There's a hint of amusement dancing at the corners of his mouth. "And what are those options?" he asks.

"Before I tell you, swear to me that you're in. No backing out," I reply.

"Okay." He places a hand over his heart and raises the other. "I swear."

I struggle not to grin. "You'll have to choose between

downing a tumbler of whiskey or getting dragged onto the dance floor."

"What if I can't dance?"

"It doesn't matter. Those are the rules."

A few minutes later, Byron surprises me. He's a fantastic dancer who enjoys his tumblers of whiskey and a few other beverages.

"You set me up," I shout over the music. "You can dance."

He laughs. "Yeah, I can."

By dawn, I've had a few ginger beers, while Byron has had even more. We dance until my sore leg feels numb.

"We should get back." I try to keep him still. He's been dancing for hours.

"Back where? To your place? Don't you live in Trench Town?"

"Yes, but the Myrtle Bank Hotel is just as close, in the opposite direction."

"So, is this good night? " He leans in, pressing against me, and I realize my ginger beers were nowhere near as potent as the whiskeys, the white rums, or the John Crow Batty drinks he's consumed.

"What if I walk you to the Myrtle Bank Hotel? I want to make sure you're settled before we say good night."

"Or good morning." He laughs. "Can't we just take a cab instead?"

"Byron, we're in Trench Town and it's almost sunrise. There are no cabs here."

"Oh, all right," he says, awkwardly kissing my cheek. "Thank you. I really needed a night out."

There's a sleepy but pleasantly handsome look on his face. "Good. I feel better, too."

The walk to the Myrtle Bank Hotel takes longer than I expected. When we reach the empty lobby, I ask the receptionist for the keys to his suite. "Let's get you upstairs."

"Thanks, Zinzi," he says quietly before asking the desk clerk to call a cab for me.

"Let's get you settled first."

He staggers toward the elevator, but I steer him toward the staircase, explaining that the exercise will clear his head and prevent a crippling hangover. He shrugs and buys into my reasoning, and we stumble up three flights and down a hallway until we reach his suite. Once inside, I lead him to his bedroom where Byron crawls into bed without changing out of his clothes or removing his shoes. I decide to leave him that way. "We'll talk soon." I turn to leave.

"Hey, take a nap," he murmurs. "You'll be dead on your feet at work without any sleep." He turns over in bed, wraps his arms around a pillow, and hugs it tightly. "The cab will be there whenever you're ready."

I close the bedroom door, seriously considering Byron's suggestion. I'm completely exhausted, and the idea of a nap draws me in. Feeling drained, I sink onto the sofa in the living room and fall asleep before my head can touch the armrest.

Myrtle Bank Hotel, Kingston

A telephone rings. A male voice mumbles "eggs" and "coffee." I sit up quickly, wide awake, and immediately know exactly where I am, how I got here, and that it's time to leave. My plan is to slip out of Byron's hotel suite without seeing him and having to admit I fell asleep on his sofa.

I look at the clock on the wall and gasp. Ten o'clock? I'm two hours late for work! And I'll be even later when I factor in the forty-minute trek from the Myrtle Bank Hotel to Constant Spring. I rush into the bathroom, splash some water on my face, and think, *Lord, have mercy; I can't lose my job.* There's no weekly paycheck for being a full-time labor union activist.

A knock on the door startles me. I open it, and there Byron stands before me, holding two cups of steaming coffee, a smile lighting up his handsome face.

"Before you go, join me for breakfast," he says, wearing silk pajamas, causing me to chuckle. It's so very British of him.

"Thanks for letting me use your sofa, but I should be heading out."

"I've already called a car for you. It'll be downstairs waiting, ready to take you wherever you need to go."

"I am so late for work." I adjust my dress, knowing I must be wrinkled from head to toe.

Byron waves a cup of coffee under my nose. "I ordered eggs and toast," he says. "We had quite a bit of rum last night. This will help with the hangover."

"I didn't have any rum. You did," I reply, not particularly keen on breakfast, but the coffee is tempting if he ordered enough milk and sugar. "You also had a few cups of homemade moonshine, which I warned you about."

"Oh, yeah, the John Crow Batty." He hands me the cup of coffee, and I take it. "It's the strongest moonshine on the island."

"I need a lot of cream and sugar," I mention as I sit at the dining room table. The coffee is delicious, but the smell of breakfast awakens my hunger, and I indulge in the scrambled eggs, sausage, and pastries he had delivered to his suite.

We steer clear of discussing the rally during the meal. The only sign of yesterday's turmoil is the return of that look in his eyes, the anger I saw in them the night before. "I'm sorry about what happened at the rally."

"It wasn't your fault. You don't need to apologize. I'm sorry if my idea shocked you. I was mad and went a little overboard. Thank you for caring enough to help me gain perspective," he laughs, "though I have a bit of a hangover."

"Me too." I smile. "But we did have fun, right?"

"Yes, we did."

I stare at my plate and lift a forkful of eggs to my lips. Looking up, I see Byron watching me.

"A car will take you to the hotel," he says.

I take a last sip of my sugary coffee and stand up. "Then I should head out." He nods and rises to his feet. Before I realize it, he's holding the door open, blocking the way between me and the exit. I'm not afraid of what he might do. Instead, I fear what I want him to do.

This moment feels like a mutual decision. I sink into his embrace as our lips meet. We kiss softly, thoroughly exploring each other until his arms circle my waist, drawing me close to his chest. His mouth is tender and generous. When my knees begin to tremble, I take a step back.

"I believe it's time for me to go now."

"Thank you once more, Zinzi."

CHAPTER 16

———✦———

VIVIAN JEAN

The SS Talamanca *at Sea, Day One*

Tully and I spend the first few hours aboard the SS *Tala-manca* unpacking, sending telegrams, and strolling from deck to deck as the ship sails into the ocean. When we run into Captain O'Flanagan, Tully keeps his promise to Othella by inquiring about her mysterious stranger.

The captain informs us that I was the one to make the final reservations—Tully, Othella, Robbie, and I were the last names added to the manifest. "No one on board is unaccounted for, Othella," I explain when we meet her and Robbie on the Saloon Deck.

"Are you sure? Maybe, I imagined seeing him." Her eyes seem less fearful than when I saw her in Brooklyn on Pier 3.

"Good girl. We can't have you feeling out of sorts just as we sail for Jamaica." Katherine wraps her arm around Othella's shoulders. "This may be the easiest part of the journey, so let's enjoy it."

"Katherine's correct," I add. "We have much to get ready for. We'll be in Jamaica in four days."

"Five at most," Katherine says with a smile.

Tully is eager to play shuffleboard and backgammon so he enlists Robbie Barnes as his partner. I don't argue. He's still not ready to talk and I want to enjoy my first hours at sea by taking in the sights and exploring the ship. If he makes it to the dining room, I ask him to bring me a sandwich because I'm skipping today's meal. Besides, it would be much worse if we were in the dining hall, sitting at a table with strangers, and he had nothing to say to me. What better way to show everyone our marriage is on the rocks?

After leaving the deck, I go back to the cabin and decide to spend part of the afternoon sitting in the sunshine. I call a steward and send Katherine a note, inviting her to join me on the Promenade Deck. Then, I change into appropriate cruise attire. Earlier, Katherine suggested that for our first after-noon at sea, we should look fashionably smart. I put on a pleated navy skirt, a white blouse, stockings, and T-strap pumps. I feel overdressed, but Katherine had insisted.

When I reach the deck, my dream of watching a breath-taking sunset has to wait. The sky is overcast with dark clouds and has turned the sea black, with rolling waves crashing against the ship's hull. I'm grateful I didn't wear a cute hat to match my outfit. I would have lost it to the howling wind. Though I am disappointed, I find the weather fascinating. Chicago's frigid winters and sweltering summers are notori-ous. The city's spring and fall often bring a fair number of sunny days and pleasant temperatures, but a storm at sea stirs my soul.

Katherine arrives. "I don't see many people out here," she says. "Could it be because of the choppy sea?"

"It's exciting, isn't it?" I ignore her sarcasm and grip the railing.

"It's the beginning of the adventure," she says into the wind. "I must admit, I'm a bit frightened. I want to accom-plish so much."

"Oh, Katherine, you're the most prepared and talented person I know. You have nothing to fear."

She chuckles. "Maybe. Technically, Maroon communities like Accompong have historically used dance, music, and rituals to maintain their fight against colonial oppression. But I'm not on this journey just to collect information. African dance will help me create unique choreography."

The ship rocks. Katherine clutches the railing firmly, her tone unwavering. "Anthropologists contribute to encyclopedias, textbooks, and museum archival materials. Where is African culture honored?"

A sailor approaches and tips his hat. "Ladies, excuse my interruption. There's a storm on the horizon, and we're heading straight for it. The captain has asked us to inform our passengers. You will hear an alarm when being on deck is no longer safe." He tips his hat again and walks to another group, gazing at the sea.

"We'd better get inside, then," Katherine says as she steps back from the railing.

"Yes, I guess we should," I respond.

"Sorry for burdening you with my nervousness."

"Please, you don't think I'm not just as nervous? I am, but I'm only beginning my expedition. You've been working toward this for years."

"That's true." She crosses her arms, rubbing her shoulders as if warding off a chill.

The ship suddenly lurches, and we both grab the railing. The alarm sounds.

"We'd better get below," Katherine says.

We head back to our staterooms, struggling for balance with every step.

When I open the door, Tully sits cross-legged on the floor, surrounded by photographs, camera lenses, and rolls of film, holding his Leica II. With two twin beds, a writing table, and a chair, the cabin feels small. I'm as long-limbed as he is, but much thinner. Tully takes up more than half the remaining space, leaving little room for me.

"The passengers aren't allowed on deck." The edge in my voice is unmistakable. I slam the door, cross the short distance to the writing table, and drop into the chair. "Katherine and I were on deck having a conversation when they ordered us to our staterooms."

"What choice did they have? We're sailing into a tropical storm." Tully sets down his camera, folds his arms, and rests his elbows on his knees, cradling his chin in his hands. "Well, that means we'll be stuck with each other's company until after the storm."

"So, you're talking to me now? By the way, that was a harsh thing to say."

"I figured I'd say it before you did." He touches his stomach, grimacing as the ship's hull tilts and sways.

My heart sinks. "Are you seasick?"

"Is that a hint of satisfaction I hear in your tone?"

"Never. Your discomfort brings me no pleasure."

"Unlike you, dear, I don't find a rocking ship thrilling. I'm trying my best not to lie flat on the floor and weep."

"I'm sorry."

"So join me on the floor." Tully pats the space opposite him as he gathers his lenses and camera parts, clearing a spot for me.

"Stop debating and sit with me."

"Okay, okay." I rise from the chair to my knees, then angle my hips toward the floor, tucking my legs to the side.

"Now, isn't that better?"

"If you say so," I reply sourly, even though I relish his attention. "What are you doing with these photos?" I notice that most of them are of me: Vivian Jean sitting on the edge of their bed, Vivian Jean in the kitchen with Maxi drinking tea, Vivian Jean in the garden pruning flowers, and Vivian Jean at 31st Street Beach with Katherine in the summer of 1933 alongside Clifford.

There's also a photo of the three of us from nearly fifteen years ago: Clifford, me, and Tully—lined up from tallest to shortest, with Clifford on the left, me in the middle, and Tully on the right.

"Do you remember who took this photo?" I hold it up for Tully to see.

"It was Maxi, with your father's old Kodak camera." Tully takes the picture from my hands. "He still has that camera."

"Why do you have these?" I gesture to the photos scattered across the cabin floor.

"They were in my camera bag. I didn't know they were there," Tully replies defensively.

Suddenly, the hull dips sharply, tossing us sideways.

"What kind of godawful storm is this?" Tully exclaims.

"Calm down. It's just a storm." I look at him with concern. Tully has never acted this way about anything. I can't remember ever seeing him scared, except around spiders or the day he found Clifford's note. "What's bothering you?"

"Drowning," he replies flatly.

"Stop joking. What's on your mind?"

"Did you know the SS *Princess* capsized in Kingston Harbour two months ago?" Tully places the old photos into his camera bag. "Several passengers and some crew members died."

"We'll be through this storm before we reach Kingston Harbour." I lean forward and gaze intently into his eyes. "That won't happen to us. We've had enough bad luck."

"Strong winds and turbulent waters." Tully inspects his camera lenses with fingers that tremble slightly. "There's no telling what might happen next."

What's going on with him? The way he's speaking suggests something more than just seasickness. "Did you take something? I have some scopolamine tablets."

"I brought a bag of candied ginger, but it's not helping."

"Let's talk about something other than the storm or the photos. Concentrate on something beyond how you feel," I suggest.

He frowns. "That won't work."

"How do you know?"

"Because that's all I've been doing lately—feeling things. Besides, I can't think of anything else."

"I can," I say. "I telegrammed Maxi yesterday about Clifford's note."

"Oh, you did?"

"I told you I would. That note is why you can't think of anything else and can hardly talk to me."

"I'm talking to you now."

"Not with affection. Not with love. There's nothing but tension between us. I expected you at least to be civil while we're on this trip."

"You're still upset about the train ride," he says. "I was hungover. I didn't have the energy to discuss the note, your father, or any of it."

The ship tilts to one side. We brace ourselves, palms flat on the floor, our arm muscles tightening to avoid being flung across the stateroom. Tully turns an unpleasant shade of gray.

"Are you going to be sick?" I reach for him.

"No." He chews his lower lip. "Maybe." He swallows nervously. "What would Maxi know about a note from Clifford?"

"Maxi has known all three of us for decades."

"I'm surprised you didn't tell her about the day we found it."

I didn't want to bring that up. If it's true, Maxi would know, and I'd be able to see it in her eyes. "I just didn't."

He scratches the stubble on his chin. "I have something to tell you. I wanted to say it the other night, but you wouldn't let me."

I remember that moment and want to stop him again. "Go on."

"Clifford and I argued the night before he died."

That was just hours before he changed the trust fund—*a coincidence, nothing more.* How many times do I have to remind myself of that? "And this argument was about what?"

"You."

"Why would you and Clifford argue about me?"

"We went to a nightclub on State Street and had dinner and a few glasses of whiskey. We probably had a few more than we should have, but the disagreement started when he asked me to look after you if anything happened to him." Tully rubs his fingers over his mouth. "I told him that's a brother's job, and added that nothing would happen to him."

"You disagreed about that?"

"Could you let me finish?" Tully glares at his camera bag as if he can peer through the leather to the photos inside. "He claimed to know my deepest secret and, out of the blue, told me I had been in love with you—his wife—since I was fourteen."

"What did you say?"

"He was right." Tully stares into my eyes. "But it was just a boy's crush."

His bright eyes and flushed cheeks compel me to look away. How long has it been since we shared a moment of tenderness? "You had feelings for me?"

"Be serious, Vivian Jean. Please."

For the first time in ages, our eyes meet, free from malice or fear. "I am. I didn't know."

He chuckles. "Anyway, he made a big deal about my not having had a serious relationship, but I reminded him I wasn't the marrying kind."

"Okay, but that doesn't sound like an argument. You said you two were drinking and lost track of common sense, which is what it sounds like. Clifford and I barely saw you after we got married. You were on the road, traveling back and forth across the country, playing baseball for two years straight." I pretend to laugh. "When did this great love affair happen? When you only showed up for Christmas dinner and my birthday?"

"I never missed your birthday," Tully says quietly.

"A coincidence."

"Now, what did I say about coincidences?"

"Tully, please."

"Clifford kept pounding on me. He wouldn't drop it. He called me a liar. And with so many whiskeys in me, I confessed. I told him I loved you and couldn't imagine being with anyone else. Not as husband and wife."

Words escape me. How could this have happened? How could I have missed his feelings? He was a friend before becoming my brother-in-law or my husband. All I can do is slowly and methodically shake my head, pressing a finger to my temple to ease the throbbing pain in my head.

"Two weeks after the funeral, you found out you were pregnant, and the major insisted that a Hartfield man had to raise a Hartfield child." Tully uncrosses his legs and stands up. "We were married, and it was so easy to be with you. It felt like coming home to the heart I thought I didn't have."

"Oh, Tully. I loved Clifford, but I fell in love with you, too, and it didn't happen overnight. Don't you remember the first months we spent together after my miscarriage?"

He was the reason I survived after I lost the baby. He saved my life. His kindness, his attentiveness, and his understanding. His unwavering support helped me through the bleakest hours and guided me toward rediscovering myself and, ultimately, my heart.

I extend my hand. "Help me up."

He does.

Standing before him, I gently cup his chin. "I know you feel guilty about how much we care for each other, and I do, too. But I refuse to think that Clifford thought you and I were having an affair. He never said that to you, did he?"

Tully closes his eyes. "He didn't have to. He wrote it in the note."

"Your guilt for no reason will ruin us. That argument was your brother telling you to move on with your life. He cared about your happiness and didn't want you to suffer. I'll prove that he didn't write that note about us. Just wait and see."

"You believe Jamaica will fix us," he says. "I know Maxi's stories of the silk cotton tree as well as you do—the legends, the duppies, the whole rigamarole. But it's just a myth. It's magic, and I don't believe in magic, superstition, or spirits. I don't think you do either. You're looking for a way to save a marriage that was never meant to be. Jamaica, with its Obeah or silk cotton tree, won't change anything between us. Not a goddamned thing."

CHAPTER 17

———— ◆━◆ ————

OTHELLA

The SS Talamanca *at Sea, Day One*

Where is Jerry Merriweather? Robbie and I have searched every corner of the SS *Talamanca*. We explore every empty stateroom and every other room, the social club, the barbershop, and the doctor's office. By the end of the day, I don't know which way to turn, so I turn on Robbie.

"I don't care what Tobias Hartfield or Commander O'Flanagan think. I saw him, and I will find him. I refuse to start my new life in Jamaica looking over my shoulder, waiting for some lowlife to jump out of the shadows and attack me." I exhale. "I may not have set foot on the island of Jamaica before, but it already holds a special place in my heart, and I won't let any man ruin it for me."

Robbie looks at me kindly. "It's not that I don't believe you, Othella, but if he's on board, why hasn't he come after you?"

As we stroll past the barbershop on the Promenade Deck, the thought of pushing Robbie overboard crosses my mind. "Don't you dare say things like that to me," I exclaim. "He's on this ship. I'm sure of it."

"But Othella, we've looked everywhere," Robbie responds softly, trying to soothe me.

"There has to be a place we haven't searched," I argue. "Maybe he's one of those people hiding on the ship—what do they call them?"

"Stowaways."

"Yes, that's it. They know every nook and cranny of the *Talamanca*, don't they?" I suddenly feel like I might cry. "I shoulda known. I get close to happiness and everything goes wrong."

Robbie guides me to the railing. "Being happy doesn't mean something bad has to happen. There's just no sign of him."

"He's here," I mutter. "He might be as dumb as a rock, but he knows how to stay out of sight."

The ship rises and falls, then rises and falls again. I cling to the railing as a brisk breeze whips through my hair and across my face. Robbie lifts a hand, his fingertips gently tucking strands of my hair behind my ear.

The gentleness of his touch surprises me, mainly because I don't mind it. "He wants to kill me, and he'll stop at nothing to accomplish what he's set out to do. I can't let Jerry hurt me, Robbie. I just can't."

"Jerry? Is that his name? You know him?" The lines around Robbie's eyes deepen with confusion.

If I had a leather belt like the one my mother used to hit me with, I'd give myself a spanking. How could I make such a mistake? Has having friends and sailing on a cruise ship made me daft? "Can I trust you, Robbie?"

"Of course you can trust me." His face lights up. "Pinky swear, remember?"

Of course I recall that silly promise. "Let's walk for a minute."

Robbie bends his arm at the elbow and offers it to me. I slip my hand through, and we saunter on the deck as other couples parade by.

"His full name is Jerry Merriweather, and he thinks I hurt his brother—he caught up with me at Mr. Abbott's house because of that, not to steal a brooch. That's why I need to find him. If I don't, he's gonna ruin everything for me."

"His brother? Was he a brute like Jerry? Was he your boyfriend? Did he hurt you? What kind of man is he?"

My nerves feel as if they are being soaked in gasoline. One more question and I'll explode. "Yes, his brother hurt me—and I hurt him back." I pull away from Robbie, but he won't let me go. "Listen, I might've done more than just hurt his brother."

"Might have? Is he dead?"

The question I've asked myself, coming from Robbie's lips, makes my chest ache. "Yes, he's dead, but I don't know if I killed him. I hit him pretty hard in the head 'cause he'd hit me a couple of times and dragged me from one end of the apartment to the other. I couldn't let him beat me to death. So I struck him in the head with a Smokador ashtray. And I'd do the same to his brother if he came after me."

"Christ, Othella. You've been through some tough times, haven't you?" Robbie halts, running his hand over his head as if to hold back his thoughts. "What are you going to do if you find Jerry?"

"Tell him I don't have what he's looking for and I didn't kill his brother, not deliberately."

"You think talking to him will make a difference if he wants to hurt you?"

"I can't just do nothing."

"Well, then." He softly pats my hand. "There's one place we haven't looked—the cargo hold at the very bottom of the ship."

"You still want to help me find Jerry after what I just told you?"

"If I were a stowaway, that's where I'd hide. Plenty of food, water, and clothing, and other supplies are stored there."

"Are you sure?"

"What have I been doing for the past few days if not helping you? You're my girl—I mean, my best friend. Just because I know his name and why he's after you doesn't mean I'll stop helping you."

"Why, Robbie Barnes." I smile. "I swear, if we weren't in public, I'd give you a big kiss."

He looks down shyly, shuffling his feet.

"Don't go acting all romantic, Othella. It's not like you."

It's almost midnight, and I find myself pacing in my stateroom, wide awake. Robbie's suggestion was reasonable: to wait until morning and search in the cargo hold. But I'm neither patient nor reasonable. I trust my instincts. That's how I stay alive.

The boat sways as the storm, which has been looming all day, finally strikes full force. Passengers have retreated to their staterooms for the night. I can hear a few sailors moving about the decks, making sure everything is secure.

I change out of my day dress into riding pants and a collared shirt, stuffing my pocketknife into my hip pocket. My loosely conceived plan is ready to be put to the test. I slip into the corridors, mindful of not being spotted by roaming sailors, and creep down the winding staircases until I reach the lowest level of the ship—the cargo hold.

It smells bad. The stench of urine and spit makes my eyes water. If Jerry is on board—and I know he is—this is where he'll be, the filthiest, darkest, and creepiest level on the damn ship. I can hear the rats scampering, rodents darting from one spot to another as I pray that my Oxfords aren't in their way.

Candlelight flickers in the distance. I move toward it.

"Jerry," I whisper. "Jerry Merriweather. Is that you? I know you're down here."

"What the hell?" His gruff voice stops me in my tracks.

"It's me, Othella." Squinting into the shadows, my vision gradually adjusts to the dim light. Jerry sits on a cot in the corner, surrounded by a half wall of crates.

"Who's there?"

"I said, it's me, Othella."

A laugh that sounds like a foghorn bounces off the walls. "Girl, you've got some nerve. Coming down here looking for me?"

"Why haven't you tried to find me?"

"I wasn't in a hurry to find you."

"Why not?"

"Because I'm not here to harm you."

"That has to be a lie." I watch him and reconsider my decision to confront him alone. He's twice my size. "If you're not here to hurt me, why are you on this ship?"

Jerry reaches for a nearby crate as if it were a nightstand and picks up a sterling silver cigarette case. He taps one cigarette out and lights it. I wait, not wanting to rush him. Plus, his puffing gives me a moment to consider what to do next and whether Jerry is telling the truth.

"Did Tony Schaefer send you to follow me? I betcha he did, didn't he?"

"Perry always said you had a good head on your shoulders." Jerry takes another drag from his cigarette. "Yeah. Tony sent me. He said you owed him an old man's pocket watch. I'm here to take it back to Chicago."

I laugh out loud. "Tony's outta luck, sending you all this way for nothing. That old man, Major Thomas, didn't have a pocket watch."

"Come on, Othella, I saw you at that party. You took it from the major's daughter, so hand it to me."

"I don't have it."

"Then where is it?"

"Don't worry. I know where it is." A lie. I hadn't thought about that pocket watch since Mr. Abbott's party.

"Then get it and bring it to me." Jerry swings his legs off the cot and stomps out his cigarette with his bare foot. "Look, the only reason I'm here is to make sure you finish the job Tony hired you to do."

"And if I do, who's gonna pay me the dough Tony promised?"

"When I have the watch, I'll telegram Tony, and he'll wire you the money."

More lies Jerry expects me to swallow. "And what about you and me? You're not gonna try to avenge your brother?"

"No way. Tony made me swear to leave you be. If any harm comes to you, I can kiss my ass goodbye."

Liar, liar. He's still gonna try and get payback because of Perry. I can smell it. But if he wants that pocket watch, he'll also go after Vivian Jean, because if he was watching us at the party, he knows I gave her back the pocket watch. "The smell down here is awful. I can scarcely breathe."

"The cigarette smoke helps," he says. "You want one?"

"No. Let's go upstairs. There's nobody outside with all this wind."

He pulls on a pair of boots. "Can we get it tonight?"

"We can make plans upstairs. On the deck."

We climb the multiple flights to the Promenade Deck and head toward the bow.

"I'm curious," I say. "What's the story behind Tony Schaefer and Major Thomas? What makes this pocket watch such a big deal?" I ask a question I already know the answer to.

Jerry lights up another cigarette. "They used to be business partners."

That's what Robbie told me. So, it must be true, and maybe they are still partners. "What kind of business?"

"Before he became a banker, he owned funeral homes all over the Black Belt. During Prohibition, he was a rum runner. Perry and I drove his trucks, hauled crates of bottled rum from South Florida to Chicago. When the banks started collapsing, Major Thomas invested his money in jewels. That pocket watch is worth a fortune."

Robbie didn't have that information. "Why would he flaunt the pocket watch out in the open by giving it to his daughter to wear around her neck? It should be locked away in a safe."

"Don't ask me. I don't know nothing but what Tony tells me."

"Is that who you are these days? Just a gofer for Tony Schaefer? Don't you want to have something of your own?"

"What you mean?"

"Why don't you give me one of those cigarettes and I'll tell you."

He reaches into his pocket and ducks down low 'cause of the wind to light two cigarettes. "Here you go. Now what's your idea?"

I take a long drag from the cigarette. "Forget about Tony. Let's cut a deal with the major. He has the pocket watch and plenty of money and can set us up. You won't need to go back to Chicago. You can go anywhere you like in the world with enough money in your pockets."

He braces his back against the railing. A dark shadow falls over him. "Tony warned me you'd try to get me to turn on him. Like you turned on Perry."

I want to swallow, but I have no spit in my mouth. "To tell you the truth, I think Tony had something to do with your brother's death. I hit him, but I didn't kill him. He talked to me as I walked out the door."

Suddenly, Jerry stops talking. He swings me around and pushes my back against the railing. He has a grip on both my shoulders and he's leaning in, making it difficult for me to keep my feet on the ground.

"What's wrong with you?" I hiss.

"You're lying to me. Lying about everything. About not

killing my brother, about knowing where the pocket watch is, about betraying Tony. You just want to save your own behind."

"Let me go. You're hurting me."

Jerry laughs. "I'll just take the watch from the major's daughter. Neither she nor her husband looks like they'll give me any trouble."

"That's not what Tony wants you to do."

"Tony's not here, and I'm not dumb enough to let you go because of him."

My back arches over the railing and my feet barely touch the deck. He's gonna push me over, and I'll drown in the Atlantic. Nothing left of me except memories of the girl I was. Nothing about the girl I want to be.

"Come on, Jerry. You want that pocket watch more than you want to hurt me. And you don't want to make an enemy of Tony."

"A minute ago, your idea was to throw Tony aside and work with Major Thomas. What happened to that plan? A lie? Like most everything that comes outta your mouth?"

Jerry's large hand wraps around my throat before I can scream.

The pearl-handled switchblade is in my back pocket. My mother's voice can't help me now. What am I gonna do?

Jerry spins me around, but our feet tangle. We stumble, and I end up with both arms wrapped around the railing and don't intend to let go. He won't toss me overboard. The man is surprised by our new positions and loosens his grip. I drive my knee into his groin, putting all my weight behind it. He hunches forward, if only for an instant, blinks, and then rushes at me. I hunch down and spring up. He is so off-balance when I drive my body into him again that he falls over the railing, his eyes wide, his mouth forming an O of shock as he tumbles over and over until he splashes into the sea.

Madness inspires madness.

If I hear my mother's voice one more time, I might follow Jerry into the sea. Where was she all those years when I desperately needed her? The disembodied voice inside my head is unbearable, a cruel reminder of the help that never comes— the help I need now.

CHAPTER 18

ZINZI

Trench Town, Kingston

Two days since we kissed. Two days since I last saw or spoke to him. On the first day, I worked, did my job at the Constant Spring Hotel. I stayed busy. Then, yesterday, a telegram from Accompong put Byron out of my mind for a little while.

A note from my mother, Momma Hazel Green, written by one of my brothers, Raymond, the eldest, because she never bothered to learn how to write, let alone send a telegram. She surprises me with a request: She wants me to guide a group of tourists to the Cockpit and Accompong—Americans on the SS *Talamanca* from New York City, arriving in Kingston this very week. She promises I won't have to stay in Accompong long, but she would be immensely grateful if I could do her this favor.

So many questions. Why call it a favor? Who are these people? Why me? I am not a tour guide, though I do know the Cockpit inside and out.

There has been some distance between my mother and me that has nothing to do with miles. Something broke between us years ago. Sometimes I, naïvely, blame her fear of my love for mermaids, but that was never the reason. I didn't believe in the magic she hid in her cloth pouches and woven baskets. I didn't believe in the potions, the herbal mixtures, or the talismans.

My relationship with my mother is like a river flowing toward the sea, but not a direct path—barriers exist. Dams. Broken promises. A young girl's need to have someone to blame, as the ones she loved so eagerly kept dying.

It's the last sentence that makes it impossible to say no. "This is Raymond. Momma is very ill and needs to see you."

I tuck the note in the top drawer of my dresser. I'll figure out what to do about it tomorrow.

Allan Coombs's Office, King Street, Kingston

Sitting in Allan's office, between Raymond's note and no news of Byron, I am battling an overwhelming sense of dread.

"What did you say?" Allan asks, lifting his gaze from the newspaper he's been reading.

Had I voiced my concerns aloud? Maybe. "I'm worried about Byron."

"Why? Where is he?"

"I'm not sure where he is," I reply.

"Your concern sounds like it should stay on the other side of the front door. He's not our problem—not when we have a major rally to plan."

I understand Allan's curtness. The Kingston Waterfront protest is shaping up to be the largest of the year. Here I am acting like a lovesick schoolgirl after just one kiss when so much more is on the line. "Sorry," I apologize sincerely.

"This is the largest rally we've ever organized, and we can't afford distractions."

Allan has been on edge since the Victoria Park rally. He doesn't blame Byron for what happened, but his organization is drawing attention across the parishes. All eyes are on the Kingston branch of the labor movement, and any misstep could affect the movement throughout the country.

Allan moistens his lips. "I've been informed that there are rumblings among government officials regarding taxation and the Cockpit. Supposedly, someone in the British Parliament is advocating for a tax on rum produced and sold in the Maroon villages."

"That's ridiculous." I think of Raymond's telegram. "My people have made, bought, and sold rum only among ourselves since 1760 without a hint of taxation. It's our cultural right. Besides, not a single jug is sold outside of the Cockpit. It's not a business." I rise, my anger driving me to pace. "What does Colonel Rowe think about this?" The colonel is the leader of Accompong and is highly respected among the Maroon people, including the arrogant members of the British government. "I'm sure he has a lot to say about it. I can't imagine he'll let this happen without a fight."

"Please, Zinzi. The war doesn't have to start in my office tonight."

My voice had shamefully risen. But I've been so focused on my life in Kingston for so long that I haven't considered how the labor movement might impact Accompong. "I'm sorry."

"It's perfectly fine," Allan replies. "The government is eager to boost island revenues. My sources indicate that these are initial discussions, while some argue they are merely rumors. Nevertheless, we must remain vigilant against these tactics that undermine our people."

Covering my face with my hands, I massage my cheeks. "I'd bet anything that the source of this taxation chatter is the island's European landowners and the rum barons."

Rum barons. Another name for wealthy, influential families who dominate the rum industry and, like the Tynesdale family, also own large sugar plantations, distilleries, and export businesses.

"They are behind this tax plan." My head hurts from the

pressure in my skull. "Rum barons. How dare they attempt to punish the Maroon people?"

I sit at the long table in his office, contemplating whether to tell Allan about Byron's reckless idea of stealing his father's rum recipe, which, suddenly, doesn't sound so ugly to me.

The labor movement has taught me many lessons, but one stands out: One person's loss, pain, grief, or thirst for revenge is just a grain of sand on a beach. What the island needs and what Jamaican workers deserve are dedicated union leaders. Anything less will not suffice. One man's problems shouldn't matter, especially if that man is named Tynesdale.

The room fills with volunteers as Allan reviews his ledger, preparing to speak to the group. "The Kingston Waterfront is a crucial hub. Our demonstration will be one of the largest we've organized, focusing on dockworkers in the shipping and export industries," Allan states. "Movement organizers will travel to Kingston from every parish in Jamaica.

"Dockworkers are very frustrated with low wages, poor working conditions, and a stagnant economy. The risk of violence is significant, and the authorities at Victoria Park are ready to use force at the slightest sign of unrest." He pauses, intensely scanning the faces before him. "While we cannot eliminate the threat of violence, we must not provoke it." He locks eyes with everyone at the table. "Our aim is a peaceful demonstration, and we must commit to the necessary steps to ensure this."

The office door creaks open, and a girl hesitantly peeks in. "What is it?" Allan demands sharply, showing his irritation at the interruption. "Can't it wait?"

She swallows hard. "There's a white man outside with his limo driver," she says. "He insists on seeing Miss Green."

My heart races. My immediate thought, the only one, is of Byron. Something must have gone wrong, and someone is here to bring bad news.

"I'm sorry," I say to Allan. "I truly am." Then I dash out of the room, my new companion—dread—following close behind.

Bernard Christian Tynesdale, Byron's father, waits for me at the reception desk. He wears an ivory gabardine suit and a Panama hat, exuding fashionable arrogance with a well-scrubbed, uniformed limo driver by his side. If not for his slightly quivering white mustache, Mr. Tynesdale Senior would seem indomitable rather than uneasy in proximity to so many dark-skinned people. As I approach him, the questions rolling around in my mind are about Byron. Has something happened to him? Is that why his father is here to see me? But why would his father come to see me if that were true? He knows nothing of me and Byron. Private detective aside, that awkward introduction in the lobby of the Myrtle Bank Hotel shouldn't have led him to me. Why would he think I care? Well, I won't give him any clues about my feelings, especially those I don't fully understand.

"What brings you here?" I ask coolly.

Mr. Tynesdale scans the office as if it's infested with sand fleas. "I need to speak with you privately."

I position myself with my feet apart and my hands on my hips. "You can say whatever you want right here."

"It concerns Byron," he replies.

My determination wavers. "Is he okay? Has he been hurt?"

"As far as I know, he's just as you left him when you last saw him." From his choice of words and sarcastic tone, I can tell he knows I spent the other evening with Byron in Trench Town, and maybe that I didn't leave his Myrtle Bank Hotel until dawn, especially if the private detective Byron mentioned was on the job.

"Yes, we can step outside." I move past him, not waiting

for his response or to see if he follows. It's early evening but the streetlights are on. I stand by a lamppost.

"I'll make this quick, Miss Green. According to my private detective, Byron is trying to involve himself in the labor union movement, with your encouragement."

"No, that's not true," I respond firmly. "Byron is not easily influenced. He makes his own decisions."

"Well, that's debatable," Mr. Tynesdale replies. "I know my son is not an extremist. He doesn't get involved in causes. His interests guide his passions. Despite your idealistic beliefs, your influence over him has little to do with the labor union."

"I have no influence over him."

"I assume you think you met him last week." Mr. Tynesdale chuckles. "He's been following you since his ship docked in Kingston Harbour a month ago from Cuba."

"How do you know that?" I raise an eyebrow. "Ah, yes, the private detective you hired to tail him." I shake my head. "Well, sir, you're mistaken. Your son has been following Allan Coombs and the labor movement, not me. And if you're unfamiliar with Allan Coombs—" I gesture toward the storefront sign. "Take a look around. These are his offices. He is the leader of the Kingston labor union movement. He and Byron are old acquaintances. That's who Byron is following, not me."

He nods at his chauffeur and says, "Bring the car around." The man walks away. "Your stubbornness is forcing my hand. I will tell you what Byron won't or can't say. He's committed to taking over the family business and will run the Tynesdale Estate and its subsidiaries as they've been run for generations, and that will not include union labor."

"That sounds like wishful thinking on your part," I say. "Tell me, are you afraid of your son?"

"I won't allow him to give up his inheritance to satisfy his guilt."

"Why would he feel guilty? Maybe shame for his association with your sugar plantation, but not guilt."

I see a flash of sadness in the man's gaze, but it vanishes as he squares his shoulders and his car pulls up to the curb.

"You should ask Byron about your fiancé," he says. "The young man who died in the Tynesdale sugarcane field a decade ago. It was the same year my wife passed away. I'm sure Byron mentioned his mother, but likely nothing about your beloved. I believe his name was Marvin Banks. As I said, ask Byron."

CHAPTER 19

◆

OTHELLA

The SS Talamanca *at Sea, Day Two*

The knock on my stateroom door sounds like gunfire. I jump out of my berth and, for a moment, can't remember where I am. Then I think of Jerry—the smell of the sea, salt, and fish. I glance out the porthole. Blue water stretches to infinity. I am on board the SS *Talamanca*, sailing to Kingston, Jamaica.

The banging on the door hasn't stopped. "I'm coming! I'm coming! Wait, don't tear the house down."

After slipping on my robe, I fasten the belt around my waist, wipe the sleep from my eyes, and open the door. Robbie rushes past me. I close the door after he enters. "Excuse me, Mr. Barnes. You're in my room, and I'm not properly dressed." I'm teasing, but Robbie isn't in the mood for jokes.

"A stowaway fell overboard and drowned. A sailor saw him splash into the ocean, but they couldn't save him."

I walk to the table next to my bed, pick up the water pitcher, and pour myself a drink. I gulp down a swallow, taking my time as I decide what to tell Robbie and what to keep to myself. "Do you think it might have been Jerry?"

"That's what I wanted to ask you. Have you been in your

WHERE THE FALSE GODS DWELL   159

stateroom all night?" He suddenly covers his mouth with his fist, as if the words came out unconsciously. "I didn't mean to imply . . ."

Robbie's rambling no longer grates. Lately, I find it mostly endearing, and I'm starting to appreciate his wit and kindness. But right now, I need him to get to the point. "Why don't you ask me the question you want answered?"

"Did you find Jerry Merriweather?"

"I fought with him and pushed him, and he fell over the railing." I speak bluntly. I figure that dead is dead, and what killed a man versus what might have killed him doesn't matter much.

"He tried to hurt you and you fought back," Robbie says.

"Yes. That's what happened," I respond. "It took all my strength, but I managed to push him off me." I walk up to Robbie and want him to look me in the eyes. "As you said, the crewman said the stowaway fell into the sea."

Robbie blinks but doesn't turn away from me.

"Are you mad at me?" I squeeze his shoulder.

"Are you sure no one saw you with him?"

"I'm positive."

"Then I don't want to hear anything more about it."

"I didn't have a choice. You believe me, right?"

"It was you or him," Robbie says confidently.

I smile at him. "Pinky swear."

"So, no one else is after you now. He was the last of them."

"No one else." I decide it's not the right time to mention Tony Schaefer or the Chicago Police Department.

"And I can trust that you're telling me the truth?"

"Yes, Robbie, you can trust me," I say, and I truly hope it will be the last lie I tell him. With that, I have nothing to look forward to but sunshine, beaches, and Robbie Barnes, my best friend.

And to think, when I first met him, I thought he was a geek.

CHAPTER 20

───◆───

VIVIAN JEAN

The SS Talamanca *at Sea, Day Two*

The day after the storm, the turmoil is far from over for Tully and me. Our feelings are still raw and choppy, fluctuating between guilt and grief, love and loss, and the possibility of loving again. Mr. Shakespeare said something like, "the past informs the present." So does that mean life's sorrows return with sharper edges and at different speeds? Or does such repetition destroy the soul? And without a soul, how can you love?

Even if I prove Tully wrong about the note, will he let go of his guilt? Will his fear that his confrontation with his brother somehow led to the trouble in our marriage? And what about me? Is my only chance for forgiveness to be found in the roots of the silk cotton tree?

A crewman knocks on our door and announces dinner, but Tully and I are exhausted from delving too deeply into the painful parts of our lives.

I roll off my twin bed and jostle Tully's shoulder. "Wake up. We've got to hurry."

Bleary-eyed and licking the dryness from his lips, he asks, "When did we fall asleep?"

"I don't remember, but I'm hungry. We missed dinner last night and I don't want to miss it again."

"Neither do I."

We arrive in the dining room on the Saloon Deck and sit next to each other at a round table set for eight. Tully and I are the last to join our dinner companions, three of whom are strangers. It's a formality of cruise ships, Katherine explained before. The captain assigns passengers to the people they will share meals with.

Katherine is seated to my left, with Othella and Robbie beside her. To Tully's immediate right sits a German orchestra conductor, Erich Greenberger, and his wife, Hannah. Between Robbie and the conductor's wife is Anne Spencer, a Negro poet traveling alone.

The composition of the table surprises me. I didn't expect to dine with white passengers. Noticing my confusion, Tully whispers that aboard a ship like the SS *Talamanca*, Commander O'Flanagan makes decisions based on his preferences. He and his crew seem somewhat indifferent to a passenger's skin color. That tolerance extended to Jews, but only to a point. "He wouldn't sit a Jew at a table of whites, I don't imagine," Tully had said.

Tully blames my single-minded focus on Negro civil rights or anthropology and the study of ancient African cultures for my lack of knowledge about white people's prejudices among themselves. "Infighting doesn't interest you if it doesn't relate to the civil liberties denied the Negro by whites." Tully shrugs. "It's one of your shortcomings, darling. The world is bigger than our backyard."

He tells me this while the others discuss the storm and the stowaway who went missing at sea the night before. Then the conversation shifts to Jamaica.

"We are staying at the Constant Spring Hotel, a resort located five miles outside Kingston," Mrs. Greenberger says. She is blond, younger than me, with soft, bland features and a whispery voice.

"I plan to alternate between playing golf and lounging by the pool," Mr. Greenberger interjects. "I guess I'll explore the local markets. Perhaps I'll take a trip to the Blue Mountains."

Mrs. Greenberger laughs. "Pipe dreams. He'll be on the golf course the whole time."

Their accents fascinate me. I haven't been around people who aren't American other than Maxi. I hope I'm not being too rude, staring down their throats when they speak.

"We're traveling up to the Cockpit Mountains," Tully adds. "And the Maroon village, Accompong."

"That sounds like an intriguing trip," says Anne Spencer.

"I hear you've traveled to Jamaica before, Miss Spencer," Katherine says. "I am familiar with your articles on the subject."

"How flattering. You are correct. I spent several weeks on the island in '29, visiting several parishes and mostly villages rather than cities like Kingston or Montego Bay. It helped me connect more deeply to the people and the African cultures here."

"That's similar to the goals of my fieldwork," Katherine says proudly. "I'm exploring the history of African dance in the Caribbean by focusing on the Maroon people in Accompong."

"I saw you perform at the World's Fair in Chicago," says Anne Spencer. "You and your company of dancers were brilliant." She nods at the rest of us. "I'm so sorry. We don't mean to dominate the conversation." Anne Spencer turns to the Greenbergers. "What are your plans besides golf, Mr. Greenberger?"

"Jamaica is a short getaway before the season starts," he replies.

"Then you'll head back to Germany?" I say casually, but the Greenbergers seem surprised by my question.

"Hannah and I left Germany some time ago," Mr. Greenberger quickly adds. "After our vacation, we're off to New York. I'm an assistant conductor with the Philharmonic."

"My husband makes it seem like leaving Germany was our choice. We were exiled because we're Jewish."

Anne Spencer shakes her head. "With Hitler and Mussolini in power, I am truly afraid of what's happening in the world."

"Mussolini?" Othella speaks for the first time. I've noticed how reserved she and Robbie have been—maybe they have had a disagreement. "I'm sorry, I don't know who he is."

"A fascist ally of Hitler," Mr. Greenberger retorts sharply.

"I've heard that more discriminatory laws may take effect in Germany as soon as this month," Anne Spencer remarks.

Othella scans the table, waiting for someone else to pose the question, but her impatience grows. "What are these laws?"

"German Jews will lose their citizenship and be classified as state subjects without any rights," Anne Spencer says soberly.

"We might never go back to Germany," Mrs. Greenberger states, her voice wavering slightly.

"Now, don't even say or think that, dear," her husband says. "We'll return one day."

She touches a napkin to her lips. "Some of Erich's relatives are in New York, and my husband has a fantastic opportunity with the Philharmonic. We'll ride out the craziness for a year or two, but I feel sad that our child won't be born at home in Berlin."

"You're pregnant?" I ask, ignoring the pain in my chest.

"Yes, I'm a couple of months along." She smiles at her husband. "But I'm fine to travel—and I'm eager to return home to Germany as soon as possible. My parents and cousins live in Berlin."

An awkward silence settles over our dinner table like a cloud. Tully breaks the silence. "Roosevelt is doing the right things for America now."

"You're right. Roosevelt's New Deal is starting off strong and could make all the difference," Anne Spencer stresses. "We might get out of this Depression sooner rather than later."

"How does he feel about entering a world war?" asks Mr. Greenberger. "Will he ignore what's happening in Europe? Or in Italy with Mussolini?"

"What about if the Fascists invade Ethiopia?" Anne Spencer weighs in. "It is one of the shining lights of African civilization and he's set his sights on it."

"We should change the subject before our meal is ruined," Tully suggests.

The table guests nod in unison and the conversation takes a turn. "Miss Dunham, perhaps you might consider a dance performance?" Mr. Greenberger proposes. "I play the piano superbly, if I say so myself, and my wife is an exceptional violinist. Based on what Miss Spencer has said, we would be honored to accompany you for a recital. And I'm sure the commander would concur."

"If he agrees, I'd love to," Katherine replies, mindful of the ship's rules. "And Vivian Jean, will you join me? We can perform the duet we prepared for the World's Fair."

"Will you ever forgive me for missing that performance?"

Katherine scrunches her nose and smiles. "No."

Everyone laughs, but I know Katherine has spoken from the heart. "Then maybe I should miss this one, too."

"Touché," Katherine replies. "Touché."

*   *   *

It's a bright, sun-filled afternoon. Katherine and I are on the Promenade Deck, lounging in steamer chairs, sipping tea, and reading *Vogue* magazine and the *Chicago Defender*. Katherine had taken a copy from a Pullman porter, and I picked up the *Jamaica Gleaner* from the ship's library.

"Have you ever had to beg for food?" I ask Katherine after an hour with my nose buried in the *Gleaner*. "Or waited in a soup line, or had to stoke a stove?"

She closes her magazine. "Definitely not."

"Me neither. Maxi handles everything. Cooks my meals, makes the beds, cleans the floors, does the laundry."

Katherine's expression sharpens. "So you and your husband live in a large house, have wealthy parents, and have never faced hunger." Her tone is mocking.

"Don't tease me—I'm trying to make a point."

"What point is that?"

"These stories about Jamaica." I wave the *Gleaner* at Katherine, "The economy is in ruins, and the people are struggling. A handful of wealthy business owners control the lives of most Jamaicans, who are fighting to feed their families and to survive. There's also a hierarchy based on skin color." I pause to take a breath. "There is a labor union movement, but rallies are dangerous. Lives have been lost."

Katherine squints. "You've described every island in the Caribbean, which, like America, is grappling with racism and the Depression. The economy didn't just collapse in Chicago."

"I know that."

"Then what's going on? You act like these hardships are a revelation."

"It's just that when I read these stories, I feel like I've spent my life in a cave called Hartfield House."

"For the past few years, you've had good reason," Katherine says, with a hint of sympathy in her gaze I don't mind. "Your life has been turbulent to say the least and staying in your cave made sense."

"Why would you think that?" I reply with a sad chuckle. "That's why this expedition, this trip, is so important to me—and Tully."

"I noticed you two during dinner last night."

I lean forward in the steamer chair. "We weren't fighting or anything like that. It's just that I sometimes wish I lived in a fantasy. I dream of sitting on a veranda on a chilly evening with my husband, enjoying cups of hot chocolate, wrapped in a shawl. I want him to make love to me every night and every morning. I want to begin and end each day in each other's arms." I moisten my dry lips. "I want to have his baby."

"There's nothing medically wrong that says you can't try again for a child, right?" Katherine swings her legs off the chair.

I shake my head. "No, there's no physical reason."

"Life isn't perfect. You know that better than anyone else I know."

"I do, but something has happened recently that could destroy any chance of Tully and me having that kind of happiness."

"I really don't want to know what's going on. I told you that any issues between you and Tully can't interfere with my expedition. But when I'm not high on my horse," she smiles, "you can always talk to me."

"I know, I know."

Together, we lean back in our steamer chairs, stretch our legs, and cross our ankles. I gaze up at the crystal-blue sky and marvel at the view.

"It's a visual masterpiece," Katherine says, as if we share the same thoughts.

A crewman interrupts us. "Miss Durham, Mrs. Hartfield, I am delivering your telegrams."

"Finally, word from the outside world has arrived," Katherine says brightly.

Two telegrams are addressed to me—one from Maxi and the other from my father. I stuff both into my handbag, unwilling to share their contents, regardless of what they say. But I want to open Maxi's letter in front of Tully. We had asked her about Clifford's note, but I wouldn't read it without Tully present.

Katherine tears open her telegram, reads it, and looks very unhappy. "Some of my meticulously arranged plans have gone awry," she says. "My Accompong guide has quit before the job even starts."

"I'm sorry."

"He was injured at one of those labor union demonstrations you were reading about." Katherine sighs. "I hate to ask, but did Maxi arrange a guide for you?"

"Yes. I believe it's one of her relatives in Accompong," I reply. "I'll telegram her and confirm."

Katherine blows out a mouthful of air. "And to think I made such a big deal about you not interfering with my expedition. And now I'm interfering in yours."

"That's not the case at all and you know it. I'm happy to help in any way I can."

"I hope your guide isn't involved in these demonstrations," Katherine says. "We won't make it to Accompong without one."

"It will all work out. You'll see." I swing my legs onto the deck. "I'm heading in. I promised to meet Tully for tea before dinner."

"Okay. I'm going to take it easy for a bit longer," Katherine claims. "And later, when you're ready, you have to tell me what was in your telegrams. Your face was quite ashen."

I exhale the breath I didn't realize I was holding. "Maybe I will. Or maybe I won't."

CHAPTER 21

———— ◆ ————

ZINZI

Trench Town, Kingston

My father died from the injuries he sustained while working at the Tynesdale Estate. Every inch of him was a scab, a scar, or a burn. When he passed, my mother couldn't be consoled. She cried for days, months, years.

Some nights, as I try to fall asleep, the memories of what I have lost are so vivid, so loud, and relentless that I can almost touch the scars on my father's arms, kiss Marvin's cold, lifeless lips, or dare River Mumma to pull me under the sea.

I lie in my cot, staring at the ceiling, wishing for the darkness to end and the dawn to rise.

I roll onto my side wearily. Generations of the Maroon people fought for their freedom and survived. I moved through my grief after my father's death when I met Marvin. A joyful bull of a man, he was eager to raise a family and believed in the power of the silk cotton tree.

Maybe Raymond's message arrived just in time. Maybe Byron will be able to tell me how much truth there is in his father's words.

Maybe, as much as I don't want to, leaving Kingston for a few days to play tour guide for some Americans will give me a chance to clear my mind. Allan said he understood. Whatever Byron says about his father won't matter. I might as well go and see my mother.

Myrtle Bank Hotel, Kingston

The sunset spreads over Kingston Harbour like a fading rainbow. I sit on the veranda at the Myrtle Bank Hotel, watching Byron as he watches me. "The other day, your father visited Allan's office." I pause, waiting for Byron's reaction, but he shows none. "He said you misled Allan and me about your motives for joining the labor union movement. He claims you've been keeping track of me for a while, since shortly after your return to Jamaica several weeks ago."

"My father believes the only way I could be interested in the labor union has to be about something other than the union."

"Like a woman?"

He shakes his head, dismissing my supposition. "Did he mention the tax?"

"On the Maroon people for the rum made in the Cockpit? Yes, he brought it up."

"He's behind the push by government officials and other plantation owners."

"That's not all he had to say." A chill runs down my spine. "Did you know a fieldworker at Tynesdale Estates named Marvin Banks?"

Byron's jaw muscles tighten. "He was your fiancé, and yes, I knew him, which I assume my father told you." He lights a cigarette, his hand shaking slightly. "I met him the season I worked the sugarcane fields at Tynesdale. We were mates."

"Were you with him the day he died?" I fear I'll lose control of my voice but I manage to avoid screaming and keep talking. "Was it your machete that took his life? Why didn't you tell me you knew him?"

"I—I didn't know he was your fiancé at first."

"You're lying. How could you not know?"

"Because you never said his name when you spoke at the rallies I attended. And he never referred to you by name when he talked about his fiancée."

"I still don't believe you," I say, my voice icy. "If you knew him, you would have known about us. That's just who he was."

"The woman he loved he called Mermaid."

Marvin knew of my love for flowing water and River Mumma. He understood my fear of enclosed spaces. He knew everything there was to know about the girl I was then and the woman I aspired to be. He called me Mermaid, a creature capable of conquering her fears, loving generously, and escaping any prison that might hold her, with the help of water and fins.

Hearing his nickname for me again after so long nearly brings me to my knees.

"Did you know about Marvin and me on the day you saved me from arrest? Was it some misguided attempt to make amends? Tell me—when did you find out that Marvin's Mermaid and I were the same?"

"It was my father and his private detective. They told me."

"Do you even care about the labor union movement? Why are you here? To tell me more lies?"

"Zinzi, please. I swear. My father will do or say whatever he can to keep me under his thumb. He told you lies and half-truths. He wants you not to trust me, for he knows if you don't, neither will Allan Coombs. He wants you to be afraid of his power. That's why he's leading the discussion on taxation against the Maroon people over rum. He's a bully: putting police officers in his pocket, sabotaging rallies, and arresting labor union organizers and volunteers." Byron exhales. "His first step is to have you arrested."

"Why me? Why not Allan or any of the organizers?"

"Bernard Tynesdale knows I care about you and believes you influenced my support for the labor union movement."

The air on the veranda rises toward the sky and disappears into the clouds. I try to swallow, but there's nothing in my throat. "I can't be arrested. I couldn't bear being trapped in a jail cell."

The lines across his forehead deepen. "Trust me. I'll find a way to stop him. But I can't do it yet. I need more time and for you to be patient."

I sense he's not saying something. "What do you want me to do?"

"Don't go to the Kingston Waterfront rally. Leave town."

"Run away? The Waterfront rally is too important to miss."

Byron leans forward, elbows on the table, palms pressed together. "Consider my father's threat a promise. He will have you arrested."

The hotel's veranda is too crowded, and our conversation is attracting onlookers. Or it's my imagination. Either way, I need to leave. "I can't sit here. Can we go for a walk?"

"Yes, sure." Byron asks for the check, although I don't recall ordering anything. Soon, we make our way through the lobby when a crack of thunder explodes. Then lightning and a downpour begin.

"Let's go upstairs to my suite," he says. "We can sit on the balcony and watch the rain."

We climb the stairs in silence, lost in our own thoughts.

In his suite, he stops in the small entranceway. "I hope you know I didn't want any of this to happen. Since we met, I've felt a connection to you that isn't only about the labor movement."

He's talking about the kiss, and if not, I'm thinking about

it. I feel a flutter in my stomach, a kaleidoscope of butterflies making themselves known. "Oh you do?"

Byron looks down at me with gentle eyes. "I've known you for a week, but I want to know you better and longer." He chuckles shyly. "I think I'm falling in love with you, or maybe I'm already in love."

Rarely in the past ten years have I been at a loss for words. In this moment, I am speechless. I have spent most of my thirty-two years either in love or afraid of love. I cherished my father, my fiancé, and the Cockpit, along with the thatched-roof hut where I grew up. I loved everything from tilling the soil during planting season to digging for root vegetables in the fall and picking ackee fruit, Jamaican cherries, and strawberries in late spring and early summer. But love can destroy as much as it heals.

That's why I fear it, and that fear has kept me safe for a decade. Byron, with his passion, determination, quiet strength, and even his anger—damn him—takes my fear away. Without knowing how, I find myself in his arms, sharing a kiss that is so passionate, so consuming, so sensual I forget why I waited so long for another kiss and now, that kiss is not enough. I want to feel his body pressed against mine, his lips on my throat, my breasts.

Passionately, my arms wrap around his neck. He has one hand on my waist, and I don't notice where his other hand is until I feel his palm gently cupping my chin. I forget about time, sugarcane, and fear as we make the kind of love I had given up on, a feeling I haven't experienced in too long. Since leaving Accompong, I have been with other men. My body craves what it craves, but with Byron, I discover something more intimate and profound—something deeper than I can or want to define.

Afterward, we lay in his bed, naked, our bodies glowing from the love we've shared. Admittedly, however, I don't recall how we got to the bedroom or where we left our clothing.

Curled against his body, I decide that I might as well give him my answer.

"All right—"

"All right what?" he says with surprise, squeezing me tighter.

"I'll stay away from the rally, but your father is dangerous."

"I am my father's son, but I won't let him jeopardize the family business because of his inability to change." Byron inhales deeply. "I'll make it right, Zinzi. Trust me."

CHAPTER 22

VIVIAN JEAN

The SS Talamanca *at Sea*

Tully and I sit on the edge of one of the twin beds in our stateroom. The telegram, open in my hand, stares ominously at me.

"What did Maxi say?"

"Ask your father. The Major will explain," I read.

"Ask your father?" Tully's voice echoes. "What does that mean?"

"How should I know? It doesn't make any sense."

Tully lets out a sigh. "Show me the telegram." He extends his hand, and I pass it to him. He skims the note, frowning. "You're right. It doesn't make sense."

I had hoped Maxi would shed light on the mystery surrounding Clifford's note. She's always come through for me before. But this time, her reply only deepens the confusion. What would my father know about Clifford's note?

Tully might not believe in coincidences, but I'm starting to think he wishes for them just to escape the misery. "Read your father's telegram." Tully stands up, walks to the stateroom door, and presses his head against the steel, with tension evident in his every muscle.

"Perhaps it's not merely a coincidence that the telegrams arrived simultaneously." I raise the envelope. "Let's hope that after I open it, this whole thing will be behind us. Then you'll need to find another reason to be mad at me."

"Stop putting it off. Open it and read it aloud," Tully suggests.

I set aside Maxi's brief telegram and read my father's message, making sure my eyes don't skip ahead. Tully and I will discover what my father wrote at the same moment.

> *Dear Vivian Jean, I will meet you at the Appleton Station, the stop before Maggotty. The train will drop you off there, and I'll be waiting. You'll be happy to hear that I've already arrived in Kingston. I had the chance to fly on an airplane. What an experience! I hope to share it with you and Tully someday. Also, I received a message from Maxi that requires a more complicated response . . .*

My breath is trapped in my throat and I can't go on. I close my eyes and cross my fingers and toes, as if it will help make my father's words easier to digest.

"If you don't hurry up," Tully urges, "I swear to God . . ." He sounds dramatic, but I share the emotion.

I swallow and continue.

> *Maxi invited me to read Clifford's note. She also told me about your questions. I will discuss it with you when I see you, which will be very soon. And I know this— the truth will be hard for you to hear, and I genuinely regret that. The truth is often difficult. Your loving father, Major Thomas.*

Tully sits beside me on the twin bed. Instead of asking for the note, he takes it from me.

"What do you think the note means now?" I ask.

He rubs his eyes wearily. "As far as I'm concerned, nothing has changed."

"How can you say that? Everything has changed. Maxi and my father know why Clifford wrote the note and to whom he wrote it."

I feel like I'm on a merry-go-round. As soon as I step off one horse, I climb onto another without any time to recover. I squeeze my eyes shut. Tully can't be right about the damn note. But what if he is?

"We'll find out everything when we meet your father."

"So, let's get ready for dinner. It's our last night on board and it's black tie—the commander's orders."

"Oh, right," I murmur, lost in a trance. "There will be dancing and champagne."

"And a lot of whiskey," Tully adds.

Our final night aboard the SS *Talamanca*, dinner will consist of items I dislike. The food is too heavy and has a fishy smell, whether it's beef or baked chicken. The champagne is rarely cold enough, the potatoes are lumpy, and the bread is stale. As for the musicians, every other note they play sounds off-key. But since it's the last night at sea, do I have a choice? I must attend.

I wear my best outfit, the same mint-green sheer chiffon I wore at Mr. Abbott's reception. Maxi had reminded me that I had also donned it at my twenty-ninth birthday celebration. I danced the night away in Tully's arms while the quartet played a captivating tune. With my heart racing, Tully and I forgot about the two-step and lost ourselves in a delicious rhumba.

The lively rhythms and Tully's graceful movements were

magnificent. Clifford only danced the waltz. I enjoy the waltz, but the rhumba pulses through my veins.

Everyone is already chatting when Tully and I reach the table. Erich Greenberger thinks everything he says deserves attention. Anne Spencer brings up topics I must research in the ship's library, so I remain quiet to avoid embarrassing myself. Even Othella and Robbie, who usually appear sullen and downcast, are annoyingly cheerful. They are falling in love, which is tough to witness. The only love match I care about is with the man, ordering his second whiskey, sitting next to me.

After a glass of warm champagne, the meal continues as I relax, but I'm not the only one savoring the last night aboard the SS *Talamanca*. Katherine laughs at one of Tully's baseball jokes. The poet Anne talks about Ethiopia's struggle against fascism with Erich. Hannah, the German conductor's wife, keeps rubbing her round belly to soothe her unborn child between bites of buttered potatoes while inquiring about dessert, particularly the apple pie. I feel a pang of jealousy, having lost Clifford's baby before I ever experienced any cravings.

I turn to Othella and Robbie. Although I don't want to watch them, I can't take my eyes off them. Robbie is more earnest about the budding romance than Othella, but she's not as far behind as she used to be. She keeps glancing at me, giggling, and playfully rolling her eyes. It's amusing how she can appear and act like a child one moment and something else the next, but I can't quite pinpoint what that something else is.

Tully takes my hand. "Is Katherine dancing tonight?"

"Yes, she is," I reply.

Just then, Katherine signals to Mr. Greenberger and Hannah. The three of them leave the dinner table and head for the corridor outside the dining room. When they return,

Erich walks up to the piano with his wife beside him, her violin tucked under one arm and her bow in the other. Katherine steps into the center of the dance floor and bows deeply. Slowly, in a silent room with no music playing, she begins to move, her body a fearless instrument of poise and elegance, spinning one way and then the other in an effortless series of steps, turns, and poses.

Erich strikes the first chords, and I immediately recognize the opening overture: Mendelssohn's *A Midsummer Night's Dream*. Mademoiselle choreographed a solo to it. Watching Katherine perform the piece now, in her strappy, thick-soled pumps and her white dress instead of pointe shoes and a tutu, makes the dance even more radiant.

As the final note fades, the dining room erupts in applause, and the passengers rise to give the trio a standing ovation. This prompts couples to rush to the dance floor, encouraging the Greenbergers to keep playing.

"We haven't danced together the whole cruise," Tully says, standing beside my chair. Erich continues to play the piano, with Hannah accompanying him.

"Would you care to dance with me?" I ask softly.

He looks down at me, smiling. "Yes, I would."

"Why?" I ask.

He cocks his head. "We won't have another chance to dance together in Jamaica. And that dress," he says, as his gaze sweeps over her, "you wore it last year. We danced the rhumba."

"You remembered."

He sighs. "I remember."

CHAPTER 23

— ⋅◆⋅ —

ZINZI

Kingston Railway Station

The awe. The excitement. The wide-eyed wonder. Even a hint of fear in one young woman's eyes—possibly the smartest reaction. These are the faces of the travelers I seek as I walk past the ticket counters and cargo holding spaces toward the waiting area on the ground floor of the Kingston Railway Station. This is where my group has been instructed to wait for me, their guide from Kingston to Cockpit Country, the home of the Maroon people and the village of Accompong.

The journey begins for them at the train station, near the waterfront at the western edge of downtown Kingston. A two-story structure, the Kingston-to-Montego-Bay railway station is Georgian in architectural style and made of brick and stone, with a touch of elegance in the mahogany staircase that leads to the stationmaster's quarters. Arched doorways and windows, wide eaves, and overhanging roofs offer little protection for passengers from the sun and daily rainfall.

Stylish yet weathered, built in 1845, it has been repeatedly patched and mended after hurricanes, rainstorms, lightning strikes, and the brutal heat that melts even stone in a decade or so, but the Kingston Railway still holds up.

I haven't been inside the station in ages—since my last trip to Accompong a few years ago. I can't even recall how long exactly. I wonder if the Americans notice the remnants of old-world beauty? Will they appreciate the artistry of the wooden tracks and the steam locomotive engine, or the winding path as we twist around and upward into the cool, jagged jungle of the Cockpit?

I spot them precisely where I asked them to gather. There are three women and two men. At first glance, they are some-what of an unusual bunch. The riding pants, pith helmets, heavy lace-up boots, and knapsacks are too creased, starched, and shiny. The price tags are still visible, even though I can't actually spot any—they are there. I next note the line of sweaty, shirtless load bearers nearby, carrying their stream of crates, suitcases, and equipment—far too much to take in.

With my gaze back on the group, I see that they don't ap-pear particularly brave for such a dangerous journey and ex-tended stay. I have been told they will be in Accompong for at least a month or longer.

The Cockpit is a rugged, forested region with steep-sided hollows and a striking maze of sinkholes, ridges, underground rivers, and caves. It is known for its jagged, weather-carved limestone landscape, which made it a perfect stronghold for escaped, enslaved Africans who resisted British colonial rule in the 17th century and to this day—the Maroons. That's why I know it so well. The ins and outs of this region were my home, and my father taught me how to survive in Cock-pit Country. Too bad he never figured out how to live through the cruelty of picking sugarcane on a Jamaican plan-tation.

The first person I meet is Katherine Dunham, the leader of the group. She is much younger than her reputation suggests. And yes, she has a reputation. Once I received the leader's name, I asked around, curious about this independent-minded American Negro. Interestingly enough, several important people in Jamaica, including Colonel Rowe, leader of the Maroon people and a citizen of Accompong, know of her. She and her party will be his guests on his property during their stay. Hopefully, her ego will be flexible enough to follow directions.

I introduce myself, and Miss Dunham explains that the group consists of anthropologists, a biologist, a camera operator, and an assistant—none of them are tourists. I don't understand why she says this because I made no mention of any of them being tourists.

Miss Dunham announces the names of the rest of the members of her party: Vivian Jean Hartfield, her husband, Tobias Hartfield, but call him Tully, and their two assistants, Robbie Barnes and Othella Montgomery. Something about this girl, however, is different. She's young, but she doesn't look her age. Not so much older but she seems experienced. She's round and pretty, but her gaze moves deliberately and doesn't miss a thing.

Dunham goes on about her credentials, mentioning that her travel fellowships from the Julius Rosenwald and Guggenheim Foundations cover the entire cost of her journey. I wonder why she needs to impress me, but the train will begin to board soon and it's my turn to speak.

"I have a few announcements, so please bear with me," I interrupt her flow of details.

"Sorry, of course," responds Miss Dunham, gesturing to the group. "Everyone, come closer. This young woman has some important updates before we board the train."

"My name is Zinzi Green and I will be your guide to Accompong." The Hartfield woman gasps audibly, and Dunham silences her with a wave.

"Continue, Miss Green," she instructs as the other woman looks awestruck but obeys, closing her gaping mouth.

"The Cockpit stretches across the center of the island and is full of sinkholes, dense forests, and caverns. There are plenty of tropical plants and plenty of tropical insects and other animals. It is the most dangerous region in Jamaica." I pause for emphasis, and from the wide-eyed terror in the young girl's eyes, I have one believer. "Your survival relies on you keeping aware of your surroundings. When we arrive in Maggotty, we'll get our mules and set off for Accompong."

"Mules?" the young girl inquires. "What is a mule?"

I hold my chuckle in my throat. "Your name is Othella, right?"

"Yes, ma'am."

"A mule is an animal that results from crossing a horse with a donkey, but it has a gentler nature," I explain. "Now, let's get ready. We have a three-hour train ride ahead."

Suddenly, Mrs. Hartfield steps forward eagerly. "It's such a pleasure to meet you. I feel like I already know you."

I look at her sideways. "What do you mean?"

"Your last name is Green," Mrs. Hartfield says with a grin. "My maid is Maxi Green. She was raised in Accompong but moved to America in 1915. She arranged for you to be our guide."

"Your maid?" I cross my arms over my chest, blocking a possible embrace I suspect from the way she leans toward me. "Mrs. Hartfield, I'm sorry, but I don't know a Maxi Green. My mother asked me to do this."

"Call me Vivian Jean," she says. "But you're too young to remember her. I'm sure your mother does. Can you believe I never asked Maxi the name of the family members she reached out to?"

Getting a closer look at Vivian Jean, I see she is stylishly dressed in the latest riding pants fashion, but she's as thin as a rail. I can guess it's not because she starves herself. She is simply excitable, and she speaks quickly, like flames fleeing from a burning building.

"There are many Greens in Jamaica," I say. "But I don't know of a Maxi Green in my family."

"Are you from Accompong?" Vivian Jean persists. "You see, she arranged for our guide—I mean, you—and she said it would be one of her relatives, or that's what I thought she said. . . ." She grimaces with embarrassment. "I'm sorry, but she's not only my maid."

"I don't know her," I reply gruffly, then remember I should soften my tone. "When we get to Accompong, you can ask my mother if she does."

A train whistle sounds, and a wave of anxiety settles in my stomach. My thoughts shift from Katherine Dunham, Vivian Jean Hartfield, and the other members of the Dunham expedition to the challenges of recent days. The last thing I want is to leave Kingston. The labor movement needs me, and I need it. Allan said he understood why I had to go, but do I?

The train whistle sounds again.

"Let's move," I say. "The train won't wait forever." I glance at the load bearers and urge them to hurry. I stay on the platform until everyone and everything that needs to board the train gets on the train. It takes a while because the expedition has many crates, boxes, and supplies. This isn't merely a weekend excursion. Forget a month, they've brought enough provisions to stay in Accompong for a year. I wish them well, but if the spirits allow, I'll return to Kingston before the expedition unpacks.

There is too much history for me in Accompong, and it's not the kind you sing about around the firepit or recite in a ritual.

I'll see my mother. She is ill, after all. I just can't stay long—I can't stay long at all.

CHAPTER 24

OTHELLA

Kingston-to-Montego-Bay Railway

I read aloud from the United Fruit Company travel brochure:

" 'The main line of the Appleton Estate railway departs from Kingston at noon each day and travels west through Spanish Town, Old Harbour, and May Pen before continuing through Bal-la-cla-va.' "

"Balaclava, that's it, Othella," Robbie says supportively. "Keep it up."

"Give me a minute." I stare out the glassless train window, listening to the crunch of the wheels on the broken iron slats. Cackling chickens roam the train, competing with the braying beasts in the caboose. Seated across from me are partially clothed islanders smoking hand-rolled cigarettes and chewing on sliced fruit.

The clickety-clack noise grows louder as the train ascends on wobbly tracks, winding around hills and jagged cliffs, passing through valleys and swaying near limestone rocks and fields of banana trees. The air is filled with the scent of

186 Denny S. Bryce

ripe fruit—bananas, mangoes, and coconuts. My mother once bought a coconut in Chicago—how it got there, I never knew—and we ate it in the kitchenette after she used a large knife to split it open. If this is to be my new home, knowing how to use a big knife seems smart because my switchblade is half the size of my mother's coconut cutter.

It's strange to think I can never go back to Chicago, not with blood on my hands. The train lurches to the side: *What am I doing here?*

This town, Accompong, is a village, and I have never seen a village before. It surely has no jazz music, dance halls, gin and tonics, or satin sheets. Not that I'd ever slept on satin sheets, but there was always a chance that might happen in Chicago.

Then there are my clothes. My T-strap pumps, sheer chiffon dresses, and plunging necklines are out of place in the jungle. And heaven help me, I have only one pack of cigarettes, even though the islanders on the train are smoking—but those hand-rolled cigarettes aren't my brand.

"Come on, Othella. Read a little more."

His voice pulls me from my panic. "Okay, Robbie, I'm reading, I'm reading." I bring the brochure closer to my face. The print is small, but I love the smell of the ink. " 'Eventually, this train will pass by the Appleton Estate.' " I pause. "What is that?"

Another jarring shift occurs, and it feels like the train is about to derail. Sitting next to me, Robbie seems to share the same concern as he turns an unhealthy shade of brown and green.

"It's a sugar plantation," he says between rough swallows. "The largest in this parish, after the Tynesdale Estate."

"A sugar plantation?"

"Sugarcane grows in fields like corn. By the time you see it in the grocery store, it has already been processed," Robbie explains.

I think about this for a moment, my eyes squinting in concentration. Then I unfold the brochure to the last page and read, " 'We'll arrive in Maggot Town.' " I frown at Robbie. "Now, that's a disgusting name."

"It's pronounced Maggotty," he assures me.

"All I hear is *maggot*."

I wince, my body twisting in disgust. The smells of bananas and other fruits have given way to the stench of animal droppings and the sweat of several Jamaican passengers in baggy, unwashed dungarees, straw hats, and without proper shirts. Beneath the foul odors lies a sweet, sugary scent reminiscent of the molasses my mother used when she ran out of white sugar.

"Robbie, what will I do in this village? Should I stay with you all day? Will we live in the same house? Are you going to teach me about the plants and animals from that book you read about the Caribbean jungles?"

"You'll spend part of the day with me and I'll teach you about plants and small animals, but we'll also work for Miss Katherine and Miss Vivian Jean. Whatever she asks us to do, we'll do it."

"You should call them Katherine and Vivian Jean. That's what they told me. You should do the same." I stare out the window again. There is little to see besides rocks, green leaves, and brown bark. "I hope I'm going to like living in Accompong."

The train hits another bump, and I worry that everyone on board will be tossed into the jungle. I grab Robbie's hand, and his fingers intertwine with mine. He touches my cheek gently, lifts my hand to his lips, and kisses my knuckles.

"Don't worry. We'll be there soon enough."

Why did a few words from Robbie make such a difference? The uncertainties fade away and I rest my head on his
shoulder. "I'm tired. You said soon, but how much longer?"

"Miss Zinzi said it would take three hours with all the
stops the train makes. We have at least another hour to go."

I close my eyes and let myself daydream. Katherine has described the African dances we will explore in Jamaica as
primitive yet inspirational. Our ancestors danced the same
steps we are about to learn to honor their heritage. I won't
need a crystal ball to know that whatever dances the Maroon
people perform will be nothing like the Lindy Hop, the fox-
trot, or the shimmy.

I jerk upright.

"Are you feeling okay, Othella?" Robbie asks, his voice
gentle with concern.

"Did you bring any Cab Calloway records? Mr. Hartfield
has recording machines, so he must have a gramophone or
phonograph too, right?"

"I don't think so. Even if it plays, he might reserve the needles for recording," Robbie replies, looking at me with something like pity.

I am livid, but my anger quickly fades. It's not his fault
that I am rethinking everything.

"When we arrive," he begins, "we'll freshen up and take a
nap. I'm sure Katherine and Vivian Jean won't mind if we
rest for a bit before the hard work begins."

"No matter what that hard work turns out to be," I state
with a hint of unhappiness.

"I understand why you're feeling this way."

"If you think my mood has anything to do with what I
told you last night about Jerry," I whisper his name, "it has
nothing to do with that. I'm worried I won't like it here. I'm
terrified I won't enjoy anywhere other than where I've been.
I've spent too much time picking pockets, gold-digging, and

being a floozy. Sorry, if I never mentioned the floozy part before."

"It's okay. You already told me."

"I'm just worried I won't fit in in Jamaica."

"You should have more faith in yourself," he replies. "Everything you've dreamed of will be yours if you want it badly enough."

"You live in a fairyland," I exclaim. "You got parents? You told me you were a numbers runner and did some bad stuff, but you haven't told me much else."

"I have parents. They live in Ohio. Yes, I've done some things, but mostly I've read books, picked snap beans and corn, and milked cows. I come from a family of farmers, you know. I grew up on a farm."

"Why did you leave? Did they die?"

"No, they're alive and kicking. But I got into some trouble helping a white woman and had to leave home. When I got to Chicago, I met Major Thomas, who helped me."

"Major Thomas took you in just like the reverend did me after my mother died." I don't mention Jerry's comment about the major being a bootlegger. Robbie might already know, but if he doesn't, I don't want to be the one to tell him.

"The reverend? You hardly mention him, or the orphanage. I don't mean to pry, but it seems like I am, right?" He smiles shyly.

"No matter. I'll tell you about the orphanage and the reverend one day." I shrug. "Or maybe not. It's just that I can never go back to Chicago. I have to stay here, in this country. Are you gonna stay with me? No, don't answer that. I know you will. You'll never leave."

He laughs. "If you want me to stay with you, I will."

"Sounds to me like you don't have many other places to go, just like I don't."

"If you say so."

A deafening noise erupts as rickety wheels screech over rickety tracks. I hold on to Robbie and gaze out the window. "How much longer before we reach Maggotty and the mules?" I ask.

"I told you five minutes ago. Another hour or two."

I close my eyes and recite in my head: *I hope I like Accompong. I hope I like Accompong.*

PART THREE

———◆———

THE COCKPIT:
SEPTEMBER 1935

CHAPTER 25

———◆———

VIVIAN JEAN

Appleton Station, Jamaica

The train arrives at Appleton Station, the last stop before Maggotty. Tully and I grab our handbags while the load bearers take everything else. We leave the others on the train, letting them know we'll rejoin them in Maggotty. The Appleton stop is where my father promised to meet us. He wrote that he'd be waiting for us here, where the air is thinner and cooler than in Kingston Harbour.

"Where is he?" My heart races with near panic as I scan the station. "He said he'd be here." I hold Tully's hand, hoping my father will appear quickly and tell us what he has to tell us, then vanish like a cloud in the wind. "Do you see him?" I ask Tully, tugging on his hand.

"He'll be here. Be patient. He'll be here."

Tully sounds like he can predict the future.

"Mr. and Mrs. Hartfield, is everything okay?" It's not the voice I was hoping to hear. Zinzi Green, the guide who insists she isn't related to Maxi, has approached us.

"Excuse me, the train will leave the station soon. If you're not on board, I'll be unable to come back for you until to-morrow. This group can't travel through the jungle after dark. And you can't travel to Accompong by yourselves," Zinzi adds.

"We're waiting for my wife's father," Tully replies.

"Is he staying in Appleton? It's difficult to travel about in these small villages unless he's lodging at one of the sugar plantations." Zinzi's tone carries an unusual hint of accusation. "He ought to have met you in Kingston."

"You're right," I respond. "He should have."

Zinzi glances from me to Tully. "What do you want to do?"

Everything has worked in our favor up until now. The boat docked on time, and the train arrived on time despite the worn wheels, the old tracks, and the shabby train cars. Why did he want to meet us here? Why couldn't we have met on Harbour Street?

"We should go with Zinzi," I say to Tully. "We can't wait for him and risk putting the entire trip off schedule."

He nods, grabs our bags, and follows Zinzi back toward the train.

"Look. Is that his car?" Zinzi points at the road. "Is that your father, Mrs. Hartfield?"

A limo driver opens the car door and Major Thomas steps out.

"That's him." I squeeze Tully's arm.

"We'll be on our way," Zinzi says sharply. "We won't be able to wait for you in Maggotty. Please get there quickly. We only have one more stop before we reach that village."

"Okay," I say to Zinzi as my father joins us. "I thought you weren't going to make it."

"You shouldn't have worried." He smiles.

He greets Tully, and I introduce him to Zinzi Green. He shakes her hand before she hurries to reboard the train. I notice he shows no reaction to her familiar last name.

"Sir," she addresses my father, "our next stop is Maggotty. We'll travel by mule from there and upon arrival, must leave promptly to reach Accompong before dark."

"No need to explain, Miss Green. I understand. We'll join you in Maggotty before your scheduled departure. We won't be late."

Moments later, we find ourselves in the back seat of the limo: Major Thomas is seated behind the driver, I am in the middle, and Tully is by the window. My father offers Tully a cigarette, which he thankfully refuses. I just want him to get straight to whatever he has to say.

"Regarding the note that Clifford wrote, he liked jotting down messages. He enjoyed surprises." My father has always viewed Clifford differently from the way I did, as if he knew another version of my childhood friend and later husband.

"Father. Please just tell us about the note," I urge him. "What did Clifford mean?"

"We know what he meant," Tully adds roughly.

"What Clifford meant was to stir up trouble," Major Thomas responds, mirroring Tully's tone.

"Trouble for whom?" Tully questions.

The car speeds along the dirt road, bumping over rocks and ditches.

"You think the note has something to do with you and Vivian Jean, don't you, Tobias?" the major states soberly. "Do not worry. It's not about you and Vivian Jean."

Tully grips the seat in front of him as if he needs help to keep upright. "You are going to tell us the truth, right?"

My father adjusts his position to face Tully and me. "It's about Maxi and me. Clifford found out about us."

My throat goes dry. "You and Maxi had an affair?"

"No, not an affair," he says, his gaze steady and unwavering. "Maxi and I have been in love since I met her."

I look out the window, watching the jungle fade into the distance. All I see is a blurry landscape as a strange pressure builds in my chest and throat.

"Vivi, I didn't mean to—"

"Shut up!" I yell. "Shut your damn mouth."

Maggotty, St. Elizabeth Parish

Maggotty is a bustling town with a train station, a market, shopping carts, and small shops. Additionally, there's a corral that emits a foul odor, spreading over the city like rancid butter. The station is not small; it's sturdy, made of stone, and features a steeple and a bell. It reminds me of the churches in Chicago on Wabash or State Street, except without the red brick or wood siding.

The load bearers adjust the crates, suitcases, and bags they carry as my father's car stops near the mules lined up across from the train station. Tully and I exit his limousine, but I don't look back as the automobile drives away. I walk over to the group and join them in gazing at the animals.

"No one mentioned mules." Othella is upset, frightened, or both. "Do you remember Zinzi mentioning these animals?"

Robbie clears his throat. "She did. She also mentioned the Jamaican boa, various species of deadly spiders, including the scorpion, and the most dangerous spider—one that sounds like a fruit."

"The banana spider," Othella chimes in.

"And don't forget, the water isn't without danger," Robbie adds. "There are poisonous sea urchins and crocodiles." He stares at the so-called beasts, his eyes slightly watery from the stench. "But I don't remember these creatures."

I study the mules, or "the beasts," as Zinzi has called them, with their four short legs, oddly shaped heads, and long snouts.

I am not as upset as the others seem to be. They provide me with a welcome distraction, keeping my mind off my father and his confession, though he didn't sound sorry for the pain he and Maxi have caused. My head hurts. Too many emotions bouncing around inside it. Instead of thinking about my father, I will master riding Zinzi's beasts.

"Do I have to sit on that?" Othella asks, scrunching her nose.

Zinzi rides over on her mule in the saddle, sitting tall and unfazed. "There's one for each of you."

"So we can't refuse," Robbie replies.

"Not unless you want to walk three miles to Accompong," Zinzi says, "through the jungle, over rocks, cliffs, and limestone quarries. By the time you reach Accompong, if you survive the jungle in the pitch-blackness of night, covered in bugbites and with a snake's fangs embedded in your flesh, then sure—you are welcome to try it."

Katherine whispers in my ear, "Why is she so unpleasant?"

"It's because we're a handful," Tully responds on my behalf.

I notice him watching me, anticipating my reaction and wanting to ask questions: How are you feeling? Are you okay? Do you want to talk?

But I'm not ready for any of that. What I want now is silence. I lift my gaze to the cloudless sky. The sun shines brightly over the Cockpit, casting patches of light mixed with impenetrable darkness. "I've been here before."

A loud squawk erupts from the treetops. "What is that?" Othella asks. "It sounds like someone is screaming."

"No," Zinzi replies. "It's a bird, not a person—a yellow-billed parrot."

"Do they bite?" Othella glances from the trees to the beasts. "I'm not getting on that thing." She slides behind Robbie, peeking over his shoulder at the mules. "They must bite," she says. "Their teeth are huge."

I watch her, hoping to find Othella's anxiety amusing, but I can't. I am reeling from what I've just learned about the two people whose love, affection, and opinions have shaped me from childhood to adulthood, through marriage and then marriage again, through sorrow, and heartbreak.

"I'd be more worried about falling off a cliff." Tully moves close to me, staying within arm's reach since we exited my father's limo. I'm unsure how I feel about the gesture because I don't want to feel anything. Not yet. Not now.

"They all have saddles," Katherine notes.

"Yes," Zinzi says, grasping her mule's reins. "Let's get going."

The load bearers forge ahead of us, jogging barefoot and shirtless. Sweat cascades down their bodies as they balance towering stacks of luggage, steamer trunks, and crates atop their heads and on their backs. I wish I could run with them. It's the only thought that matters to me at this moment: how desperately I want to run.

The Mule Trail, Cockpit Country

More than two hours have passed, and we are that much closer to Accompong. I should feel exuberant, the excitement rolling off my brow like raindrops on a spring day.

Instead, sitting in the saddle atop my beast, I am thrust back through time, thinking about what I took for granted over the past thirty years: the love and affection from Maxi that I always counted on, the absence of warmth from my mother that I accepted, and my father's controlling nature that I tried to appease. I have missed so much: the signs of his brutishness and the anger my mother suppressed, which turned into tolerance and indifference when she looked at me.

What other signs did I miss?

Just the other evening, the night I returned to Hartfield House from Mr. Abbott's, I rushed inside and hurried up the stairs, searching for Tully. I thought my father had left when I dashed down the grand staircase, still looking for my husband, but I caught sight of my father and Maxi from the corner of my eye. Standing in the doorway, Maxi had her arms crossed over her chest while my father held the door ajar. He stood close to her, speaking with a pleading urgency in his gaze, and then, over Maxi's shoulder, he spotted me. Immediately, he stepped back and shut the door in Maxi's face. I didn't pause for more than a second. I was eager to find Tully and too upset with my father to let curiosity distract me. Tully needed to know that the major was at it again, interfering and mucking things up.

Now, as I picture him and Maxi in that doorway, I wonder how many other times I've seen them like that and brushed it off. How many times was the truth of their affair right in front of me, just an arm's length away?

Each time—every time—I assumed they were talking about me, debating what Vivian Jean needed, how to do better for Vivian Jean, defending Vivian Jean. How often did I see them side by side, and the conversation was not about Vivian Jean? Were the affectionate glances I thought were meant for me, the sweet smiles I cherished and the embraces I longed for merely placeholders for what they were eager to share with each other?

All those times I saw them overflowing with love and joy had nothing to do with me.

"Another two miles."

I blink. Who said that?

It's Tully, responding to Othella's question about how much longer we must remain in the saddle on the beasts.

"Riding a mule over rough terrain is tough on the bones," he says. "I swear, I didn't know I had muscles in certain parts of my body." His chatter aims to provoke a reaction from me. He can't deceive me. Everyone else in my life has, but not Tully. Not now. And I'd thank him if I felt like talking, which I don't. Not yet.

CHAPTER 26

──•◆•──

ZINZI

The Mule Trail, Cockpit Country

How can a girl dream while riding in a saddle on a mule's back? Or maybe it's not a dream, but a memory that invades my thoughts as we get closer to Accompong. The more vivid it becomes, the more I recognize Momma Jayden and the day I discovered one of my mother's secrets.

The clouds hang low over Cockpit Country. While my mother and I till the soil in the heat of an August dawn, the sky suddenly bursts open, drenching us in a summer downpour. She mutters a curse, grabs my hand, and pulls me close, balancing a bushel of corn on her head as if it were a silk scarf. Despite wading through puddles of mud and fallen branches with her protruding belly—she was with child, or children, carrying twin boys, as we later learned—she moves effortlessly.

We arrive home to the thatched-roof cottage where I was born, only to find a guest waiting at the doorstep: a gray-haired elderly woman sits on a three-legged wooden stool, blocking our way.

The rain pours down in buckets, soaking us to the skin, but my mother does not shove the old woman aside or pull her indoors to escape the rain quickly. No, instead, she growls at the woman.

"What do you want, Momma Jayden? Why are you here? I don't let anyone into my hut when my husband isn't home."

"I want some of your blessed herbs," Momma Jayden states firmly, refusing to step aside. Gripping my mother's skirt, I glance up at the woman. The twinkle in the elderly lady's eyes calms me, assuring me that I have nothing to fear from her.

"Please," Momma Jayden pleads. "I need some of your salves, herbs, or precious oils. I'm injured and need healing."

"You hush now," my mother replies, looking around warily. "Why do you bring up such things in public where anyone might hear? What's wrong with you?"

"Then let me inside your home," Momma Jayden insists.

My mother releases a frustrated sigh, followed by a flick of her hand, signaling that the old woman must hurry through the entrance. Once inside, Momma Jayden wipes her face, removes her cover-up, and shakes the water from her dress. I gasp at the sight of the ugly scars and burns covering her arms and legs. My mother doesn't seem surprised. She tells Momma Jayden to sit on the stool by the door. Then she goes to the box in the corner that I'm not allowed to touch. When she opens it, a mix of gardenias and some very unpleasant odors fills the hut.

"Thank you. I need a potion to ward off the misfortune that plagues me," Momma Jayden says, her voice heavy with tears.

"Can you do this for me? I have never spoken of what I know. I will never speak of what I know."

My mother sucks her teeth. *"I will pray for you when the moon is bright and full."* She pulls out a small basket from behind a larger one and opens the lid. *"Until then, take this."* She hands Momma Jayden a cloth pouch, which the woman takes and clutches to her chest.

"And now, listen to me," my mother begins. *"Don't come back here. Trust the herbs. They will take care of your troubles."*

That was the day I learned about my mother's mastery over herbs and plants, and that she can harness the knowledge of the sacred silk cotton tree, the dwelling place of spirits, African ancestors, and the enslaved dead. Some villagers say she can also communicate with the duppies, the spirits of the departed. But these are secrets that can never be spoken. For in Jamaica, it is a crime to be an Obeah woman—and that is what my mother is: Obeah.

Accompong, Maroon Village, Cockpit Country

Standing on the final precipice outside Accompong, the village looks the same as when I last saw it. Numerous gardens of yams, plantains, bananas, various fruits and vegetables, along with small sugarcane fields, separate the scattered wooden houses topped with thatched roots made of bamboo and palm leaves.

The sacred silk-cotton tree stands in the center of town, the keeper of memories and centuries of history. African culture and heritage breathe through its roots, limbs, and leaves.

This is what my mother preaches—sacred trees, duppies or ghosts, and Obeah. She isn't alone in these beliefs. The entire community shares them.

I'm the outsider. My beliefs are grounded in practicality rather than myths, ancestors, or superstition.

"Is this it?" A voice breaks into my musings.

"Yes, Miss Dunham. This is Accompong. Colonel Rowe's yard is at the foot of the village. You can see it at the bottom of the hill."

"His yard?" Katherine frowns.

"His property," I explain. "His houses and the surrounding land."

"It's very large."

"There's a separate dwelling for the women in your party and another for the men. Later, they'll find a place for the married couple. I don't believe the Hartfields were initially included in the letter the colonel received from Melville Herskovits."

"No, they weren't," she answers, perched on her mule, looking out over the land, her gaze shifting from the hills to the lowlands to the huts. "How'd you learn so much about me and this expedition?"

"My mother's place is next to the colonel's yard." I point to the thatched-roof hut where I grew up.

"Oh, they're neighbors."

"In some communities, that would be the correct definition. In Accompong, and for Colonel Simon Rowe the elder, the entire village is his neighbor, and proximity to the leader's yard doesn't give anyone special status."

"That seems odd."

"That's the tip of the iceberg." I chuckle. If she only knew what Accompong has in store for her, it might even shake some of the confidence she shows.

We continue our descent. Our line of mules, with their side-to-side gait, shuffles down the hillside with sure-footedness.

It takes another twenty minutes before one of the colonel's lieutenants meets us and introduces himself. Lieutenant Clerk is a new face to me. He was probably just a boy when I left. The young man leads us and the load bearers to a corral, where we dismount from our mules. I suggest that the group gather their luggage or knapsacks holding the personal items they'll need for the night.

"Why does this feel like a military base?" Katherine asks as we gather the bags we will carry to Captain Rowe's main house. "What war are the Maroon people fighting?" she asks with humor in her voice, an inappropriate tone to my ears.

"You do know the history of Accompong and the Maroon people in the Cockpit?"

"Of course I do." She pauses. "They were enslaved people who rebelled and fought for and won their freedom in the 1760s and have lived in the Cockpit since then, as free people."

"Yes, that's it in a nutshell," I say.

As we walk to the main house, which is a bit far from the corral, I feel like Katherine's summary was too simplistic. She sounded as if she were reading from a book. "You'll find that there's more to the legacy, now that you're in Accompong."

"Like what? Tell me, please."

Vivian Jean trots up to my other side. "I'd like to hear it, too."

I have the attention of these ladies, which I am not sure I want, but there is so much history of the Maroon people not written by white men.

"During the rebellion of 1760 under Tacky, a Koromantee chief, the Maroons aided the English. By 1795, the Maroons of Trelawney Town rebelled."

Katherine grunts. "Koromantee, and Trelawney Town?"

"Trelawney Town no longer exists. Neither does Scotts Hall, Charleston, or Moore Town. Over time, the Maroon numbers dwindled. One hundred years after the first rebellion, sixty Maroon families resided between Accompong and the other communities. Now, Accompong is the last Maroon community." I stop, gesturing to Katherine and Vivian Jean that we should slow down, as the others are lagging behind. "Over the years, the Maroon people have had to fight over and over to keep their freedom. A military mindset has been a part of the Maroon culture since it began."

I think about Byron's father now. He intends to wage another kind of war against the Maroon people: taxing the villagers of Accompong for making rum. "There will always be battles to fight, wars to win, and freedom to defend."

"Who are the Koromantee?" asks Vivian Jean.

I am not ready to give her the whole definition of the word, "You'll learn more about them as you get to know the Maroon people."

We arrive at the colonel's main house. An impressive man, although short in stature and not much of a talker, he welcomes us with an assertive presence, skipping lengthy greetings and unnecessary smiles. He swiftly establishes his authority, which does not include directly interacting with village visitors. I sense Katherine's disappointment. She expected open arms and welcoming hugs and kisses upon her arrival in the village. She'll find that gaining the trust of the Maroons won't be without its obstacles, even with Melville Herskovits's endorsement in her favor.

The colonel's oldest daughter, Iris, serves as the hostess. After introductions, she ushers the group to a long table at the side of the house, where a meal is set. I can smell the heat of the peppers. Even at Edna's Diner, the menu didn't offer as many peppers as I see floating in the savory stew made with pimento, coconut oil, and many different peppers. A side bowl of rice won't shield the tongue as much as the Americans will require.

I warn Katherine Dunham's team in a whisper, "Careful. The stew is made with African seasonings. It's very spicy."

"Will they think we're rude if we don't eat it?" Vivian Jean asks.

"We don't want to get off to a bad start here," Katherine adds quietly. Then she raises her voice. "This looks delicious, Colonel, Iris. Thank you so much."

Ten minutes later, after Katherine insists that everyone eat up, she, Vivian Jean, Tully, and the two youngsters, Robbie and Othella, are wiping tears from their eyes, snot from their noses, and coughing up half a lung.

They are not suffering alone—even I'm sweating.

After dinner, the group regains its energy. Their enthusiasm for being in Accompong can't be suppressed, even though they should be exhausted after a long day of travel. Iris claps her hands to gather everyone's attention and announces, "The living quarters won't be ready until tomorrow night." She forces a smile. "You can rest anywhere in the yard that you find comfortable."

Disappointment hangs in the air, evident from the groans and sighs. The women from the Dunham party seem particularly uneasy. They long for a restful night's sleep. I feel the same. Meanwhile, Iris is quick to act. She seizes one of Katherine's bags and strides into the house but stumbles, causing the bag to burst open. With an excited gasp, Iris removes a large, square object from Katherine's suitcase. "Is this one of those phonographs?"

"Yes, it is."

"Do you have any records?"

Katherine seems hesitant. "I would really like to listen to some of your music, Iris."

"We've heard about portable phonographs, but I've never come across one." She sets the device down on a nearby stool. "What type is it?"

Katherine looks distressed. "It's the RCA Victor Special Model K."

"Do you have any records?"

"I have a few," she grumbles, not pleased by what is happening.

Mr. Hartfield doesn't pick up on Katherine's signals and helps Iris open the portable phonograph.

"Let's put on some music so they can listen," Othella says with a glance at Iris and the others. "Where are the records?" She digs around in a sleeve-like slit in the lid and removes a few records.

"I'll crank it up." Mr. Hartfield glances at his wife, who nods in agreement.

"It's battery operated," Katherine says solemnly.

Between Iris and Othella, they take possession of the records and the phonograph. The next hour, we listen and dance to Duke Ellington, Cab Calloway, Benny Goodman, and Billie Holiday. For a few minutes, it's like we are at one of the nightclubs on Harbour Street or the lounge at the Myrtle Bank Hotel.

Sitting next to me, Katherine has a weary expression on her face. "And I repeat, I was hoping for African native music and some dance rituals. Instead, it's a Saturday night on State Street in Chicago."

"I bet you've never been to the Savoy Ballroom," Othella chimes in, snapping her fingers and shifting her torso in her seat to Louis Armstrong.

Katherine shrugs. "I've been to the Savoy many times."

Tully raises a record and waves it in the air. "Look what I found." He puts it on.

Cab Calloway's distinctive voice bounces through the night as "Minnie the Moocher" plays. When the call-and-response chorus begins, everyone sings, "Hi-de-hi-de-hi-de-ho," including me. Othella dances the Lindy Hop, gracefully moving into the two-step with hips swaying and body spinning. She tries to coerce Robbie Barnes into joining her, but he declines shyly. Then Katherine takes Vivian Jean's hand and leads her into an open spot near the whirling Othella. In moments, the entire Dunham party, including Tully, is dancing and attempting to teach Iris and Lieutenant Clerk how to shimmy their hips. The only two abstaining from the festivities are Colonel Rowe and me. He doesn't look pleased with what he's witnessing. Though, how could I tell? His expression is the same as when we arrived.

With all the revelry, I seize the moment to slip away. I'm sure my mother has heard the music and the commotion and wonders what is happening in Simon Rowe's yard. Or she has guessed I have arrived and is patiently waiting for me to come home.

CHAPTER 27

OTHELLA

Accompong, Maroon Village, Cockpit Country, Day One

Familiar music fills the air. New friends dance the Lindy Hop and shimmy to Cab Calloway's searing vocals. The chorus shouts back and forth at the top of our lungs, "Hi-de-hi-de-hi-de-ho."

"Minnie the Moocher." It never crossed my mind that I would be dancing and singing to Cab Calloway on my first night in a Jamaican jungle.

It's almost perfect. I just need a gin and tonic to wash the taste of those hot peppers outta my mouth and an Italian beef to fill my empty stomach. I only had two swallows of stew. The first spoonful, I was hungry and swallowed it quickly, but the second was a mistake. My impatient nature got the best of me. If I had just waited another second for the spices to hit the back of my throat, that second swallow would never have happened.

Tully keeps the turntable spinning and plays at least six records, most of which he has played twice. He announces the last dance, and we kick up our heels until he closes the lid of the portable phonograph. Afterward, I collapse onto a stool, sweaty and ready for bed, wherever we're supposed to rest our tired bodies.

"My legs feel like melted butter," I say to Robbie with a laugh. He joins me at the end of the long table, away from Iris and her family, who are still chatting with Katherine and Vivian Jean about American music and dance. "My backside hurts, too."

"You've been dancing for an hour. I'm not surprised you're sore."

"It's not only the dancing. I blame my aching ass on those mules." Robbie's cheeks turn red like a juicy ripe tomato, and he ain't all that light-skinned. My language must have shocked him.

"Do you need—do you need," he begins, but becomes lost in his thoughts.

"Just tired, but wasn't that fun? Do you think every night in Accompong will be this much fun?"

"I doubt it. Look at Miss Katherine. She isn't happy with this rigmarole."

"What do you mean by rigmarole? I don't think she's un-happy. She was dancing. And call her Katherine."

"Okay. okay. She might've been dancing, but she's here to conduct fieldwork, which she's very serious about. I read one of her papers. She's not playing around. She's gonna keep us busy, and tonight didn't go the way she would've preferred. Least that's what I'm thinking."

"I don't see it that way," I respond. "She just likes to dance. I do, too. It doesn't matter what kind of dancing, as long as there's music that lets our feet, hips, and bodies move to the beat. It's all about having a good time."

I feel slightly disappointed by Robbie's attitude, but I wave it off as Iris summons us inside the main house. She directs us to a large open space where we're given rolled-up cloth, which I assume we can use as a pillow or sheet. It's cooler than I expected in the jungle at night, and I search for a spot to rest my head and use the sheet to cover myself against the chill.

With Robbie nearby and the others around us finding their spaces for slumber, I'm almost settled when Colonel Rowe suddenly appears in the archway, startling me. From the first time I saw him, I thought of Reverend Nathan, purely because of his appearance, nothing about his behavior. He's quiet, standoffish, and uninterested in mingling with the visitors from America.

"What is wrong? Every time Captain Rowe is nearby, you act all cockamamie."

"No, I don't," I say, but I do.

"What's bothering you?"

"Nothing. Go to sleep. You say we're gonna have a busy day tomorrow. We should get some rest."

I shoo Robbie away. There's something I don't wanna tell him about.

When I first laid eyes on Captain Rowe, I almost screamed. Then I thought about running at him and knocking him in the head. But how would I look if I did something crazy like that? So, instead, I clenched my fists and pulled my arms behind my back to keep myself from doing anything. After that, we sat down and ate that pepper stew, and Iris found the phonograph. I didn't think about Rowe and Reverend Nathan while I was dancing.

Robbie notices things like that about me. I want to tell him the story but know what he'll say. Whatever issues I had with Reverend Nathan won't trouble me no more. He's in the middle of America, while I am on a Caribbean island with no plans to return to Chicago. I want to believe he'd be right in his thinking. So, lying on the floor, I pull the cloth up around my throat and close my eyes, but the memory of the last time I saw Reverend Nathan won't leave me be.

I should never have gone to the church. I should have known

he was the same no-good son of a gun he'd always been. But I'm muleheaded. I thought this time it would be different.

AME Fellowship Church on 24th Street, Chicago,
A Week Earlier

> *It is not a dream. It isn't happening again, but I remember every detail, and it's as clear as crystal. I ran from the apartment I shared with Perry, desperate because I couldn't find my money and couldn't keep searching because Perry might rise up from the floor, and I wouldn't get out of that apartment alive. I needed help. I needed cash and headed to the first place that came to mind—and it wasn't Tony Schaefer.*

I take a puff of the lit cigarette between my teeth. My leather-trimmed suitcase is clutched in one hand, and my purse is squeezed under my armpit as I reach the corner of State Street and Wabash, just a block from the AME Fellowship Church.

The sun has dipped behind a cloud, but the August heat lingers. Sweat trickles down the front of my polka-dot dress into my brassiere, soaking my breasts and ruining the bodice. I take another drag of my cigarette, blinking smoke from my eyes and breathing in the scent of jasmine and rose petals. A nearby fragrance shop reminds me of how Perry would prepare me a bath. Pour in sweet-smelling perfumes and read to me while I lie in the tub. He'd even light a candle. A sweet side of him, but it only surfaced on his better days, which were never frequent enough.

If Perry hadn't died, he would never have forgiven me for hitting him in the head with that standing steel ashtray. Something twists in my chest.

Breathe, Othella. Breathe.

The church's steeple reaches high into the sky, while the brick façade glows bluish-white in the sunset. I don't recall ever seeing it that color before. Reverend Nathan used to tell me that the church was built on a small hill so it couldn't be missed from dawn to dusk, whether the day was sunny or cloudy. "There's no way to avoid the Lord," he would say. "He reigns from on high, almighty and all-powerful."

I light another cigarette and quicken my pace. A few minutes later, when I reach the church, I drop the remnants of my cigarette on the ground and extinguish it with the toe of my spike-heeled pump.

As I step inside, I am not surprised that nothing has changed after three years. The pulpit still sits at the end of the center aisle. Above the altar, Jesus Christ continues to hang on the cross, gazing down at the congregation with that same expression. The wooden benches, though empty, smell of linseed oil. The stained-glass windows are unchanged as well. I used to stare at them for a long time, marveling at how the colors of things seemed to shift. Tree leaves appear blue, swirling through the sky, while at night, stars drift from the moon like falling snowflakes.

"Can I help you?"

I recoil, instinctively lifting my hands to guard my face from the incoming punch, but the voice isn't Perry's. It is too high-pitched. I push away the anxiety swirling in my chest and meet the gaze of a scrawny kid wearing a stiff-brimmed cap and baggy dungarees.

"Who are you? And where'd you come from?" I ask roughly.

"Right over there." The boy points. "Around that corner, ma'am."

"Don't call me *ma'am*. Makes me sound older than I am."

"Yes, ma'am," he replies with a smirk.

Ignoring the stubborn child, I say, "I'm looking for Reverend Nathan. Is he in the rectory?"

"Follow me." The boy takes off, and I follow.

Finding myself in a familiar place, I shorten my stride. I'm in the hallway lined with framed photographs, one featuring the round-faced Miss Lucille, the reverend's wife. She should've been a better woman. She should've looked out for me when her vile husband put his hands all over me. How come she never noticed? How come I never fought him off?

I guess I had no steel-standing ashtray to fight off the beast.

"Hey, boy. That's the door over there, isn't it?"

"See? You didn't really need my help after all."

"I suppose not," I respond.

I knock on the rectory door, and a deep voice invites me inside.

Reverend Nathan sits behind the same long wooden desk, which is as large and pudgy as ever, though the crescent-shaped patch of hair that circles his head has turned completely white, and his eyes are red and watery.

"Othella! My girl, how I've missed you. Miss Lucille missed you, too." He maneuvers around the desk and approaches me like boiling water, arms flailing and lips bubbling.

I turn my back and place my suitcase near the door. When I turn back, holding my bag tightly against my chest, I allow the hug to happen. If it weren't for my circumstances, I'd never have returned to the AME Fellowship Church with the handsy reverend, his ignorant wife, and its basement orphanage. "Thank you."

"What for?"

"For seeing me."

"How could you think I wouldn't want to see you?" His arms flap in my direction. Good Lord. He's coming at me for another hug. I move fast, a quick sidestep and a spin, and I successfully evade a second attempt. I plop down onto the chair across from his desk.

"I need your help. I might have hurt a man—after he hurt me."

"A dangerous man, I assume."

"No more dangerous than other men I've known." I can't conceal the accusation in my voice.

The reverend's eyes flash. He knows who I'm referring to but shows no sign of shame on his black face. "So, you're here only for money?"

"I need cash for a fresh start in a new city," I say, expecting a quick *okay, yes, dear, of course, baby girl, whatever you need, precious*. But instead, my request lingers in the air like a bad penny as the reverend shifts around like ants crawling in his pants.

"Oh dear. I'd love to help you, Othella, but I can't give you any money until Miss Lucille returns. You know how she keeps an eye on every nickel and dime, and she won't be back until morning."

"I need the money now. My train leaves at midnight, and I've got to be on it," I exclaim. "Since when do you obey your wife's wishes and whims? You were never that considerate when I was around."

His eyes darken. "But you haven't been around for three years, sugar. And things change, but I might reconsider if you'd give me the pleasure of having a meal with me before you get on that train."

"So you ain't gonna give me no money unless I hang around with you for a spell. Like in the old days?"

He shrugs, his bald head shiny with sweat. "Then you'll have to wait until Miss Lucille comes home, first thing in the morning."

I jump to my feet, kicking the chair and sending it tumbling to the ground. "I can't wait until morning. I need to catch the midnight train! And I don't need to have a meal with you."

"I'm sure there are plenty of men in town who'll give you what you want." The reverend rises. "Sorry I can't help you."

"So, just like that, you're gonna say no?"

"You heard what I said. If you wanted to stay for a meal, I might scrounge up some change for you."

"You ain't nothin' but an old bastard." I think about the Smokador ashtray and wish to give Reverend Nathan some of the same medicine I gave to Perry.

Standing in the doorway and glaring at the old man, I feel the heat of hatred in my blood. I spot a lamp on a table by the door. I grab it and hurl it across the room. I don't know if it struck him or not. Doesn't matter—I don't plan on seeing him again anyways.

On the street again, all I can think about is how much I want a cigarette.

But that was a week ago. Not today. Not now.

CHAPTER 28

———— ◆ ————

ZINZI

Accompong, Maroon Village, Cockpit Country, Day One

The hour is late. A strong breeze sweeps through the Cockpit, rolling over the hills and into the valleys and caverns. My nerves tingle. It's been a long while since I've been home. But this visit is my mother's doing, not my decision. She asked me to bring the Americans to Accompong, to leave the labor movement for a few days, just for her. I wonder if she even knows them—the Dunham expedition.

I stroll up the short pathway to my mother's hut and am surprised. She is outside, snapping peas while sitting on the same three-legged stool Momma Jayden sat on those many years ago.

"I thought you'd be cleaning up after dinner in a house full of family. Are the twins inside?"

"Mi wondering when you were gonna come this way." Her voice is the usual mix of gravel and honey. "Mi been watching you since you came up to the colonel's house with all those people."

"Good evening, Momma Hazel." I use her full motherly

name. It's been so long since she's heard my voice. I owe her the respect. I kiss her on the cheek. She looks different. She looks old. I know she's been ill, but most Maroons are ageless.

"It's about time you came home. You haven't bothered to visit your momma in ages." She looks past me. "Who are those people who were with you in the colonel's yard?"

"The Americans from Chicago. You sent me a note, Momma. Or Raymond sent it to me. You asked me for a favor."

"Don't quibble. Mi know about the note, and mi know the colonel has told the village about Katherine Dunham and the dances she wants to learn."

"Oh, by the way, I should tell you that Vivian Jean Hartfield was very insistent that her maid—her name is Maxi Green—is a relative of ours," I say, rolling my eyes. "I told Mrs. Hartfield I've never heard of her. And I didn't go into any detail about Father's side of the family because I don't know enough about them."

My mother grunts, which is about all the reaction I am getting from her on the subject. With her gaze fixed on the houses next door, she's more interested in what's happening in the colonel's yard.

"The Dunham party will spend the night in the colonel's main house. Their living quarters aren't ready but will be tomorrow."

"Oh, that's right, the colonel is hosting them," she says. "Besides, you haven't seen me in over a year. We should spend time together, just the two of us." She closes one eye and stares at me with the other, and I can't determine if it's a wink, a twitch, or a wince.

"You look thin. And what have you done to your hair, curled on your head like some girl who doesn't know the Cockpit—a girl who belongs in Kingston, dressed in floral dresses and store-bought shoes?"

"Momma, please. Can we discuss my hair and shoes later?" I glance at my hiking boots. "I'm here for only a day or two. And I don't wish to have any disagreements with you."

"A few days?" She drops the peas in the basket. "I told Raymond what to write, but it wasn't my idea." She lowers her voice to a whisper. "A duppy told me to bring you back home. Mi never would have asked on my own."

"Please don't start with that. You know it's forbidden even to say that word in Accompong."

"Mi just telling you what happened." She pats her knee. "And why you think mi whisper." She raises a brow. "Come down here so mi can see you up close."

I kneel in front of her. She takes hold of my face with both hands. "Tell me about your life in Kingston. Why you've stayed away from Accompong for so long? Mi know about you and the labor union movement. Are you in love with Allan Coombs? Or does someone else have your heart?"

Now, that is a question I will never discuss with my mother. "I spend my time with the labor movement and working at the Constant Spring Hotel. You already know this."

"You and Mr. Coombs, peas in a pod? There is nothing more between the two of you but this union work?"

"That is correct, Momma. Can we stop talking about this now? I'm tired."

Sleeping at my mother's house may be the hardest part of being home. I forgot how she can be. Even when she's unwell, she insists on having things her way. She wakes up before the sun rises, banging pots and pans as she prepares the morning meal, yelling for the chickens to gather in the coop or for the goat to get ready for milking. But I am not alone, it appears. The colonel's house has the same lack of regard for sleeping in after a long journey, and shortly after I am forced out of my bed, Katherine and Vivian Jean stand at the front entrance to my mother's hut.

They look absolutely desperate.

"Is there something you need?"

My mother peeks around a corner, tying a scarf around her head. "Mind your manners, Zinzi. Tell those girls to come on in."

"You heard her." I step aside and gesture for them to enter.

"Call me Momma Hazel."

They walk in, looking around, comparing the colonel's yard to this one, I imagine. My mother's house is spacious but has only two rooms, and a cloth partition conceals the sleeping area in the corner of the largest room. Katherine and Vivian Jean are polite, but their eyes widen. The colonel's yard offers many more amenities: carved furniture, wooden planks instead of beaten earth for the flooring, and no woven grass mats scattered about like here. The colonel's walls have art pieces, beaded belts and headbands, machetes and hunting tools, and above a main rafter, as a sign of legacy, hangs an honored weapon from long ago—a powder horn.

Apart from four machetes and some gourds, I would never call them art. The only wall ornaments are garden tools and more machetes.

"Mi just made breakfast. Sit. Sit," my mother orders.

Katherine and Vivian Jean obey, but I can appreciate the flash of concern in their eyes.

"Don't worry, breakfast won't be anywhere as spicy as last night's stew."

We take our seats. There isn't a proper dining table inside, but there is more seating outside near the firepit my mother uses for cooking. I help my mother fill some bowls with sweet potatoes, taro, saltfish, and johnnycakes.

"Thank you so much. It feels so much less hectic here," Vivian Jean says.

"You asked my Zinzi about Maxi Green?"

Vivian Jean looks away shyly. "She's Jamaican and from Accompong, but she left many years ago."

"Zinzi told me you thought your maid, Maxi, was related to us."

"I'm sorry. I did think that, but Zinzi set me straight."

"Zinzi thinks she knows everything," Momma says, "but she doesn't know everything about her father's side."

I lean forward on my stool. "I know enough."

Momma hisses. "You don't know this story." She hobbles around, picking up bowls. "Maxi was exiled for betraying our community's morals."

Vivian Jean half-chuckles. "I would have never thought her capable of such a thing. . . ." She seems about to continue but stops. "What did she do?"

Seated nearby, Katherine takes Vivian Jean's hand. "It's okay. Whatever happened is long past."

"That's all you need to know," Zinzi's mother interjects. "The rest is a family matter."

"You can't just leave it like that, Momma Hazel. We're too curious about what happened."

My mother scowls. "Okay, since I'm sick, I wouldn't want the story to end with me."

"Momma," I groan. Sometimes, she can be dramatic.

"Let me tell it," she begins, "She was loose and kept heading to the beach to meet sailor boys. And you remember when Momma Jayden came here that last time?"

"Yes, I do," I reply.

"Well, it was to help that girl Maxi, her niece, get off the island."

"Why would she need herbs to get off the island?" I ask.

"Don't brush aside the power of herbs and potions," my mother says sharply. "She slept with a man she met on the beach, bringing disgrace to her family. Worse, she never showed remorse. Banishment was the only option. Momma Jayden wanted to protect her, to cleanse her spirit, and ensure safe passage for her voyage."

I had to ask the question. It has been on my mind for years. "Then why didn't I ever see Momma Jayden again?"

"She went with her to America. She was her talisman."

"Maxi never mentioned her." A sad expression grows on Vivian Jean's face.

"She died shortly after they arrived in New York City," my mother says, having taken the bowls and using a pitcher of water to rinse them over a large bin.

Katherine clears her throat, drawing attention to the awkwardness of the moment. "We will move into our quarters later today, and this afternoon, Iris will be taking us to a ritual at the silk cotton tree."

"Katherine is very excited about this ritual, which we may be able to participate in, but I was wondering," Vivian Jean says, staring at her hands. "Can you tell me about the Obeah women or men in the village? I'd love to speak with them. Of course, I understand the practice of Obeah is very private. But I need to—want to know more about the silk cotton tree. Maxi said that the silk cotton tree is a powerful gateway."

My mother scratches her nose but I'm not interested in hearing her or these women get lost in the superstition of Obeah. "My mother is tired and needs her rest. We can talk about the sacred silk cotton tree, the myths and Obeah some other time."

"I would love to hear more, especially about the silk cotton tree." Vivian Jean's voice is high-pitched and her anxiety shows in every movement.

"It's all superstition," I say.

"You don't know what you're talking about, Zinzi."

My mother's harsh tone embarrasses me. "Then, please explain what I'm missing?"

She exhales sharply. "All right, then. I'll say this about the tree: It is a portal between this world and the next, but it's not for just anyone who visits Accompong. It is a place where our ancestors are present and can help guide us, the Maroons, on our journey in this world and the next.

"Why is the silk cotton tree so important to you? What do you seek from it?" my mother asks Vivian Jean.

"Maxi told me about its power. I've read books and articles by Melville Herskovits and others on the beliefs surrounding it and its importance to generations of Maroon people."

"That does not answer mi question."

"Momma, please."

Vivian Jean sighs. "My interest in the tree is just part of what intrigues me about Accompong and ancient African dance. The rituals and the spirituality of the people are the focus of my work here."

"Yes. But I think you want more than that, eh? You want to meet the ghost of our ancestors that guard the portal."

Vivian Jean's chuckle sounds hollow. "Yes, the duppies."

"Shush, girl!" my mother's voice suddenly booms, startling everyone in the house. "Zinzi, you didn't tell these folks nothin', did ya?"

The Dunham party looks at my mother and me with wide-eyed bewilderment.

"Sorry, Momma." I signal for the group to lean forward. "It's forbidden to say that word in Accompong. Never use it in front of any of the villagers. Or anyone in the Cockpit."

Vivian Jean frowns. "We know that Obeah is illegal."

My mother rolls her eyes and hisses. "You keep that word to yourself, as well, girlie."

"Don't worry, Momma. These Americans aren't here to chase superstition or talk to ghosts."

"Oomph. We'll see."

The following day, everyone's living quarters are ready. Othella and Katherine have one of the colonel's huts, while Vivian Jean and Tully are in another. Meanwhile, my mother somehow becomes involved in where Robbie will stay, and now he's nearby, living in the home of my oldest brother, Raymond.

"Mi surprised you came home." She sits on the stool, weaving a mat. "You've been so busy helping strangers, you forgot about your mother."

"Momma, I'm helping Jamaican workers. That's what the union is doing."

"You're lost. You can't navigate the hills," she warns, shaking her finger at me. "Your connection with the ancestors has faded. You won't survive without it, Zinzi."

"Momma, please. I don't want to upset you, but the ancestors are not concerned with me."

"And why do you think that? Are you afraid to admit mi right? You no longer practice our rituals, you no longer share our beliefs, but you are just as much a Maroon as me or any of your brothers and sisters. Mi don't understand how you can turn your back on your culture, your heritage."

"I haven't turned my back on Jamaica. I just don't believe in magic or superstition."

"Jamaica belongs to the British, not the Maroon people. We belong to no one else." My mother forces herself to her feet. "You're not happy in Kingston. I can see it in your eyes. You think I'm old. Have you looked in a mirror? The circles under your eyes are as rugged as the Cockpit."

"Thanks, Momma. Your kind words are helpful." I can't help but feel as if I've been slapped in the face. She'd never do such a thing, but her words are just as hurtful. I dash out of the hut, just needing to get away—not only from her words but also from the truth behind them.

CHAPTER 29

VIVIAN JEAN

Accompong, Maroon Village, Cockpit Country, Week Two

It happens on the tenth day in Accompong. I am visiting Katherine and Othella in their living quarters on the colonel's yard when Iris comes puffing into the house with exciting news. "Tonight there will be a dance," she announces gleefully.

"That's too good to be true." Katherine dramatically slumps against the wall, and she's not overreacting. Since our arrival, the villagers have resisted her requests for anything and everything, from conversation to storytelling or an innocent chat about herbal remedies, let alone a dance. Katherine has struggled to connect with any villagers, much less receive an invitation to dance. I can see how distressed she has become in just a few days. The reason we are here is dance. She can talk all she wants about potions, artifacts, or mat weaving; the purpose of our expedition is African dance, history, legacy, the music, the movement, the bridge to ancient Africans.

Aside from Iris, our conversations have been limited to

Momma Hazel, who I sense doesn't like us, let alone trust us with Accompong's secrets.

Very few villagers acknowledge our presence, regardless of how much time we spend wandering around the market and attempting to converse. It has reached the point where Katherine asked me to tell Tully to stay in our hut. "I think his cameras are frightening the villagers. The recording devices might be too much civilization for them to take in."

She doesn't say this in front of Zinzi, mind you. Our guide might find the remark condescending and feel obliged to give Katherine what for.

Meanwhile, I'm struggling to sort out my thoughts. I never knew how much my father could hurt me. I never knew how indebted I was to Maxi. She saved my childhood. But at what cost? My relationship with my mother? My father? I've been so consumed by that sorrow that I haven't given Katherine's mission the attention it deserves. I haven't even learned as much as I need to know about the sacred silk cotton tree and how I can reach the duppies, or the one duppie I pray is tangled in the roots of the tree. Maybe tonight's dance will bring me back to my senses, and I can talk about the other reasons I'm here, including the secrets I keep. I return to Iris, who is excitedly detailing the night's festivities. "We have the fiddler coming in from White Hall, there will be rum, and tonight we dance the set dances of the parade."

Katherine starts pacing, hands on her hips and taking deep breaths.

"What are set dances?" I ask to distract her, recognizing her excitement and my curiosity.

"I have no idea," Katherine replies absently. "I am a little disappointed. This dance has nothing to do with the Koromantee war dances." She turns to Iris. "Where will it take place?"

"The small pavilion—but don't come too late or you'll be in the back rows," Iris explains, before adding, "Don't come too early, either. You don't want to seem too anxious, and strangers in the front row are bad juju." Iris curtsies and hurries off, shouting, "See you tonight."

"It's going to be hard to wait for the night to fall." Katherine starts pacing. "Everyone must take notes."

"Will that draw attention?"

Katherine nods. "You're right. This is the first of many invitations, but we must document every step—the sounds, the patterns."

"How? Didn't you say there can't be any more photographs or motion picture cameras?" Othella reminds us from the archway where she has been standing quietly. "If we're not writing, and Mr. Hartfield—excuse me, Tully—can't use his cameras, then how?"

"Count on your memories," Katherine says emphatically. "Every one of us has to be there, too, even Tully. He can use his camera, the Leica II, for a couple of shots, but he must be careful, take them before it's completely dark, and use no other recording equipment."

"I'll have my journal, and you and Othella can take notes, too. But we don't want to have our heads bobbing up and down the whole time, either. So, commit to memory as much as you can." Now, Katherine's excitement is contagious, but my mind still isn't functioning the way she needs it to. The way I thought I wanted it to.

My spirit is too weak. Always a reed caught in a wind tunnel, snapping at the first gust. No matter how much I try not to dwell on my troubles or avoid focusing on what I wish weren't true versus what I want to be true, I fall prey to it—weakness of spirit, mind, and character. How could I love Tully more than I ever loved Clifford? Where did my grief go so quickly? Was it my fault his baby died?

My life is slowly being stripped away, piece by piece. At least Tully knows Clifford's note wasn't written about us. Funny, I almost wish it was. My father and Maxi, all those years of lies?

Christ, this merry-go-round will destroy me.

Othella is speaking, and I make myself listen. "I'm very good at memorizing things. My mind works like that. It's something that has helped me tremendously. I see a room once and can remember where every item belongs. It's like I have a camera inside my head."

"That is a skill," I say emphatically.

"A photographic memory," Katherine adds with a touch of jealousy.

"Yes, Katherine, that's exactly it," I concur. "Do you think there's anything we need to do to prepare?"

"We just have to show up," Katherine replies. "No one has seen them performed since Professor Melville's earliest visit, but he's no dancer.

"We'd better remove our riding pants and boots and wear lightweight dresses and sandals."

"She did say it was in the open pavilion."

"I don't have a dress like that," Othella replies with a sigh.

"Oh, you can wear one of mine," Katherine suggests.

"I'm twice your size."

"I have a trunk full of dresses, all types and styles. We'll find something."

"We should all go together," I say.

"And stay together as a group." Katherine takes Othella's hand. "Let's hurry, I haven't opened all my trunks and it might take a spell to find the right clothes." She turns toward me. "Will you need anything?"

"I have plenty. And I need to tell Tully about tonight," I say, heading to the door. "I'll see you later."

"Count on it."

*   *   *

Katherine wishes to follow Iris's instruction by arriving neither too early nor too late, but waiting makes her jumpy and cranky. Her tongue is so vicious that I think I see a tear in Robbie's eyes. And the boy, though a gentle spirit, is not weak-minded or a complainer. Sadly, however, I'm almost glad about her bad mood. It distracts me from thinking about me.

After screaming at us to hurry and stop wasting time, we follow Katherine—Othella, Robbie, Tully, and me—to the open pavilion.

It is already filling up with villagers of all ages, some with familiar faces but mostly strangers. Tully lifts his moving picture machine over his head until he finds an elevated spot, a mound of dirt, for a better view.

"Help me up," Katherine orders.

Tully doesn't change his position, holding his machine with both hands. "I'm already losing the light."

Katherine huffs loudly. "All right, then. I'll stay here. Is everyone taking notes?" she shouts to the rest of us.

I wrap my arm around her shoulders and squeeze. "This is just the first of many dances, Katherine. We'll be here for weeks. So, let's just take in this moment. Maybe even enjoy ourselves." I anticipate her shaking off my arm, but she surprises me.

"You're right," she replies. "I'll try."

Some villagers offer friendly smiles, while others are openly curious, as if we haven't been marching around Accompong for the past week, trying to get to know them and talk to them about rituals, history, and African legacies. Other villagers are outright hostile. Katherine, as she has been since our arrival, remains oblivious. She can't or refuses to see that to some, we are intruders, outsiders, and unwelcome—these villagers may never change.

A commotion in the center of the pavilion grabs our attention. Colonel Rowe is pushing through the crowd with his wife, his daughter, Iris, and a man who must be the fiddler from White Hall by the look of the musical instrument in his hand.

The fiddler is middle-aged, and some villagers call him *yella man*. I can see it's not because of his skin color. He's black as night. It must mean something else. He hobbles on a crippled leg, shifting his weight from side to side as he appears to tune his fiddle.

Whatever the colonel intended by charging to the center of the crowd is forgotten as a group of old and young women and baby girls come center stage wearing white kerchiefs on their heads.

A jug is placed in Robbie's hands, and he quickly passes it to me, looking horrified. Glancing around, I notice others sipping healthily from their jugs.

"It must be the white rum," Katherine remarks.

I sniff the mouth of the jug and nod, and before anyone can stop me, I take a long swig and lick my lips. "It tastes good."

Tully laughs. "Save me a swallow."

I am so stunned by the sound of his laughter that I indulge again, taking an even longer drink. When I look back, thinking I'll get another playful reaction, he's looking through the lens of his motion picture machine. I pass the jug to Katherine.

"Are all the women here wearing something on their heads?" I ask her, although I can see that the answer is yes.

"Of course, we are capless," Katherine replies with a shrug.

"At least we got the dresses right," I say. They also wear loose-fitting dresses tied at the waist that fall below their knees. The men circling the dancing women wear blue denim or faded khaki trousers or go barefoot. The only ones in sandals like us are the prominent members of the village: the council members, their immediate families, the shopkeeper, and several young dandies, as Zinzi informed us one afternoon when she took the time to show us around.

"Are you getting all of this, Othella?" Katherine looked sharply at the young girl whose eyes were wide but not empty. I could see her taking in every speck of information that came within her gaze. Katherine saw it, too, and gave me a raised eyebrow. "Maybe she can do as she claims."

"I think so."

A hush suddenly falls over the crowd, but only for an instant. Music of some sort—anharmonic chords, squeaks, and thumps—mix together.

Six of the women dancers are not just old, they are quite elderly, and the men dancing with them are young. "I wish I knew the meaning of this dance."

"Look at that." Katherine gestures toward a wrinkled, profoundly hunch-backed woman who suddenly straightens and ties her kerchief more tightly around her head. She then takes the colonel's hand, who appears out of nowhere, and twirls him into an embrace.

"Just like a seasoned ballerina," Katherine notes happily. The women's skirts rise as their kicks become higher and higher, their bodies move sensually, arching and dipping, joined by the men whose hips circle around and around, creating an almost dizzying effect.

Or maybe it's the white rum.

There is more fiddling, more rum, more dancing with high kicks, backbends, and rum. Time passes, and the lines blur between the set dance and the dancing villagers. We stay until the end, exhausted, slightly drunk, and wearing broad smiles.

As Tully and I bid farewell to Katherine and Othella, Katherine turns to me, her breath sweet with the scent of rum. "As you said, this is only the beginning." She heads into her living quarters, barking instructions to Othella about writing down everything she remembers before she falls asleep. Nothing must be lost. Nothing.

CHAPTER 30

─ ⬥ ─

OTHELLA

Accompong, Maroon Village, Cockpit Country, Week Two

I impressed Katherine Dunham. I could absolutely squeal with delight!

After the set dance, I wrote down everything I observed, as she ordered, recalling the smallest details from when the music began to the dancers' clothing, hairstyles and, in that case, the white kerchiefs. I noted what they wore when they lifted the hem of their skirts, sashaying their hips all around the pavilion. When I showed her my journal, she said I was a natural, not just because I had this photographic memory but because I saw dance and dancers and translated movement, passion, and exuberance—her words—in such a way and with such thoroughness that she almost didn't need her notation system. She quickly admitted that the last part was a bit of a stretch. "My notation system is unique, and you will learn it flawlessly, but you've already demonstrated your talent in this area."

I'm accustomed to swinging, bobbing, and shaking my tail feathers—not evoking the spirits of the African ancestors. Of course I don't say this. I just nod my head, look at the diagram, and act as if I know what all the symbols mean. It's just that she trusts me to learn it. My skills of observation—that's what she calls them—and my natural talent for dance make my job totally doable. That and this photographic memory she keeps beaming about.

This is great news, but I am secretly thanking my lucky stars that Tully documents everything with his camera or motion picture machine. So, even though she acts like I'm the only one to rely on, I'm not.

"The notation system is a way to record dance movements through symbols or written instructions," she says, explaining it for the umpteenth time since she showed it to me. "Dance is essential to the Maroon culture, and I intend to capture footwork, gestures, and torso isolations, which are central to Afro-Caribbean dance traditions, without losing authenticity. It also documents the timing and rhythm, along with drumming and oral chants, and even symbolic gestures that hold spiritual or ancestral meanings. Researchers and future generations will be able to re-create these dances accurately."

I ponder this for a long moment. "Is it similar to sheet music for a jazz band?"

"Exactly, Othella." She hands me another journal. "We're going to work very well together."

A week later, Katherine Dunham puts me to work. "I'm trusting you. You're responsible for the notation system." She might rethink that trust if she knew my only responsibility for as long as I can remember has simply been to survive.

"Every breath I take is influenced by movement and sound. Whenever I'm onstage or in a dance studio, I become immersed in the rhythms of the music and the breath of sound, feeling more alive than ever," Katherine says one morning as we walk toward the silk cotton tree and the market.

"I understand what you mean," I tell her. "I feel the same way when I dance. It's as if nothing else matters except my body and the music."

"Dance is always present," Katherine continues, "whether or not a musical instrument is playing."

Katherine Dunham loves to dance, and I could listen to her talk about it for ages. The sparkle in her eyes and the words flowing from her mouth take my breath away.

"You're a quick study, too. Over the past few weeks, you've picked up some movements from the African dances demonstrated by the Maroon people." She pats me on the shoulder. "I've seen you practicing."

"Oh, you have," I reply shyly yet proudly. "These dances are quite different from the ones I performed at the Savoy Ballroom. None of them resembles the Lindy Hop, the fox-trot, or the shimmy." I pause. "Okay, maybe the shimmy."

Katherine nods in agreement. "You're right about that."

The market isn't large, but it offers fruits, vegetables, and cloth wraps that can be fashioned into dresses. I'm pleased that Katherine seems tired of wearing riding pants and shirts every day. "You know what?"

"What, ma'am?" I ask politely.

"You have what it takes, Othella, a flexible torso, spine, and pelvis, and can isolate your limbs. You're talented," Katherine says, looking deeply into my eyes. "When we return to Chicago, I want you to take dance classes with me."

"Are you serious?" I exclaim. "Oh my. I would love that. Thank you, ma'am. I will, I swear I will."

I feel like floating across the sky and dancing on Lake Michigan without a boat. My chest swells with delight, and I wish my jubilation could last forever. But it can't—I told Katherine a lie. I will never take a dance lesson with her, for I will never return to Chicago.

CHAPTER 31

— ✦ —

VIVIAN JEAN

The Sacred Silk Cotton Tree, Accompong, Maroon Village,
Week Three

I feel like a shadow.

Maxi and my father—my father and Maxi. Everything I've seen but refused to acknowledge. When they were watching me, judging me, pretending to care while looking after me, was that genuine? Or was I merely an excuse? Someone they could use to conceal themselves?

That was then; this is now.

There are days when I barely catch half of what is said. I drift away for minutes at a time. Thank goodness for the recordings. Otherwise, I would be failing at my purpose. But I feel like I'm in limbo, waiting for a response to the telegram I sent to Maxi Green after Maggotty.

Then the wait is over. Three weeks after we arrive in Accompong, it is finally delivered.

There is only one place where I want to read it, and only one person I want by my side. So, I lead Tully to the sacred silk cotton tree after dinner. It is late enough that the marketplace isn't crowded, except for a few stragglers and hawkers covering their goods with thin pieces of cloth and setting up their beds nearby for the night.

Tully has brought a straw mat from Zinzi's small thatched-roof house for us to sit on. He carefully checks the area for spiders or other bugs. Finding nothing, he arranges the mat. I sit cross-legged on it while Tully faces me with his legs also crossed.

"I got it today," I tell him. "A letter from Maxi. Yes, a letter, not a telegram. That's why it took so long."

I hold the unopened envelope for him to see, flipping it over and back again.

"You don't want to read it by yourself?" Tully asks.

"Why should I?" I snort. "We are in Jamaica partly because of Maxi and Clifford's note—and because of what you thought it meant and what I wouldn't accept it could mean. Neither of us expected her and my father's secret to be part of this, so I want you here to share this moment."

> *My dearest Vivian Jean,*
>
> *I couldn't be the first to tell you. Your father had to be the one; he only told you part of it from what he tells me. So, I will fill in the missing pieces. But understand, this isn't me writing to seek forgiveness. I'm writing to explain how love changed me and made me who I am.*
>
> *I was very young when I met your father, and falling in love with him came easily. He was handsome and bold in his American ways, and he promised to give me a better life. This was what I longed for, dreamed of, read about in books, and heard of while I swept floors, mopped hallways, and did my chores at the Jamaican hotels where I worked—so many different hotels in Kingston, Montego Bay, and everywhere in between.*
>
> *He and I were lovers in Jamaica, but despite all my prayers, I never expected him to ask me to come to America. When he finally did, I thought God had given*

me a gift. Once I agreed to come, booked my travel, and stepped off the ship in New York City, I had no idea about you or your mother. Yet she was exactly the same person upon my arrival as she is today. Your father's many infidelities and lies had already taken their toll on her.

But I was young and blindly in love—a fool who refused to give up her gift. Your father hired me as a maid and a nanny in your parents' home. I thought about returning to Jamaica, but after a few months of caring for you, you became my priority.

I fell in love with you and devoted myself to raising you. I ended my relationship with your father, but it took longer than I thought to finally break the bond between us. I even returned to Jamaica once, but my longing for you drew me back. This doesn't excuse what we did, though I wish it could.

Now, regarding the note Clifford wrote. It was addressed for your father to read. Clifford discovered our betrayal long after our relationship had ended. He overheard a disagreement between your father and me, and he confronted your father not only about the affair but also concerning his business dealings in Jamaica. Later, I learned from you that this was around the time Clifford arranged for you to oversee your trust fund. He wanted to protect you.

I know there are other reasons you feel you need to seek Clifford's forgiveness. He loved you deeply, as much as he loved his brother. Clifford will speak to you beneath the silk cotton tree, but my hope is for you and Tully to finally forgive yourselves for falling in love.

Losing Clifford and then his child is a grief you may never fully recover from, but you've found the love you deserve. I wish for you and Tully happiness, joy, and peace.

With all my love, Maxi

* * *

It takes a moment before I can speak. I fold the letter and carefully reinsert it into the envelope. Then, I shove it into my pocket, take a deep breath, and gaze at the night sky. When I finally open my mouth, I mean exactly what I say. "I can't forgive her now, but I do know I will never forgive him."

"She didn't ask you to," Tully replies, settling back into a cross-legged position.

"I understand. But why would he continue this for so long? Why inflict so much pain on the women in your life? Why not just be honest?"

"He's selfish. What he wants outweighs anyone else's desires."

"He must hate women." The thought makes me feel sick. "He has destroyed my relationship with my mother, and now, with Maxi, and I think he tried to wreck us, too. That's more than selfishness.

"After I lost the baby, I felt like I was drowning. It was as if my heart had shattered. I thought I would always carry a part of Clifford with me. Losing him was hard, but losing his child? The only way I believed I could survive was by pushing both him and the baby away as if they never existed. But you were there and you brought me happiness and smiles. Then the note was found, and it seemed you wanted to destroy us because you thought our love couldn't be real."

"I know, Vivian Jean. I know. We almost wrecked ourselves. We can't blame him for our own choices." He folds his legs in front of him. "And I'm not sure about your mother either. She may have hardened herself against love long before Maxi came into the picture. Your relationship with Maxi will only be ruined if you allow it to be."

I cover my eyes with my hands. "I can't forgive her. I just can't."

"Okay, then, don't forgive her. Kick her out of your life.

Forget her feelings for you and your feelings for her. Forget everything she's done for you over the years—you should be able to do that."

"I'm not in the mood for your sarcasm, Tully."

"Am I being sarcastic? I don't think so." He claps his hands together and holds on. "She says they're no longer a couple. The relationship ended a long time ago. She did that because she loves you."

"Does she? Can something like that ever really end?"

He shrugs. "If you want something to end badly enough, it will end."

Seething anger rises within me. "How can you be so calm? My father made you marry me after Clifford passed away. He knew Clifford was aware of his relationship with Maxi. Don't you feel betrayed? Why aren't you angry?"

"We're talking about betrayal, selfishness, and deceit," he states. "How can I judge Maxi or even your father? Not when I was ready to believe I betrayed my brother. I selfishly admitted my love for his wife. I aimed to upset him, to hurt him; my big brother, the doctor—the ideal husband, the perfect man my parents treasured. I was envious of him. I drank too much and let that envy take over." He shut his eyes, and although I couldn't see them, I could feel his tears. "So, why am I not angry? Perhaps it's because I'm weary of blaming others for my decisions."

He reaches out and takes my hand. "And your father didn't force me—I wanted to marry you."

Tears fill my eyes as I look to the sky, hoping to hold them back. But there are no stars; the night is empty—no light, no sparkles. How could such a thing happen in Jamaica? It is an island without stars, a phenomenon that only occurs when it rains. Yet, there is not a single drop of moisture in the air or a breeze. No rustling of the leaves on the silk cotton tree, only the rise and fall of Tully's voice in my ears.

"I can't just let it go."

Tully tilts his head. "We can't change your father, Maxi, or your mother. We can only do what we can to help ourselves."

"You sound so wise and mature."

"Is that a problem? I actually like the sound of mature Tully," he replies.

"I came to Jamaica seeking forgiveness from the silk cotton tree and the duppies. I wanted Clifford to forgive me—and you, too."

"I understand that," Tully says. "But can we repair our relationship?"

"Do you want to?"

"I do."

"Do you love me?"

He squeezes my kneecap. "Yes, I love you."

"I love you, too."

"So, there's hope for us."

"Yes, there is. Plenty." I kiss him on the cheek, and for the first time in a long while, he doesn't pull away.

CHAPTER 32

ZINZI

Accompong, Maroon Village, Cockpit Country, Week Four

As I run from my mother's house, tears stream down my face. This is why I don't visit. But she's getting her way. I can't leave Accompong, not with this tension between us.

I take a mule to Maggotty to send two telegrams, one to Allan, apologizing for being unable to return for the upcoming demonstrations. I must stay in Accompong longer than I originally planned.

The second telegram takes longer to write, even though its message is shorter. Instead of quickly jotting down what I need to write, I walk around the small telegraph office, pacing back and forth. Finally, I hand the message to the woman operating the telegraph. It reads:

> Byron, I won't be returning to Kingston for two weeks.
> My mother is very ill. Zinzi.

It's all I write because otherwise, I might say too much.

* * *

A few days later, I leave the house early, wearing a loose-fitting cotton dress tied at the waist, socks on my feet, and thick-soled boots. My knapsack rests on my back and my machete in hand. I am ready to hike into the jungle. I follow a familiar path, the same trail I used to take with my father, searching for water, wild pears, or strawberry trees—the sweet fruit of my childhood.

Sunlight filters through the palm leaves. Branches graze against my arms and legs, but I continue for more than an hour until I reach the clearing. It is a beautiful, open area, a dry sinkhole, an old campsite of the Maroons where my father often visited as a child and brought me for picnics and swimming. Encircled by steep limestone ridges and enveloped in thick vegetation, my joy comes from the river, though that may be too strong a term for the stream of water that glimmers in the broken sunlight.

I unlace and remove my boots and socks, strip off my dress, and sink into the rippling water, floating on my back for a while and swimming until my body feels limp. I walk from the water onto the riverbank, open my knapsack, take out a folded cloth, and stretch it over the ground. Then I lie in the sunshine.

After a short time, a sound from the bushes draws my attention. I grab my dress and slip it over my head. A large creature moves through the dense forest. Not a mongoose or a crocodile. Still, I take one cautious step, but I'm not afraid. I know who I hope it might be. I told my mother where I'd be right after I received his telegram.

"Who's there?"

"Zinzi. It's me." Byron steps through a tangle of bushes.

"My God, what are you doing here?" I say, smiling broadly because I know the answer. "How did you find me?"

He strides into the clearing, hatless, with disheveled hair, a sweat-soaked cotton shirt, and a knapsack slung over his broad shoulders. "You always ask so many questions. You knew I was coming."

"Not true. I just hoped." My tone is terse and teasing all at once. "After receiving your telegram, I told my mother where I'd be. All she had to do was give you directions."   ·

"She did a decent job, but I also know my way around the jungle. I was raised in the Cockpit. The Tynesdale plantation is not far from here. Besides, you left an easy enough trail to follow."

He sweeps his hair back from his eyes. "It's been four weeks and I needed to see you. Did you miss me?" He hooks his fingers on the belt of his pants, giving him a boyish air of uncertainty.

"I'm glad you came," I reply.

"You are? I hoped you would be."

I feel my dress clinging to my wet skin. I step closer to him. "Well, you're right."

"You should stop looking at me that way or I will want to make love to you again."

"I can't stop." I slide my arms around his neck. "Kiss me."

He does, and this clearing in the jungle becomes our refuge.

Our intimacy is rich in tenderness and emotion. I mirror Byron's fervor, clinging to him as he clings to me, his fingers digging into my back, his muscles tense. I hold him in silence as we revel in each other's touch, warmth, and comfort.

Our clothing came off so easily that it feels awkward to dress again in front of each other, especially with the jungle surrounding us. I pull on my socks and step into a boot, but there's a change in Byron's mood. His silence is sullen, his movements jerky, and the crease between his eyebrows has deepened. I brace myself for the conversation I know we need to have about Bernard Christian Tynesdale.

"My father has lost his mind."

"What happened?"

We still sit on the cloth I stretched out on the ground. "He has a new policy. Any worker—man, woman, or child—who is found in attendance at a labor union rally will be fired."

I sit upright. "My God, what is he thinking? Even with the awful conditions, people need to work in this economy. That's monstrous," I exclaim. "Who will he get to replace the field-workers he lets go? Will he put unskilled laborers in his sugarcane fields?"

Byron takes my hands in his. "It's not just the Tynesdale Estate. He's formed an alliance with six other sugar plantation owners in St. Elizabeth Parish. They've agreed to support him and one another in enforcing the policy. He claims they also provide financial backing to hire detectives and constables to monitor attendance at the movement's activities. He even said he'll hire scabs, strikebreakers, to do the work. He'll even ship scabs here from Cuba."

"Damn."

"He wants me to stop playing around. No more labor union talk. No more dining in public with labor union activists." He smiles. "I told him to go to hell."

"Good for you, but how does that stop him from destroying lives?"

Byron runs his fingers through his hair, his eyes dark with rage. "I can't let him get away with this." He stands and paces. I rise, too, watching him as he stalks back and forth. But I can't keep silent.

"No matter what he does, he won't stop the labor movement," I say defiantly. "We will work harder. Recruit more volunteers. The movement will only grow bigger and stronger. We won't be stopped."

Byron clenches his fists. "I believe you believe that," he pauses, "but my father is relentless and greedy. To stop him, I need to play his ball game."

"What game? Steal the rum recipe?"

He chuckles and shakes his head. "No, that won't work. He'd squelch that story. He owns too many people, including newspaper reporters.

"But I've found another way," he says. "During Prohibition, while I was out of the country, my father formed an alliance with some American rum runners out of Chicago. Now, he has a new deal with the same partners. And it's legal—but that doesn't mean ethical."

My nerves feel like they're coming apart. "You learned all this since the last time I saw you, four weeks ago?"

"I can hire detectives, too." He takes my hands. "Let's sit down." He helps me return to our spot on the ground. We face each other, sitting cross-legged.

"Okay, I'm ready."

Byron exhales. "I've known about his illegal rum business during Prohibition for a while. There was no ban on liquor or rum in Jamaica. My father's new business supplies distilled rum to his Chicago partners. They handle bottling and distribution in the United States. It's a huge deal. To make it work, he has to increase his rum production. The deal won't work if there's a labor union. This business venture gives him the capital to resist the labor movement, and his attack on the Maroons shows he'll do anything to make a profit. But I'm going to put a wrench in his plans."

"How?"

"It's complicated."

"I understand complications."

He caresses my hand. "I know that."

"What have you done?"

"I met with one of his partners. Actually, both of them have been in Jamaica for a couple of weeks, secretly meeting with my father. Bernard doesn't want the other plantation owners to get wind of his plans." He pauses. "Turns out I can be just as unscrupulous as my father. I reached out to one of these men and made a deal to put more money in his pocket rather than my father's."

"Earning his trust—"

"Yes." He chuckles. "By playing the part of the spoiled son, who wants his father's business for himself."

"What did you do, exactly, Byron?"

"I've been feeding this fellow shipping schedules and some financial information. Making it seem as if I'll do anything, even partner with him, to delay major shipments."

"Don't your actions also ruin the partner's business interests? What happens when your father finds out? I thought he was ill. I thought he was dying!"

"That was a lie to get me to come home. He has health problems, but they aren't killing him."

"Christ."

"Amen." Byron takes my hand and we start down the path. "This man is greedy. More so than even my father. He's making deals with rum distillers in Cuba and all across Jamaica. He wants money and power." Byron sighs deeply.

"What's wrong? Is he dangerous? Has he threatened you?"

"He asked to meet you."

I let go of his hand, stopping on the path lined with rock formations. "Why me? I have nothing to do with your father's business."

"He doesn't trust me. Meeting with you, my girlfriend, the labor union activist, who has prompted me to betray my father . . ." Byron shrugs a shoulder.

I don't miss the *girlfriend* comment but move on quickly. "I hope I'm not the reason you're doing this."

"No." He cups my chin and kisses me. "Not the only reason, but will you help me?"

"Oh God, Byron." I pause, thinking of all the reasons I should say no—all the reasons Byron should walk away from this dangerous plan—but the look on his face. He's desperate to do something, anything to stop his father. "When do you want me to do this?"

"So, you'll meet with him?"

"Yes, I'll meet him."

He exhales his relief, which I can feel in my chest. "In a week, maybe two. You'll need to come to Kingston."

I chew my lower lip. "I can do that."

CHAPTER 33

———•◆•———

OTHELLA

Accompong, Maroon Village, Cockpit Country, Week Five

Most of my days are spent either writing dance notations for Katherine or digging in the dirt with Robbie while being eaten alive by various bugs—both large and small—and surrounded by leafy plants, dirt, and heat. Still, I can't shake the feeling that every day is a test.

I feel utterly exhausted all day, every day. I swear, some days I lose track of time.

If I were back in Chicago, I'd be in bed all day, sipping gin and tonics—and staying up all night, doing the things I promised to stop doing.

But Accompong is not Chicago.

Everyone is at Momma Hazel's hut tonight. She invited us over for dinner. Vivian Jean, Tully, Katherine, Robbie, Raymond, her eldest son, and her two youngest boys, Elise and Sammy, the twins, and me—we are all here. Zinzi is the only one missing.

She left two days ago, and her brothers are very concerned. Her sick mother doesn't seem worried. She mutters about knowing where Zinzi has gone and keeps saying not to worry about her. "My daughter is grown and can care for herself," Momma Hazel says. "After all, she lives in Kingston. City girls know how to stay out of harm's way."

I couldn't agree with her more, but I keep that thought to myself. In fact, I'm starting to like Momma Hazel. She keeps giving me things to stop my bug bites from itching, and she's awfully feisty—I like that in old people.

Despite being sick, she loves to give orders. She orchestrates meals like Miss Lucille dished out Bible verses—with severity and precision—and she doesn't cook much either; she barely lifts a finger around a pot or a pan. She directs, which she does from her throne: a three-legged stool in the middle of the room.

The hut lacks a stove, so meals are cooked outdoors over a cookfire. There is no dining room or dinner table, just places to plant your behind and hold a plate in your lap. This evening's feast includes goat, callaloo, yams, dasheen, and sweet potato. The flavors overwhelmed me after the first night—I don't trust most of the meals. Zinzi did give me some pointers on how to recognize the peppers that would cause me the most discomfort.

I really miss my Italian beef.

With a plate in hand, I find a spot near Robbie, as usual at mealtime, and begin picking at my food while listening to the others' conversations.

Katherine is upset with Colonel Rowe. "He refuses to discuss the Koromantee war dances with me. It is one of the main reasons I included Jamaica in my schedule," she explains.

I look at Robbie, confused. "The Koromantee includes many aspects, such as the Maroon language, rituals, and dance."

Momma Hazel grunts. "Come by tomorrow, Katherine. I'll introduce you to Miss Mary and Teddy. But here's what you need to know about the Koromantee. It's a British word for slave, slaves from West Africa, various regions, also known as Akin, mostly from Ghana, who rebelled, but they were enslaved."

"I thought that was the Maroon people," Tully says.

"The Maroons were formerly enslaved and won their freedom, and signed a treaty with the British." Momma Hazel waves her hand. "Mary and Teddy will explain more when you meet them."

Katherine's eyes light up. "That sounds lovely. Thank you."

Tully raises his hand. "Us too," he says, waving at Momma Hazel. "Vivian Jean and I are facing the same issue." He sounds lighthearted, but his eyes plead for help.

Vivian Jean doesn't join him in his petition. She has changed a lot since her father gave her a ride to Maggotty, not nearly as talkative as before. Something terrible must've happened that day between her and her daddy.

I chew on a piece of goat meat, trying to swallow without choking.

Then Zinzi's mother laughs, a sound I haven't heard before. But when I look up, I understand why there's a big smile on her face. It's not so much because Zinzi has surprised us by returning; I wager it's the look on her brothers' faces that has tickled Momma Hazel. The man at Zinzi's side has caused their faces to turn gray and their mouths to drop open.

I smile, too, because like them, it's been some time since I set eyes on a white man.

"Hi, everybody. This is Byron. Byron Tynesdale." Zinzi's brothers, Raymond, Elise, and Sammy can't seem to keep their mouths shut. Now, they are so slack-jawed that I recall my mother chastising me, saying, *Close your mouth before you catch flies.*

Then I think about it for a second and realize why they are experiencing a second shock—it's the man's last name.

"Oh, right," I say, recalling my chat with Robbie. "That's the name of a sugar plantation that makes rum."

"This is her friend from Kingston," says Momma Hazel. "He came by mi house a few days ago."

"Oh, so that's where you've been, Zinzi," I say. "Spending time with your friend?"

Robbie clears his throat, signaling me to stay quiet, I guess. I shrug and pick up a piece of sweet potato to nibble on. "With two more mouths to feed, there won't be any seconds," he whispers seriously. He loves the food, unlike me—and must fear he'll lose out on a second helping.

I smile at him while watching Zinzi's friend, Byron Tynesdale. He reminds me of Chicago—nightclubs, whiskey, and cigarette smoke.

The conversation after the shock lessens becomes jovial, easy, and I think maybe this Byron isn't so much Chicago as everywhere else in the world. He's been to so many places, listening to him go on and on, and watching the light in Zinzi's eyes; well, I haven't seen this side of her. I like it. They suit each other.

After dinner, we take a walk around Accompong. "Does anyone smoke?" Byron asks.

My hand goes up. "I do, but I've run out," I reply. "Do you have an extra pack you could share?"

He reaches into his knapsack and pulls out a carton. "Here you go."

"The whole carton?"

"I've got plenty at home."

Zinzi's eyebrows knit together as she gives him a nod of appreciation. "He's a generous guy."

"Thank you. Thank you." I haven't smoked a cigarette in so long that I nearly weep.

When Robbie walks me to the yard I share with Katherine, I smoke three cigarettes in quick succession. "I'll see you in the morning at dawn," he says. "Tomorrow, we'll be hunting for dung beetles and flower beetles."

I wince. "Do they bite?"

Robbie smiles. "No, they don't bite."

He gives me a kiss on the cheek, something he does every evening after dinner since we arrived in Accompong.

Tonight, I kiss him back. "Until tomorrow, Robbie."

CHAPTER 34

——— ••• ———

VIVIAN JEAN

Accompong, Maroon Village, Cockpit Country, Week Five

Early in the morning, I leave my hut with my husband by my side to collect oral histories from Accompong's storytellers. I ask the questions, take the notes, and Tully photographs our subjects or records them with his motion picture machine.

Momma Hazel and her friends, Miss Mary and Teddy, have been incredibly helpful in securing interview subjects from among the Maroon villagers. The only quibble I have is that Mary and Teddy are always armed with a pouch of herbs, some pungent spices, and a few bottles I describe as potions, to help influence those who need a better reason than hospitality to speak with us. But however our good fortune comes to us, I am pleased that we now have many more villagers lined up than we'd hoped for.

On the outside, Tully and I appear to be functioning normally—no quarreling or snappish words directed at one or the other. On the inside, we remain on unsteady ground, mostly because of me. The distress in my heart feels like I'm carrying half the jungle on my back.

I don't know if the silk cotton tree can fix me, let alone us. My belief in communing with Clifford's ghost is as much Maxi's as mine. "It will help rid you of guilt, talking to Clifford," she said. But I can't trust Maxi. She and my father cost me my mother's love. Regina must've always known about their affair. I don't even have to hear her say it. Looking back, it was clear as crystal.

With these thoughts racing through me, I know they are affecting my contribution to Katherine's expedition. It's noticeable, and not just to me. I sense Katherine's frustration—and her concern. Today, she finds me in Tully's makeshift darkroom, where I like to hide away, and insists—or, I should say, demands—that I join her to learn how to play an authentic African musical instrument.

"It is my goal for the day," she states.

"I have several interviews arranged."

"I believe Tully can manage them. I'll ask Robbie and Othella to help him."

"I'm not sure that's the best idea."

"It is a brilliant idea," she says emphatically. "Besides, what good are you doing hiding in the dark? It's midafternoon. The sun is still shining and the village is alive with activity." She sighs. "Vivian Jean, your sulking must cease."

Given no choice, I do not resist.

The "goombah" is a hollow block of wood covered with sheepskin that has been stripped of its hair and produces a sound Katherine describes as "gay and grave." She then remarks with a smile that fails to reach her eyes, "Sort of like your mood lately."

How can music be more than just sound? I wonder, but I don't ask. "I've had a lot on my mind."

"None of which you have chosen to share with me, your friend and leader of this expedition. I wish you thought I could help."

I close my eyes. "I'm sorry. I don't mean to be this way—there's a lot I'm too afraid to tell because it's embarrassing and—" I look into her eyes. "Scary and foolish."

We are heading toward the pavilion where I've spent numerous evenings recently, taking part in ceremonies, dances, rituals, celebrations, and activities that have both thrilled and mystified me. "Is this where we'll learn to play the sheepskin instrument?"

"I may have exaggerated a little. I seriously doubt we'll be permitted to handle the goombah during this ceremony. Tonight, it's a sacred instrument. You see, we've been invited to a Koromantee war dance ritual."

I see the sparkle in Katherine's eyes. This is something she has been looking forward to since we arrived. She's been seeking out an opportunity to see it, to participate in it, but she was denied at every turn. The reasons were never clear. She was beginning to believe she would never witness one of the most authentic ancient rituals of the Maroon people, passed down from those brought to and enslaved in the Caribbean from West Africa who fought but never won their freedom.

"How did the invitation happen?" I ask.

"It seems that the Koromantee war dance is not just another dance performance. It is an invocation that calls upon ancestral warriors, Cudjoe, Nanny, and Tacky, who fought against colonial forces to free their people. There will be drumming, chatting, and a procession to connect the living to the warrior spirits of the past."

"Like those I might find beneath the sacred silk cotton tree?" I ask.

"That is why you came, isn't it, Vivian Jean? The silk cotton tree—in the middle of town. The spirits of the tree. You believe in all of it, don't you?"

I don't respond.

"Who is it you need to speak with?"

I still don't answer. I stare at the dirt beneath my feet.

"It's not about fieldwork. That you would share with me—it's personal."

I look at her even more intensely but remain silent.

"You'll tell me if you still need to after this ceremony."

My shoulders relax. She's backing off, and I will tell her—just not yet. "If the war dances are held because of an adversary's threat, who are the Maroons raging war against now?"

We have reached an area of the pavilion, and others have already started together. We take our seats, not in the back or the front but in the middle of the group already in place. "Who is the war dance meant for?"

"Talking to Zinzi the other day, she told me that some sugarcane plantation owners are mounting a campaign to legalize taxing the Maroon people for the rum they make and consume in the Cockpit. For centuries, the Maroon people have operated independently from Britain and its policies and taxes. Colonel Rowe intends to ensure that this autonomy continues."

"And it begins tonight with the Koromantee war dances."

"Oh, did I mention that this is a proper Maroon ritual, and the ceremony lasts until dawn?"

"So, we'll be here all night?"

"Yes, we will."

"I didn't tell Tully."

"I told everyone we are the only two who were invited."

"I understand your invitation, but why me?" I ask.

"You'd have to ask Momma Hazel. She has a lot to do with this ceremony," Katherine explains.

No wonder it takes all night. The entire village is in attendance. The drums, the goombah, and the chanting soar, and the freedom of movement is intoxicating. Such abandon of spirit that Katherine has put aside her notebook. There are no photos to document this experience. It's felt in the heart. In the soul. That is where the memory of the ancestors come to life within each of us. I start to giggle. I do believe the atmosphere has caught me off guard, or has simply caught me. I feel a warrior spirit inside me, bursting to be set free.

Katherine holds my hand. "This ceremony," she gestures across the pavilion, "is the living embodiment of rebellion and identity." She taps her foot to the frenetic rhythm of the drums.

"Do you want to join them?" I nudge her.

"I always want to dance," Katherine says, squeezing my hand. "And since we have adversaries, a war dance is for us, too."

"Yes, it is," I reply, more seriously than I meant to.

"Maybe a war dance will show them their place. With the spirit of Cudjoe, the mighty warrior, they will think again about standing against us. So, yes, we should dance."

"And we aren't being sacrilegious."

"It's not a religion. The Maroon people call upon the heroes of their past to give them strength, cunning, and victory in the present."

"All right, you've convinced me. Let's dance."

Katherine stands up gracefully, while I get to my feet with less elegance.

I kick off my sandals. "Do you think we can do it?"

"Do what, dance?"

"Yes, but dance until dawn."

"Finally, you understand me," Katherine says.

I stomp my bare feet, striking the hard ground stroke after stroke, jump, jump, jump. Then I circle my hips and drop my head forward, look up at the sky and down at the dirt, then up at the sky again, and twirl and twirl. Stomp. Stomp. Stomp. I sway from side to side, my hip thrusting toward the ocean, then toward the mountains; my body tumbles down and rises up. I don't know if you call it dance or something mythical, something spiritual, but it has control of my limbs, has control of the center of my body, and just lets me do whatever comes next without thought, without choice. It's freedom. And the ancestors are watching.

Only the stars can tell how long we danced, but my spirit feels so free. I am not concerned about time or exhaustion; my feet might be. I stumble, and Katherine steadies me with a firm hand.

"I want to shout this to the moon."

"What? Tell me."

"Art and history bring balance to our world, Vivian Jean. Humanity cannot survive without acknowledging its past. We stagnate if we don't honor and study the creativity that has thrived through generations."

She twirls away from me. "Without dance, music, and our ancestors' wisdom, we wouldn't survive."

"I understand."

She twirls back. "Do you? Understand? Then answer my question."

"Which one?"

"Do you believe in Obeah?"

I let my head tilt back and gaze at a sky blanketed with more stars than I've ever seen. "Yes, I believe in Obeah, in the duppies, in the sacred silk cotton tree and that it can heal my wounds."

She opens her arms, and we embrace. "I do, too."

And once more we are dancing.

CHAPTER 35

OTHELLA

Accompong, Maroon Village, Cockpit Country, Week Six

Water pours from the sky, hard and fast, crashing into the earth like a locomotive slamming into a brick wall. I sit up in my cot, wide awake, peering out of the small hole in my hut where a window would be if I lived in a civilized town.

Massive sheets of rain tumble from the endless black sky. Thoughts of Noah's ark cross my mind. If the rain never stops, will Accompong float away? Will I be washed out to sea? How far am I from the nearest ocean?

The rain crashes against the ground: splat, boom, splat, boom. I hide my head under a thin cloth, hoping the noise will cease. I remain this way for hours, curled into a ball, trembling and praying until exhaustion overcomes my fear and I fall asleep.

Silence awakens me. My first instinct is to peer through the hole in the wall. Is the hut a raft now? Am I floating on a river?

Surprise! Accompong is dry. Aside from a few puddles, dawn's sunlight has already burned off any water that might have pooled.

I quickly get dressed and leave the house, calling out to Katherine to let her know I'm heading out early to gather bugs. I want to talk to Robbie about the rain. What does he think of the storms, the heavy downpour, and the howling winds?

"Honestly, it's not that much rain."

"It's not raining that much?" I exclaim in horrified disbelief. "You must be crazy."

He laughs. "It's the season. We should expect sudden heavy rainstorms, strong winds, and hurricanes. These intense bursts of rainfall are nature's way of releasing the earth's tension—that's all."

"We didn't have hurricanes in Chicago."

"It's just a lot more wind and rain—similar to the storm on the SS *Talamanca*, but on land instead of at sea."

I feel as though he's laughing at me, and for the first time in a long while, I don't have much fondness for Robbie Barnes.

A few days later, I'm over my hurt feelings and have forgiven him. I am also getting used to Accompong's heat, mud, mosquitoes, and even the occasional snake slithering through the grass. Just don't let me get cornered by one of those giant rats the Jamaicans call mongooses. I'll have to pull out my switchblade.

On the other hand, I believe Momma Hazel likes me. She has come to my rescue, giving me ointments and herbal potions—Obeah magic, I call it—for my insect bites, irritated skin from so much sweating, and the sore back I've developed from helping Robbie dig in the dirt for plants I've never heard of.

Accompong is no heaven, but it's better than the hell I was dealing with in Chicago, minus the gin and the Italian beef. Especially now that I've discovered I have so many talents. Not only the dance notation for Katherine, but I have something for Robbie, too. I can draw. Details, details, details. I guess I love them.

"Today, we're going to study limestone karst formations," Robbie begins each day we're together with a lesson. It feels like being back in school.

"Karst what?" I ask as we walk through a valley filled with the Cockpit's limestone karst topography—fancy words for sinkholes, caves, underground rivers, and steep, rugged hills. Robbie also describes the region as having limited seasonal water, a lie he repeats to taunt me after that scare when the deluge of rain terrified me.

"Today, we're checking on the pimento trees," Robbie says, explaining that the dried berries from these trees produce allspice. "Zinzi's mother uses it in almost everything she cooks. Tomorrow, we'll focus on the Jamaican mahogany trees. There are many species in the Cockpit." There is so much to learn, but that memory of mine helps. He shows me the hardwood trees, wild ginger, agave plants, and orchids that thrive in limestone. He's always adding definitions for terms like ecology, caverns, sinkholes, and topography. I admit his ramblings are sounding less and less annoying.

Robbie takes notes while I sketch, and he switches to a new topic. "The wood from the pimento tree is used in jerk cooking. And you have a talent."

"What do you mean?"

"You never damage a single specimen while digging for tiny seeds or delicate plant parts."

"Are you praising me?"

He laughs. "Yes, and you don't need magnifying glasses. Your eyesight is as sharp as a hawk's."

"Thank you. I also credit my long, slender fingers. They are nimble and steady." I wiggle them, proving my point. "Didn't you know? In Chicago, they called me the queen of the fingersmiths?"

"That sounds like an appropriate nickname for you even in the Cockpit."

"I agree." We laugh for a few minutes but don't stray far from the task at hand. It's good to have fun while you work, especially a different kind of fun than I'm accustomed to.

This is one of those days when I feel like Robbie is someone I could fall for, or maybe I already have. Sure, we've been flirting since we first met at Mr. Abbott's house, then on the train and the SS *Talamanca*. He has learned a lot about me, even the nasty bits about Perry and Jerry, or at least as much as I dared to reveal.

Pinky swear. I can trust him. We're best friends.

We kiss, too—sometimes a lot. But that's it, and boy, is that ever different for me. It's romantic. He never paws at me or demands anything from me. Robbie is what folks call a gentleman.

"Don't worry. We've got all the time in the world."

Who would've thought that Robbie Barnes and I could be sweethearts?

CHAPTER 36

OTHELLA

Accompong, Maroon Village, Cockpit Country, Week Seven

It's dinnertime at Momma Hazel's, and ladies' night with Vivian Jean, Katherine, Zinzi, and me. Robbie is finishing a paper on the giant swallowtail butterfly, while Tully has set up a darkroom in Colonel Rowe's main house and is developing his photography.

I look forward to a night of gossip, rum, and picking over my dinner plate, searching for something I can swallow. I've gotten so good at it that no one notices I scarcely eat anything other than sweet potatoes, and only if they haven't been dipped in the stew. My other treat is the hard bread, but only as long as it hasn't been sprinkled with pepper sauce.

After we finish dinner and clean up, Zinzi takes me aside. "How would you like to come to Kingston with me tomorrow?"

I'm surprised by the invitation, but more so by my reaction. "Everyone else turned you down, huh?" I say playfully, because I don't know if I want to go.

"I wouldn't have asked you if I didn't want your company," she replies.

"I'm supposed to go with Katherine to a town meeting in the morning, and then Robbie and I are heading to the market in Maggotty for supplies."

She looks at me sideways, but she's not mad. "I checked with everyone and they agreed, it's okay with them if you want to go. In other words, it's up to you."

I couldn't believe I was hesitating, but I think I've grown attached to the Cockpit, Robbie, Vivian Jean, Tully, and Katherine. I might miss something important if I'm not around.

On the other hand, I only caught a glimpse of Kingston, a Jamaican city, rushing from the SS *Talamanca* to the train station on the day we docked. This time, I might be able to listen to some live Jamaican music that's not a ritual. Maybe go to a nightclub. Maybe some restaurants serve steak and mashed white potatoes. Real food, not mashed leafy vegetables, yams, and saltfish with peppers that burn my mouth. "I'd love to go."

Kingston Harbour and Myrtle Bank Hotel, Kingston

We had to ride the beasts again, but I had done quite well the first time with the mules, and this time is no different. In fact, the journey is the same, except that when we arrive at Kingston station, there's a limousine waiting for us.

"This is nice," I say as I slide into the back seat next to Zinzi. "So, what do you have planned for the day? Is there any chance we can go shopping? Robbie gave me a few dollars to spend."

But small talk doesn't seem to be on Zinzi's agenda. "I didn't tell you everything last night, and it's bothering me." Zinzi lets out a sigh and then a shudder. "Let me tell you the truth."

"Okay."

"You remember my friend Byron, who visited me a few weeks back?"

"Of course. He gave me a carton of smokes."

"He's trying to stop his father, the plantation owner, from taxing our rum in the Cockpit, which is also a way to get under Byron's skin about the labor union movement."

I shrug, because this part of the gossip I don't pay much attention to. It just doesn't interest me. "Okay," I say, watching the scenery.

"Othella, look at me."

Suddenly, Zinzi sounds very serious, and I face her, doing as I am told.

"I need your help. Byron's father has some business partners, Americans, and one of them is promising to help us change his father's mind about the movement and the tax on Accompong's rum. This man is from Chicago and wants to meet me. He doesn't quite trust Byron, and this meeting will prove he's trustworthy. I'm pretty good at judging people, but my approach is to ask them a thousand questions, and this man is not the type to ask too many questions. Everyone says that the way your mind works, always picking up on the small details, you'll be able to tell Byron and me what kind of man this fellow from Chicago, your hometown, is. We know better than to trust him, but I think you can help us."

My chest tightens when I hear *business partner*, let alone *hometown*.

"A man from Chicago?" I say hoarsely. "Major Thomas? Vivian Jean's father?"

Zinzi shakes her head. "No. Vivian Jean's father has nothing to do with this. Byron put the man's name in the telegram he sent me the other day."

We hit a bump in the road, and Zinzi places a hand on the

seat in front of us. Then she swallows and says, "His name is Tony Schaefer."

I stare at the door handle. The car is moving, but not too fast. I could jump out, land on my feet—or close to it—and then run, disappearing into the crowded sidewalks of Kingston Harbour, never to be seen again.

Damn. "Schaefer? I know him."

"You do?"

"Did you mention my name to him?"

"I told Byron to tell him I might bring a friend, but I wouldn't think he'd tell him who, because I wasn't sure you'd come. But you know him?"

"He's a mobster, Zinzi. A no-good, thieving, killing, gambling, Chicago mobster," I practically yell, suddenly feeling that I might be losing my mind. "You have heard of them, haven't you? And Byron's father is doing business with the mob!"

"I've heard of Al Capone, the Chicago syndicate, Johnny Torrio, the Chicago outfit. Mobsters take vacations, too." She inhales deeply, calming herself. "Fact is, I'm not telling you the whole story. Byron knows this guy is no good. He also knows his own father isn't a good man, either. They used to be in the rum-running business together during Prohibition. Now, they're a legal business and making enough money to bring down the labor union before it can catch hold and, as a side project, they'll destroy what's left of Accompong." Her voice quivers, but she isn't about to cry; she's just mad as hell.

"This situation would be a funny coincidence, except it's not funny."

"My mother would say the ancestors planned it."

"I can't meet this man, Zinzi. He'll kill me dead on the spot."

"Oh my God. You know him *that* well."

"I used to work for him."

She tilts her head. "I had a feeling about you the first time I met you."

"What was that?"

"You weren't a college girl, not because you aren't smart; you're too smart." She chuckles weakly, then covers her face with her hands.

I hope she doesn't start crying, but she's not a crier. That's something I knew about her from the beginning—she's strong-minded, like me.

"You'll have to stay in the car. I'll have the driver take you back to the train station. You get home. Private detectives are working for the Tynesdale Estate, and I wouldn't want you to be added to their list." She sighs. "I need to think of something. Byron is gonna get himself killed."

"He has to know Schaefer's a cheat and a liar. And greedy, too." I almost slip and mention he hired me to steal Major Thomas's pocket watch when I notice the limo has stopped.

"Is this where you're supposed to meet him?"

"Yes." Zinzi is staring into space and looking trapped.

I think about Jerry Merriweather falling into the sea. "You know, I have a feeling Tony knows I'm here. So, I might as well help you out. See what I can learn from him. Tony won't harm me in a public place. Besides, your boyfriend gave me a carton of cigarettes." I mention that last bit to help her feel better about getting me into this pickle. But I truly believe if Tony Schaefer is on the same island as me, he'd find a way to find me sooner or later. Might as well be now. When I'm expecting it.

The Myrtle Bank Hotel is the finest hotel I've ever set foot in. It has that breezy island feel I heard some of the ship's passengers talk about. Every door to every room is open, the wide windows are never shuttered, and everything feels airy and spacious. This must be how Jamaicans design their hotels, with plenty of palm trees, potted plants, gardenias, verandas, porches, balconies, and lots of bamboo and lampshades.

Zinzi guides me through the hotel lobby to the veranda. We draw quite a few stares, not just because of our skin color. We aren't dressed in fashionable clothes—we're in our Accompong outfits: riding pants, loose-fitting blouses, and thick-soled boots. Neither of us has on a flowing dress or an oversized straw hat like the other women.

We sit at a small round table, and Zinzi immediately waves off the waiter. Around us, elegant women sip tea or rum punch from frosted glasses. The men smoke thick cigars while the women hold fire-tipped cigarette holders, watching the smoke swirl into the air.'

Zinzi suddenly stands. "I'll be right back."

"Where you going?" I ask, not wanting to be left alone with so many people staring, but she doesn't return to her seat. There's a worried look in her eyes. "Don't take too long."

"I won't, but Byron needs to be here now. I don't understand why he's not," Zinzi says, worry showing on her face. "I'm gonna have the front desk ring his room."

I watch her leave, sitting on the edge of my seat, tempted to follow her. She isn't out of sight for more than a few seconds when he appears.

Tony Schaefer, as always, is immaculately dressed in baggy tan trousers and an open-collared white shirt—except he isn't wearing a hat. His blond hair, now mostly red, is much longer than the last time I saw him, and his pale skin is almost brown. Looks like he's been on the island for quite some time.

"I had to see you with my own eyes. Othella Montgomery."

My lungs are empty.

"Alive and well, I see," he says, grinning.

"How else could I be?"

"And still with that slippery tongue." He chuckles. "Where's my pocket watch?"

"Didn't Jerry give it to you?"

"I ain't seen that boy in almost two months. Far as I know, he might be dead."

His remark is enough to freeze the blood in my veins. He knows Jerry's dead. How he knows, I have no clue. "Maybe he is. Maybe he's not. I haven't seen him since Chicago."

He sits in the chair beside me. "Girl, you're lyin.'"

"The only way you'd know I'm lyin' is if you've seen Jerry and he told you otherwise."

"Could be. Could be." He laughs. "Let's not discuss either of the Merriweather boys. They've served their purpose."

Tony leans his elbows on the table, his gaze fixed on my face. "You should be shaking in your boots. Why aren't you scared? Or maybe that's your problem—you're not smart enough to be afraid." He bites his lower lip, eyes still locked on me. "I love how you always look as pretty as a picture and just as clueless at the same time." Scooting his chair, he closes the distance between us and adds, "You're just a scared little girl pretending to be tough." He retrieves a pack of cigarettes from his breast pocket. "A man fell overboard on the ship you took to Jamaica."

Oh Christ. "Yeah, I heard there was a stowaway on the *Talamanca*. But I didn't know him."

"You sure? I was thinking it was Jerry who was the stow-away who drowned."

My mouth dries. I force a confident smile despite the dread gnawing at my bones.

"Don't look so glum, sugar," Tony says, still grinning and showing off his sparkling white teeth that seem like fake pearls and diamonds. "I ordered you a gin and tonic. I bet you haven't had one in a while."

I gaze at my hands, delicate and slender fingers capable of creating beautiful drawings, digging holes in the earth, and examining insects and plant parts without causing harm—the skilled hands of the queen of the fingersmiths.

"No, thank you, Tony," I respond. "I don't need a gin and tonic, but I could use a smoke."

CHAPTER 37

————— ✦ —————

ZINZI

Accompong, Maroon Village, Cockpit Country, Week Seven

Byron is late. I stand in the lobby of the Myrtle Bank Hotel, nursing a headache that has worsened since Othella and I left Accompong. My mother professes that the pressure from the waves and wind causes my pain. These headaches are a harbinger, a warning sign that a hurricane is approaching, and my body senses it. Changes in the wind, sunlight, clouds, and the violence of the sea course through my veins, rest on my skin, and sink into my bones. My mother describes my abilities dramatically, but they aren't real. It's a theory she has conjured. I wish she would stop telling these lies to the villagers. But Momma Hazel doesn't care about me being stared at while the village waits for doom to fall from the sky.

When Byron arrives, I don't ask questions like what took you so long. Instead, I hurriedly lead him to the veranda where Othella has company. It can only be Tony Schaefer sitting across from her at the table. He holds a cigarette at the corner of his mouth, blowing smoke rings into his unblinking eyes. I immediately think of a snake slithering through the grass.

Byron speaks first. "You've met Othella, I see."

"That's right. She's a real doll."

I don't wait to be introduced. I extend my hand. "My name is Zinzi Green."

"Tony Schaefer, sweetheart. Did you say your name was Zinzi or ZZ?"

He quickly makes me regret shaking his hand.

"You had it right the first time. It's Zinzi." I don't bother to wait for him to invite me to sit. I've already decided I don't like him, and so much so, I don't feel up to faking politeness.

"Oh, okay," he replies. "I was just talking to my old friend from Chicago. We go way back."

"I'm not sure how far back that might be," I say, "she's nineteen."

I glance at Othella. She nods almost imperceptibly, and I know she is okay for the moment.

"The only reason Othella is here is that she trusted me. So, Byron," I turn to him, "are you sure this man is someone you can trust?"

"Nobody talks to me like that," Schaefer interrupts gruffly.

"You'd better calm down, sir." Byron's tone is firm, and the man from Chicago flinches slightly. After a tense but brief silence, he adds, "So, what else do we need to discuss now that everyone has met?"

"We're still on track," Schaefer responds. "Our deal is working. A large shipment of Tynesdale goods will be lost at sea, and your father will lose his shirt. I'll step in, save his business and reputation. Oust him, and you'll take over." He lights another cigarette. "That'll open up the international trade for me, which doesn't interest you. Our dealings will end. You'll be the local good guy who brings the union to Tynesdale Estates. And I'll have my hooks in so many different pies, I'll end up happy as a lamb."

There isn't much more to say, and soon Othella and I are boarding the train back to the Cockpit. None of us was interested in spending any social time with Schaefer. Besides, he and Byron had some final touches to make on sabotaging his father's shipment.

"Did he threaten you?" I ask Othella, afraid of her answer.

"Yeah. But he's going to double-cross Byron."

"He said that."

"He didn't have to. I know the man that he is and will always be."

'Othella, I'm so sorry to get you involved. I didn't know."

"He knew I was here. It was just a matter of time before he found me, and I never would've wanted him to show up in Accompong."

PART FOUR

———————

THE COCKPIT:
OCTOBER 1935

CHAPTER 38

ZINZI

Accompong, Maroon Village, Cockpit Country, Week Eight

My stomach feels uneasy and my head throbs. I need rest, but when I enter my mother's home after the trip to Kingston, she is wide awake and eager to talk. "You are a woman of strength and conviction, ready to stand up for what you believe in," my mother says, out of the blue. "What is happening in Kingston? Are you in trouble?"

"Momma, why are you up? You should be resting."

"Don't worry about me. The ancestors will watch over me."

"Are you suggesting that they aren't watching over me?"

"Mi don't play around with words like you children from Kingston. But you're the one who said it, not me."

I collapse onto the mat next to her. "I'm very tired, Momma. We traveled from Kingston and back in one day. It was a long journey."

She lifts her head to meet my gaze. "The spirit of the ancestors tells me you are worried about Byron."

"I'm worried about Accompong, too, Momma." I lift my arms over my head to stretch the tension from my back. "His father and men like him are trying to use our community to strike out against the labor union movement."

"Colonel Rowe knows that. The Koromantee war dances have begun. We've protected our freedom for centuries, and if you had more faith, you would worry less."

"Sorry, Momma, but this is a dangerous situation. Sometimes, the ancestors aren't the answer."

"Blasphemy, as those churchgoers like to say. But that's what it is. You speaking against the ancestors is more dangerous than your man friend's father will ever be."

"I'm too tired to argue. You may well be right."

"Mi proud of you."

"Thank you?" I am confused as my mother so quickly changes the subject. "You go from scolding me to praising me. I'm confused. What brought that on?"

"You are doing something mi haven't seen you do in a long, long time."

"Which is?"

"Showing that you can care deeply about more than one thing," she says. "You loved your father, but when he died, you began to fade away. You fell in love with Marvin, and mi thought you weren't lost. But the ancestors came for him early, too, and when he died, you ran away to Kingston."

"Do you still think I'm running?"

"No," she replies. "You've been skipping, but you're ready to slow down and stay still for a bit."

"I do miss the Cockpit, but I can't stay here, Momma. Kingston is where I belong now."

"That's not what mi meant, Zinzi."

"I know what you meant," I say. "Every dream I cherished was taken from me. It's not that I don't believe in dreaming. I just feel cursed. If I stay here, I will have nothing to look forward to except watching more people I love pass away."

"But you came back when mi asked."

"Honestly, Momma, I didn't want to."

My mother waves her hand. "You still came home, and from now on, you'll come more often. Or at least I hope you will. Our family needs to have its older sister around more."

"Why did you want me to be the guide for this group? And don't tell me about the ancestors."

My mother yawns. "Mi did know Maxi. Fairly well, and mi owed her a favor from when we were girls. She didn't tell on me when I snuck into the jungle with your father." My mother raises her eyebrows teasingly. "That clearing you went to was one of our favorite places."

I gasp in surprise but then chuckle at the youthful smile on my mother's face as I help her to her feet. "That's enough chatter for one evening it's time for you to go to bed."

My mother leans on me heavily. "You're right, Zinzi. Mi needs some rest."

I kiss her on top of the head. "It's the only way you'll get better, Momma."

"Uh-huh. The only way."

CHAPTER 39

＊·◆·＊

OTHELLA

Accompong, Maroon Village, Cockpit Country, Week Eight

An unbearable heat wave climbs into the Cockpit as if it has arms and legs crawling on all fours. It travels down my back and over my head, leaving me drenched in sweat and irritable. It's late October in Chicago, and just knowing it might be cold enough for some snow on the ground back home makes me long for the city where I was born and raised. Even Robbie agrees that we wouldn't be so hot if we were in Chicago. But that's just a hint of the trouble I'm in.

The clouds hang thick and black in the sky, while a flock of birds rises from the treetops to the east, sweeping the sky to safer ground. Robbie and I walk through a field nestled between two mountains. As far as the eye can see, rows of sugarcane stretch across the landscape. He learned from one of the village elders that the plants are over fifteen years old and continue to sprout each year.

"It is one of the richest valleys in the Cockpit," he says. "The daily rains and warm sun create the ideal conditions for cultivating sugar, ginger, coffee, and bananas. These are staples of Maroon commerce, alongside breadfruit, plantains, coconuts, yams, corn, ackee, pimento, cho-cho, cucumbers, and cashews." He pauses to catch his breath. "There is so much here. I could stay forever."

He carries the two baskets of fruits and vegetables we've gathered in the valley. "You've been different since you returned from Kingston," he says.

Not only has he noticed, he is also gently asking questions about how I feel and if there's anything he can do to help.

I hesitate to respond. Our pinky swear weighs heavily on my mind. If I say anything, it would be a lie, and I don't want to face the consequences of lying. Not the absurd penalty of having to swallow a thousand needles; there aren't that many needles in all of Accompong. What troubles me is losing Robbie's trust.

"Are you going to answer me?" he asks, still walking with his baskets in hand.

I don't respond. Maybe if I stay quiet long enough, he will grow tired of waiting and leave me be. But when have I ever been that lucky?

"This has something to do with Kingston. What happened when you went there with Zinzi? Tell me—I won't judge you, Othella, no matter what it is. I want you to know that you can always talk to me."

I pick up flower buds and leaves, no longer pretending to know what I'm doing. I've learned quite a bit about botany and collecting samples. I stop digging in the dirt and glance at Robbie.

"Can we just talk about plants, limestone, or sinkholes?" I hope to distract him, but it feels wrong. "I'm sorry. I will tell you everything, but just not today. Is that okay?"

He frowns, but a smile emerges—then a lightning bolt streaks across the sky, thunder roaring behind right after.

"Robbie," I call out, scared nearly out of my skin.

He carefully places his basket on the ground. "Don't worry. We'll head back now." He holds my hands. "You're okay. Don't look so frightened."

I can't help it. I believe the lightning and thunder have scared me into telling the truth, or it's a sign from one of Momma Hazel's ancestors, telling me to stop hiding the truth from people I care about. "Chicago has followed me to Jamaica." I squeeze his hand.

"Who's here from Chicago?" he asks.

"Before Jerry fell overboard, he told me something I probably should have shared with you a long time ago, but I didn't. So, I didn't lie—I just never mentioned it. So, I haven't betrayed our pinky swear pledge—I just didn't know how to say it."

He clears a spot on the ground for us to sit. He doesn't appear concerned about the darkening sky, the lightning, or the crackling thunder. His attention is solely on me.

"Go on. Tell me what's wrong."

"It's Tony Schaefer. He's in Kingston. He's trying to hurt Zinzi, and Byron, and Accompong. He's telling them he's helping them fight against Byron's father while saving the labor union movement and Accompong. But Robbie, he's lying. He just wants to make as much money as he can and after that, he'll come after me. You see, I did something—I don't even know what—that made him so mad, all he can think about is getting even."

"Keep going," Robbie says encouragingly. "Tell me everything."

"He's not going to leave us alone. I just know it. He's gonna keep causing trouble. He can't help himself."

CHAPTER 40

———•◆•———

VIVIAN JEAN

Tynesdale Estate, St. Elizabeth Parish, Week Nine

When we received Bernard Tynesdale's invitation to join him for supper, Momma Hazel made a symbol with her thumb and forefinger and spat on the ground. I looked at Zinzi but received no sign that she understood why her mother had reacted in such a way. Or, if she did know, Zinzi kept it to herself.

Two days later, we pull up to the Tynesdale house in the cars he sent for the Dunham expedition.

It's an impressive home—a two-story stone building covered in white stucco, with an expansive wraparound veranda, large, shuttered windows, and stone columns. The sheer size makes me a bit envious.

"Are you okay, Vivian Jean?" Tully asks as we pass through the archway into a lobby as spacious as the one in Mr. Abbott's mansion.

He's been very attentive since the letter from Maxi. "I'm fine," I reply. "It's a plantation, isn't it? Probably hasn't changed much since slavery. I've never seen one in the flesh."

Just then, a dark-skinned man in a white jacket and well-pressed black pants approaches us.

"Welcome," he says. "Please follow me this way." He leads us down a grand hallway adorned with a series of paintings on the walls. The women in the portraits wear long, old-fashioned gowns embellished with lace and jewelry, while the old men sport high-collared suits and neckbeards.

We pause, and as I wait outside the dining hall, I hold my breath and finally understand what Momma Hazel meant when she spat after learning about the invitation. She may not know my father, but she sensed trouble.

Major Leonard Thomas stands with three others to welcome the Katherine Dunham expedition—the claimed reason for our invitation to Tynesdale Estates.

"Is that your father?" Katherine asks, her voice tinged with disbelief.

Tully exhales. "Yes, that's him."

Seeing my father for the first time since Maggotty and Maxi's letter makes my stomach turn. "Tully, can we go?"

My husband moves close to me, his body protecting me in case my father does something unexpected. Or I do. "We can't leave." He touches my waist. "Byron's father invited us to honor Katherine's fieldwork in Accompong and we can't abandon her."

"I don't believe the expedition is why we're here," I whisper, just before the major embraces me.

"I told Bernard to keep my presence a secret. I aimed to surprise you."

"And you've done just that," I respond.

"Katherine, it's wonderful to see you as well." He tries to hug her, but she greets him with a stiffly extended arm forcing him into a handshake. I regret not doing the same.

The other three men are introduced, but I barely catch their names as my anger consumes me.

As we enter the dining room, I discover there is a seating

arrangement. I am to sit with my father on my left and one of the two white men on my right.

"Are you sure we can't leave?" I ask no one in particular.

"No, you can't," Katherine says haughtily. "I want to see what these men are up to."

"Did you catch the name of the other man?" I ask.

"Tony Schaefer."

He is already seated and quickly begins downing a tumbler of rum. I assume it's rum; after all, we're on a sugarcane plantation with a rum distillery.

I sit and take a moment of silence to quell my anger. I notice the men—even my father—are stylishly attired in linen Panama suits with wide shoulders, long lapels, and high-waisted, pleated trousers tapered at the ankles. They look like members of a band or a street gang.

The rest of the party finds their spots at the dining table. Byron, Zinzi, Katherine, and Tully are seated across from Othella, my father, Tony, Robbie, and me. Mr. Tynesdale is at the head of the table, with his son to his right.

"So, Mrs. Hartfield, how are you finding Accompong?"

I glance at Tony Schaefer. His strong South Side Chicago accent makes him sound out of place. "How do you know Mr. Tynesdale?" Normally, I wouldn't speak so bluntly to a white man, but something about Schaefer suggests my tone won't matter.

"We're business associates. I'm a partner in his rum enterprise."

"Then how do you know my father?"

His lip curls in an unappealing manner. "He's one of our partners, too."

I glance frantically at Tully across the table. He's looking at me, but I can't tell if he caught what this man just said.

"Father, is this the business venture you have in Jamaica? Rum and sugarcane?"

"It's not illegal, Vivi."

The waiters pause our conversation as soup bowls are placed before the guests. There are more servers in the room than guests. After the soup is ladled into our bowls, I don't bother to lift my spoon before I interrupt Tony's slurping to ask him, "How long have you known my father?"

Tony looks past me and smiles at my father. "Shall I tell her, Lenny?"

"Go ahead, Tony. My daughter deserves the truth." My father's voice sounds resigned, almost defeated.

Tony wipes his mouth with his napkin. "We both worked for Mr. Tynesdale during Prohibition, smuggling rum into Chicago."

I look across the table at Tully, who hasn't touched his soup either. I don't have to wonder if he heard Tony this time. I can see it on his face.

"Are you suggesting my father was a bootlegger?" I raise my voice so the entire table can hear.

"A former bootlegger," Tony replies. "Prohibition is behind us. Now we're legitimate businessmen. Isn't that right, Mr. Tynesdale?"

"What are you talking about, Tony?" Bernard Tynesdale responds. "This gathering is meant to honor Miss Dunham and her work in Accompong." He turns to Katherine. "You've been here for nearly two months, correct?"

Katherine begins talking about the people we've interviewed, the history we've recorded, and the dancing we've watched, learned, and notated.

The soup bowls are cleared away, and the next course—a salad—is set before me. Once again, I don't pick up a utensil. I keep my voice low to ask Tony a question: "You sound proud of your partnership with my father."

Schaefer laughs. "Your father is a clever man for a Negro. No offense."

"No offense taken."

"He's not perfect. He cheated me out of some money. So I have a bone to pick with him. What better place to pick it than in front of his precious little girl?"

I dismiss the *precious little girl* remark. "Seems childish, because it sounds like you're still in business with him."

"I came to Jamaica to assist Mr. Tynesdale with a problem he's having with his plantation workers—and my personal feelings about your father don't necessarily interfere with making money."

"Shut up, Tony," Bernard Tynesdale says sharply from the head of the table. "We can discuss this subject later," he says forcefully, glaring at Tony Schaefer.

Upon Bernard's withering gaze, Tony raises a hand in apology. "I'm zipping my lips shut right now."

The reaction is as I expected. Mr. Tynesdale is not only the host but also the boss of my father and Tony. I imagine him to be the boss of his son, too. Then again, Zinzi doesn't strike me as a woman who would fall for any man who might be under another man's thumb.

"You lied to me," Byron says suddenly.

I can't tell whether he's addressing Schaefer or his father. Then he makes it clear: "Father, I thought this dinner was meant to honor Katherine and her friends, but that's not the reality, is it?"

"Byron, maybe you shouldn't . . ." Zinzi says, but he stops her with a gently raised hand.

"No, his pact with the other six plantations was bad enough, but bringing in a bully from Chicago to do what? Make you enough money to hire scabs?" He glares at Tony. "Schaefer? Is that how you'll help my father with his plantation problem?"

"Byron, you are going too far. I warned you and that girl. You'd be very sorry if you go against the family in these matters." Mr. Tynesdale's face is an ugly shade of red.

I look down at my plate. What is it about children and their fathers? Are they ever the men you want them to be?

"Well, guess what, Father?" Byron says. "Tony Schaefer isn't trustworthy. I've been giving him the schedules of your major rum shipments. He intends to sabotage one or more of your boats. He also has partnerships with plantation owners in Cuba, which I imagine neither you nor Major Thomas knows.

"He is going to bury the Tynesdale Estate. Your thirst for power and your misguided ideologies will destroy a centuries-old family business."

Bernard Tynesdale's face was like a mask. "Is my son telling me the truth, Tony?"

"I assure you, Bernard, I was not aware of any of this," my father interjects.

"I'm not talking to you, Leonard, but there is no need for me to hear Tony's response." He signals to his waiters. "Let's finish the meal. My cook has been working on it all day."

The man sitting next to me curses under his breath. Byron's speech didn't sit well with him, but judging by Zinzi and Othella's ear-to-ear grins, they are as happy as clams. On the other hand, my father has turned a shade of grayish-brown.

Dinner ends shortly after Byron's outburst. I am surprised Tony Schaefer didn't walk out with his head hanging before dessert. But he stayed, sipping on his rum, his narrow gaze full of hate and rage shifting from Byron to Zinzi, but mostly resting on Othella, for some strange reason.

When it's time to leave, Katherine catches up to me as we head for our cars. "I told you there was something more going on here tonight."

"Yes, you were right."

"Are you okay? I mean about your father? It's a lot to take in."

I slip my arm through hers. "Oddly enough, I feel better than I've felt in a long while."

Upon returning to Accompong, the group goes to their separate lodgings. Byron remains at his father's place, but Zinzi stays with us. Robbie and Othella, walking hand in hand makes me smile. Katherine also says good night to us.

Now, the only thing on my mind is the sacred silk cotton tree.

CHAPTER 41

VIVIAN JEAN

Accompong, Maroon Village, St. Elizabeth Parish

The village prepares for a severe storm. Hut doors and windows are boarded up. Machetes trim the branches off nearby trees. The winds have picked up dramatically. And though we aren't close to the ocean, others in Accompong swear they can smell the sea and its angry, turbulent nature. Lightning rips across the sky. I count to three; sure enough, thunder rumbles, shaking the trees and my heart. A hurricane is coming, but the rain hasn't started yet. There is still time.

Before heading to our hut, I tell Tully I want to visit the silk cotton tree. He points to the sky. "Bad weather is coming," he says.

"I have something to tell the tree and it can't wait, but I need to be alone to say it."

"I'm going with you."

"Please, I need to do this on my own."

He nods reluctantly and walks away, looking over his shoulder as the rain begins, the heavy drops falling like small pellets.

When I reach the tree in the middle of Accompong, I sit on the damp ground beneath the branches, my legs folded beneath me. I lift my hair off the back of my neck and twist it into a bun. I don't need to talk to Clifford. His death was an accident. His note was frustrating, but it wasn't about Tully and me. The true monster was my father's infidelity. And dear Clifford, he knew about that and maybe even my father's criminal activities.

A knot twists in my chest as pain and grief battle for supremacy. I miss Clifford. I mourn for him and the baby I lost to a miscarriage. I tell the tree how much I love Maxi Green. Despite my father's sins and Maxi's role, she is just as much a victim as my mother and me.

My father is the last thought I have while sitting under the tree. I see him in my mind's eye, as clear as day and as dark as night. When I return to Chicago, there will be a headline in the *Chicago Defender* that reads BRONZEVILLE FEDERAL SAVINGS AND LOAN'S PRESIDENT CONVICTED OF RACKETEERING.

The subheading will state MAJOR LEONARD THOMAS TO SERVE 30 YEARS.

My father will be punished for his crime, and I will mend the broken pieces of my relationship with my mother. I won't abandon Maxi Green. I will forgive myself as well. Even Tully will be loved for who he is, not for what he saved me from. But that day isn't today, tomorrow, or even the day after. It will happen just as everything happens—in time.

"Vivian Jean, you should come out from under the tree." Zinzi walks toward me, a little more than a silhouette against the darkness of the moonlit night. "The tree is a dangerous place with all that lightning in the sky."

"I hadn't thought about that." I wipe a hand across my mouth. "That was quite a speech your friend Byron gave at dinner," I say.

"He said what needed to be said," Zinzi replies.

I stand, shaking leaves and dirt from my riding pants. "I feel the same about my father."

"You didn't know he was Tynesdale's partner?"

I shake my head, walking toward Zinzi, but she sways and looks ready to crumple. I grab her shoulders just in time. "You almost fainted. You need to get home."

Zinzi smiles weakly. "I think I'm pregnant."

"Oh my God." I hold her tight. "That's wonderful. Or is it?"

"It's fine. If I am with child, the father is the man you met tonight."

"Byron Tynesdale?"

"Yes." We start walking toward our homes. "But he doesn't know. Not yet. I want to wait until I'm certain."

"You must be pretty close to being sure." I smile. "You told me."

Zinzi grins weakly. "Sometimes life is like drawing straws. You get the long stick and other times, you get the short one. I feel like I've won the game and the long stick is mine whenever I want it."

"You're in love," I say.

"Anything is possible."

We reach Zinzi's home first.

"I'll see you tomorrow," I say.

After leaving the silk cotton tree and Zinzi, I head home and slip into bed next to Tully, wrapping my arms around his waist.

"Are you asleep?" I ask.

"Only if you need me to be," Tully replies, tightening my arms around him. "Did you say what you needed to say and hear what you needed to know?"

"Yes. And don't you dare laugh." I feel his body tremble as I anticipate his response.

"No, seriously, my dear, I wasn't laughing." He rolls over

carefully, adjusting our positions so we face each other. "I'm embarrassed but something bit me." He smiles shyly. "And it hurts like hell."

I caress his lips with my fingers. "Where? Let me take a look."

"I shouldn't have mentioned it. It'll be all right." He kisses me gently. "We should get some rest."

CHAPTER 42

OTHELLA

Accompong, Maroon Village, Cockpit Country

That night, Robbie and I lay on my cot, fully dressed. I often feel butterflies in my stomach when I'm alone with him. I no longer find his long-winded chatter annoying. Now, his voice is a soothing sound that comforts me.

"You and I should stay here in Jamaica forever," he says. "Together."

"Should we stay in Accompong, or find another town on the island?" I finally feel safe enough to ask such questions. The outcome of the dinner at the Tynesdale Estate proved I can trust my new friends. They'll look out for me, but Robbie will do the most to protect me.

"I like it here," he says, rubbing my shoulder. "But there's no reason we can't travel and find the place that suits us best."

I sit up straight on the bed. Hard rain pounds down from the sky. It doesn't scare me—the wind, the thunder, and the lightning bolts—as it has before. "Okay, then, let's make a promise." I extend my hand, form a fist, and lift my pinky finger.

He chuckles. "You seem giddy."

"No one has ever said that to me before. Is it a nice thing to say?"

"It's a wonderful thing to say. It means you show your happiness with every part of your body, and it's contagious. Anyone near you will feel happy, too. Your joy cannot be slowed or stopped."

I wiggle my little finger. "Guess what I want to swear to tonight?"

"I have no idea, but I'm all ears."

"It's amusing to think about, with your handsome face overshadowed by your big ears."

He tugs at my earlobe. "Yours aren't exactly small, my dear."

"You know, I'm going to draw a picture of you with just ears. I'll erase my drawings of your precious bugs, plants, and roots, and keep only the ones of you."

"And my ears."

I suddenly feel very serious and don't want to talk about ears anymore. "You know, I keep a notebook with my sketches that I'm proud of, even though not all are meant for anthropological study. My sketches aren't perfect, but they are much better than your illegible scrawl—and each day, I get better. All this is to say, I like to draw sketches of you, Robbie, and the other members of the expedition."

"Othella, you've hidden this journal from me. Why?"

"Because I want to capture you perfectly in my drawings."

His expression shifts, and I see the words he's struggling to express reflected in his eyes. "I promise to love you forever," he says as he kisses me.

My heart pounds, and if I could describe how I feel, I would choose the word *giddy*.

I am about to tell him how much I love him when suddenly, hell storms through the door and brings a commotion so quick and brutal that I don't react right away. Not until it's too late, and then there's nothing I can do. Within seconds, Robbie lies on the floor, knocked out cold. I can only pray that he's not dead.

"You won't escape from me this time, sweetheart." Tony Schaefer has come for me. "I don't get bested by any man or woman, colored or white." Tony has a handful of my hair, and it feels like he's pulling it out by the roots. I struggle to break free, but Tony is strong. I should've known what would happen next, but I never see it coming—the fist aimed at my face. Just like when Perry hit me that time in Chicago. And now, it's Tony's turn. But then I stop thinking as the world goes black.

CHAPTER 43

———◆◆◆———

ZINZI

Accompong, Maroon Village, Cockpit Country

The pounding in my head, the pain that makes my eyes water and my jaw tense, won't quit. I don't believe my mother's claim about hurricanes and my sensitivity to them and other changes in the weather, but something is coming. Or it's the baby, a miracle for a woman my age, unmarried and just beginning to come to terms with falling in love with the man I've slept with twice.

It felt good to confide in Vivian Jean about my possible condition. As I approach my mother's home, I decide to wait before sharing the news with Momma Hazel. That will stir up a different kind of storm.

I stop as a sudden guttural scream rips through the air—someone crying out in pain. It isn't coming from my mother's house. I quickly turn and head back to where I was moments ago. The scream is coming from Vivian Jean's hut.

I rush into the house. Tully lies on the bed, his bare legs bent and his left knee pulled toward his chest.

"I was bitten on the calf by a spider and it hurts like hell."

"What kind?" I pose a question that neither of them can answer. They can't tell one spider from the next.

Tully opens his hand. "I killed the damn thing." The insect is as large as his palm, and Tully is a tall man, with long limbs and fingers.

"Give me the bug." I take the creature from him, and it's not entirely smashed. "I'll take this to my mother. She'll know what it is and how to treat the bite."

Tully is already sweating profusely.

"It really hurts," Tully repeats, with a short laugh. He notices the fear on Vivian Jean's face. "I hate spiders, but I couldn't help yelling. It didn't hurt that much when it actually bit me, but then . . . sorry for making such a fuss."

I glance from Tully to his wife. "I'll be right back. My mother will sort this out."

As I make my way to her hut, I decide that if she can't, I'll just wake up everyone—Colonel Rowe, Iris, Katherine, Robbie, and Othella.

"Who is hurt?" my mother asks as I enter the house.

"You're up. Good."

"How could I not be with all the ruckus?"

"Vivian Jean's husband was bitten by this." I open my hand. The expression on my mother's face confirms my concern. "It's a banana spider, isn't it, Momma?"

"No, not exactly. Some call it that because it travels from Brazil to Jamaica on banana boats." She walks with a heavy gait toward her basket of herbs in the corner of the thatched-roof house. "It's a wandering spider, and it's deadly."

I place the bug into my mother's outstretched hand, and my mother sets it aside. "We need something to relieve the pain and draw the poison from his body." She slowly moves from one spot to another, opening one basket after another. "Where was he bitten?"

"In the calf," I reply.

"Good. That's quite a distance from his heart." Momma

Hazel clears away a collection of herbs and jars I recognize, either by sight or by their strong aroma. There's ginger, soursop leaves, allspice, leaf of life, and guinea hen weed. She hands me the leaf of life. "You need to go now and apply this to the wound. It will help prevent swelling while I prepare the poultice."

I blink, anxiety rolling off my brow like perspiration. My mother hasn't said it, but I can feel her apprehension. Tully's life is in jeopardy.

"Go on, child. Stop staring and hurry up. Mi be right behind you," she says, glancing at the spider she holds. "Mi have that boy with the plant, Robbie, take a look at it as well. He might know something about poisons."

As I run to Vivian Jean's hut, I realize I need to go to the colonel's yard next to wake up Robbie, Othella, and Katherine. It won't be easy—not that I'm not in good physical shape or worried about the possible baby in my belly. It's the rain. It is falling hard and heavy. The wind is blowing, and the weather will worsen before it improves if the crater-sized pain in my head is really the sign my mother claims it is.

"My mother's coming. Hold this over the wound," I say to Vivian Jean. "I'm going to wake up Robbie. He may be able to help."

"Zinzi," Vivian Jean says, her voice shaking. "What kind of spider was it? Is it poisonous?"

I glance at Tully, his eyes closed and his face a mask of pain. Then I catch Vivian Jean's gaze and nod.

"Yes," I whisper. "It could kill him."

I keep my head down as the storm brings heavy rain and strong winds that could tear the clothes from my back. But I need Robbie. My mother's poultice is potent, but it isn't a cure. If there's something Robbie can tell them or help them with, I believe he'll do it. That's the boy's nature.

As I reach his hut, a kerosene lamp burns and the door stands wide open. I move cautiously forward.

"Othella? Robbie," I call, taking each step slowly. My eyes are peeled and my body is tense. Something feels wrong.

"Is anyone home?" The hut isn't large. It consists of one open space with two connected rooms. I pause to listen. What do I hear? A moan? Was someone calling my name?

I turn sharply and run toward the room farthest from the entrance. As I step through the archway, I find Robbie on the floor, groaning and holding his arm. But he hasn't been bitten—he's been beaten.

"He took her."

"Who?" I ask. "What happened, Robbie? Who hurt you? Where's Othella?" I move to help him sit up, but he's covered in bruises and cuts, and his arm is oddly bent. "Who the hell did this to you?"

I walk further in, and see that Katherine is already here. "He took Othella. The white man from the dinner."

Robbie's voice is unsteady as he says, "He hit me in the head."

"He's badly hurt." Katherine looks at me with worried eyes.

"Slow down, Robbie. Let us help you." I place a hand on his shoulder and he squeals in pain.

"Damn it," he winces. "My arm. I think it's broken."

As Katherine and I help him to the cot, I realize who Robbie and Katherine are talking about. My stomach drops. "Tony Schaefer. He took Othella."

Gritting his teeth, Robbie nods.

"How did he find us? How did he get here?"

"He must've followed us," Katherine says.

"Can you walk? You have to come with me to Vivian Jean's place. My mom is taking care of Tully. He was bitten."

"By what?" Robbie's eyes appear to roll back in his head.

"Don't pass out. Not yet. I need to get you to Vivian Jean

and my mother. You might be able to help my mother with Tully, and she can help you, too."

"I need to go after them," Robbie says. "Schaefer will hurt Othella."

"You can barely stand," I tell Robbie. "Katherine, get him over to Vivian Jean's hut, and stay with him and the others."

"Where are you going?"

"Robbie's right. He'll hurt her," I reply. "I'm going after them."

"That's not a good idea," Katherine says.

"I have to go after them."

She huffs. "Then help me get Robbie to Vivian Jean's first."

CHAPTER 44

ZINZI

The Hartfield's Hut, Accompong

The rain is relentless, with ominous clouds pouring gallons of water from the sky. However, the harder it falls, the more determined I am to do everything possible to find Othella.

It's my fault she's in trouble. I'm responsible for bringing the girl to Schaefer—Byron and me. He feels the same as I do, which I realized during our quick exit from dinner at Tynesdale Estate. When Byron met Schaefer, he knew he wasn't a good man, but he didn't know all the details of the man's agreement with his father. We were both naïve and foolish to believe anything Schaefer said. *Business partner* can mean many things. Then there was Byron's father, who manipulated our emotions, starting with the unexpected and cryptic visit to Allan's office. Then there was his pact with the six other sugar plantation owners and, finally, the threat of violence against his own workers if we publicly supported the union. Byron and I had our hearts used against us. Now I have to help Othella.

I explain this when I arrive at Vivian Jean's hut with Tully and Katherine, but Vivian Jean has other ideas. "There's nothing I can do here to help Momma Hazel. You can send your brother Raymond with a message for Byron. He can bring a doctor for Tully and Robbie."

"You don't need a doctor, miss. I'll take care of your husband," Momma Hazel intervenes. "And mi look after the boy, too. You should accompany my daughter. She can't be alone in the jungle."

"I agree," Vivian Jean adds. "Not in this weather." Then she whispers, "Not in your condition."

I can't argue with her, especially since my mother seems to be on Vivian Jean's side. As we leave, I hear my mother chanting. She has started the healing ritual. Vivian Jean pauses, giving her husband a hopeful glance, but I urge her out of the hut. "We're wasting time."

I grab a machete and some hiking gear from a large pouch in the corner of the hut.

Without mules—since the storm makes them too skittish to trust—I only know one footpath to take—the one heading toward Maggotty.

"If we don't find them on that path, when we get to Maggotty, I'll call Byron or send a telegram if the phones are down.

Wrapped in long, oilcloth coats that Vivian Jean had taken from her hut to ward off the rain, we set out with me in the lead.

We stay close together and move quickly through the jungle, densely covered with fallen leaves, branches, and mud from the wind and rain.

"We're about thirty to forty minutes behind Othella and Schaefer." I hope Vivian Jean can hear me over the storm. "We need to stop Schaefer from whatever he's planning before he hurts her."

"What if that's all he's planning?" Vivian Jean yells.

"Let's keep moving," I say, slashing my machete through vines, branches, and more, because I have no answer for her.

I might be acting on a whim and a prayer, trying to convince myself that our effort to find Othella isn't in vain. If Schaefer hasn't hurt her yet, Vivian Jean and I are ready for a confrontation—I hope. I have my trusty machete, while Vivian Jean brought one of the small shovels Robbie uses to dig up plant roots.

"I heard something," Vivian Jean shouts and we stop.

"What was it?"

"A voice, I believe."

"Quiet. Listen." I stand completely still, struggling to hear anything other than the sound of rain and wind.

Then Vivian Jean spins and begins marching back in the direction we just came from. "I heard it again."

As we retrace our steps, a pool of water seems to bubble up from nowhere. I keep an eye on it, trying to remember something my father once said. At the same time, I cup my ear, listening to the night, straining to hear what Vivian Jean hears.

"Help me."

We turn sharply to face each other. We both heard it.

"Was that Othella?" Vivian Jean asks, barely breathing.

Holding Vivian Jean's hand, I squeeze the handle of the machete in my other hand. We inch forward, careful to steady our footing, but suddenly, we're not on solid ground.

Vivian Jean screams as our hands tear apart. I feel the ground drop away beneath me. The machete slips from my other hand. I reach out, grabbing onto anything to halt my fall.

What is happening? My oilcloth coat catches on something, and I am no longer falling. Instead, I am hanging onto a branch or a rock, kicking as I search for a ledge or something solid to stand on.

One foot touches a rock or ledge, while my arms hold onto another rock or a thick palm tree root.

Blinking repeatedly, I try to clear the mud and dirt from my eyes. I hear a voice.

"Where are we? What is this?"

"Are you holding on to something, Vivian Jean?" I shout, recognizing her voice as I cling to whatever root or branch has stopped my fall. "We are in a sinkhole. I don't know how deep it is and can't see how far we've fallen. I think Othella is here, too. Can you hear us?" I call out. "Can you see us, Othella?"

A tense moment passes as I wait for a reply.

"I hear you, Zinzi. Is that you and Vivian Jean? What in the world are you doing here?"

"Coming to save you," Vivian Jean shouts.

"If that's what you came to do, then your plan isn't gonna work. Not when you're as stuck in the mud as I am."

"We'll get out," I say, with as much confidence as I can muster. "I just need to think for a second." I finally remember the story my father once told me, about how he and one of my brothers had been trapped in a sinkhole in the ground that had appeared suddenly. But it wasn't at night or during a storm, and it wasn't as deep as this one.

"How do we get out?" Othella shouts.

"Are you above us? I think you're above us."

"Yes, I climbed up. I almost reached the top."

"I thought you sounded like you were near the opening. If you can get out," I say, yelling, "go get help, okay?"

"Where's Tony Schaefer?" Vivian Jean calls out.

"Where is he?" Othella's voice is clear and loud. "He kept falling, but I never heard him hit the bottom or cry out."

"Then he's gone, and we need to get out of here," Vivian Jean says.

"Can you tell me how far you are from the top, Othella?" I ask, straining to hang on to the wall of mud and roots.

"I'm not sure, but I'll let you know. Just give me a moment."

CHAPTER 45

———◆◆◆———

OTHELLA

The Cockpit Jungle, St. Elizabeth Parish

Tony Schaefer fell into a hole in the ground and took me with him. I kicked and kicked, grabbing onto whatever I could, but he clung to me and did his best to drag me down. Yet with nimble fingers and strong arms, I grasped a vine, a root, a limestone ridge—anything within reach—and as soon as I felt steady, I kicked him in the head. Not once. Not twice. But again and again, my legs and feet pounded against him, hitting his back, shoulders, and the meaty parts of his flesh.

Then, at last, he fell, screaming into the abyss, and I thought he must be dead, which meant I was free. Except I'm still in the hole and I'm not a bird. I can't flap my wings and fly up and away. I must climb. Scale the muddy rock wall and rise toward the opening above.

Minutes pass—long, rain-soaked, mud-covered minutes. I am so tired but I refuse to stop. I won't stop. I can't stop. Too much to do to quit now. I keep climbing.

What a strong girl! I think to myself. I've almost made it to the top and am nearly out. Then the mud gives way, and I drop, falling a few feet, and then a few feet more. I reach out and grab onto a vine—a strangling fig vine—which Robbie says is the strongest.

Now, I have to climb again. I can't give in to the feeling I should give up, but I am almost—almost too exhausted to hold on. Then I hear something—someone in the jungle above me.

I whisper, "Help me."

A cacophony of sounds—screams and voices—call out my name. I recognize them—Vivian Jean and Zinzi. What are they doing out here?

I repeat my cry, this time louder: "Help me."

CHAPTER 46

——— ◆◆◆ ———

VIVIAN JEAN

The Cockpit Jungle, St. Elizabeth Parish

We were heroes for at least three seconds.

Zinzi lay flat on her stomach, her arms reaching for Othella while I held on to Zinzi's ankles. Although I might not be strong, I understand leverage. Fortunately, Othella is on the lip of the sinkhole, so she can be yanked free, and we do just that.

Then, before we can celebrate our victory, we heroes become victims of the cavernous ditch. I am not sure how it happened. I thought Zinzi had pulled Othella completely free, and I eased up my grip on Zinzi's ankles.

Then, the greedy sinkhole somehow swallows all three of us.

I cling to a root as thick as Tully's leg, my frail arms and thin fingers wrapping tightly around the vine. Is this what happens when you try to help someone out of a hole?

I slip and can't stop falling.

Now, all three of us might be lost. Tully will be heartbroken. Maxi will be sad and my father—how will he feel? Inconsolable? Or will he pack my body into a box and ship me back to Chicago like a stolen crate of rum?

"Vivian Jean! Reach up, Vivian Jean. Keep grabbing. Keep holding on to the roots above you."

Another voice joins in the chant. "Come on, Vivian Jean. Climb!"

I feel a hand helping me rise while another hand pushes me from behind.

"I don't know if I can," I mutter softly. The thin muscles in my arms burn and my skin is raw from grasping limestone rocks, roots, and clumps of mud. Then, I find myself stuck. "I can't move," I cry. "If I let go, I'll fall."

"If you don't move, you'll die." This voice belongs to Zinzi, who is below me, the owner of the hands pushing my bottom up from beneath.

I'm not sure I can do as she tells me. My head is hurting. The duppies in the silk cotton tree are talking to me. *We won't take another husband from you. The ancestors don't need him. Not now.* Tully will survive. Momma Hazel will work her magic and take great care of him.

Mud is caked on my face, lodged in my throat, and weighs heavily on my chest.

"Come on, Vivian Jean, don't give up," I hear someone say, as powerful hands hold me up.

I push myself upward. Just one more push. My foot slips, but Othella holds on tightly. Damn, she's strong, and she'll need all her strength to pull me out of this hole. Othella keeps pulling, and before I know it, I'm on my stomach, dirt surrounding me.

"Are you okay?" Othella asks.

I grin, feeling like kissing the ground beneath her. "I'm great."

"Good, now we need to hurry," Othella says. "Zinzi is still down there."

CHAPTER 47

ZINZI

The Cockpit Jungle, St. Elizabeth Parish

I grip the vine, clinging to the strangler fig as I push through the crumbling mud. It feels sturdy and supports my weight. All I need is the strength to hold on. The sounds frighten me. The sinkhole is opening, and an echo rises up the walls. It is deep and getting deeper.

Othella has freed Vivian Jean and pulled her from the sinkhole. I hear their cries of joy, but I am weakening. Who is strong enough to save me? It isn't Vivian Jean—her frail body will crumple. So, who can lift me from the swirling mud and water creeping up from the caverns and lakes below?

I am bone-tired, my limbs weary from holding on. If this is my end, I only wish to finish what I started. I dream of Byron and me sitting at the edge of a stage in front of thousands, looking out at the crowd of union employees while Allan delivers one of his brilliant speeches.

Jamaica will never forget that day. The promise of the island's future is near. The labor union will triumph. It's no longer a dream or a goal, but a reality that requires more work, persistence, and leadership.

I believe in that dream. I will write that speech. I will stand side by side with Allan and Byron. If I have a child, I will raise him to be a man like the ones I have known and loved.

My thoughts are like a boat drifting on a river, moving from shore to shore. Now, I yearn to hear my mother's voice more than ever.

"Momma, what do you think I should do? Should I stay here and hide from the world because I'm having a baby?"

"No, Zinzi. Don't give up. With all the pain you've survived in your life, I can't imagine you letting go. Hold on to that vine and bring me that grandchild. If it's in your body, I want to meet her."

"What about Byron's family? What if they find out about this baby and try to take him away from me?"

"Why would they? What old man Tynesdale cares about is sugar. You will teach him a lesson by raising a child as smart, savvy, and resilient as their mother. And I mean you.

"Stop worrying, Zinzi. Your life will be filled with love and purpose, and Byron, if he is who you want," her mother says. *"You're strong enough to face any obstacles that come your way. Just remember that you can love deeply more than once."*

Is this a fever dream, a hallucination, or a premonition?

"You need to fight for your child, Zinzi." River Mumma is suddenly in my thoughts.

"You're right," I reply. *"I must fight to survive with every ounce of my strength. I have so much to live for."*

"Zinzi, Zinzi, hold on. We're coming for you."

I hear their voices and try to follow their guidance, but I'm losing my grip. The tree roots and the cluster of limestone stuck in the mud can't support me. I am sinking.

They will have to save me again.

They do, and when I get out, it's because of Othella. She climbs down into the sinkhole until she's beneath me and pushes me up while Vivian Jean pulls and pulls.

But the sinkhole's walls are collapsing beneath my fingers.

Finally, they give way as Othella falls out of our reach, tumbling deeper and deeper.

Vivian Jean stares into the sinkhole, her eyes filled with dread and determination. "Hurry, Zinzi! We have to get her out."

"Yes. I have an idea."

I've never realized how much I remember from the countless trips I took with my father along that path. He spoke of trees, orchids, silk cotton, pimento, hardwood, bamboo, and the strength of the vines.

Vivian Jean's eyes shine. "It will work."

"We just have to try."

CHAPTER 48

OTHELLA

The Cockpit Jungle, St. Elizabeth Parish

Madness inspires madness.

These words are borrowed from my mother and never truly belonged to me. I use them as a crutch to get by, to push through, and to excuse the things I've done that I shouldn't have or should have stopped doing. Now, I see the other side. Good people are there: friends like Miss Vivian Jean, Zinzi, and my best friend, Robbie. All the wrong people are gone, leaving only the good. I'm on that path, a road for the good. I cling to the muddy walls as dirt and sand clog my nostrils and lodge between my fingers and toes. I've shed a thousand tears, but the silence in my head screams. I should have expected this. Did I kill Perry and Jerry or did I protect myself from them? Either way, if I hadn't been there or if I were some other kind of girl, none of this would have happened to me.

I should have sensed the danger weeks or months ago. Perhaps I never should have left Chicago. But with my stubbornness, naïveté, and nature, it took me a while to accept what lingered before me—plain as day, dark as night—with its tortured gaze, sweat-drenched cheeks, and large white teeth in a dazzling smile.

I can't catch my breath. I can't breathe and my chest hurts.

Why didn't I notice it before? Why did it evade me for so long? What did the Obeah woman say?

This is where the false gods dwell. Beware, or you will miss the one true God when She comes.

Or was it something I thought she said or wished for?

A rush of wind brushes against my cheek like a gentle breeze, and the sky isn't black. The moon shines brightly above. It's amazing.

Peace envelops me, calming my racing thoughts. I try to lift myself up. A hand reaches for mine, but I can't hold on. I'm falling down, down, down into the pit. As I descend, I have a clear, unburdened thought: The old woman was mistaken.

There are no false gods here.

EPILOGUE

VIVIAN JEAN

Hartfield House, Bronzeville, Chicago, A Year Later

"Tully! Tully! Where are you? Tully!" I rush through the house, calling out for him, convinced he'll pop his head around a corner any second. He must be here. He's always here.

When I catch sight of myself in the foyer mirror, I smile; the pregnancy suits me. But there's still that distance in my eyes—the haunting memory of Clifford, the baby I lost who was his, and Othella, the girl who died in a sinkhole in Jamaica after saving Zinzi and me.

Later, we learned that the Haitian hurricane or Jérémie, as some called it, hit the eastern coast of Jamaica, causing widespread devastation. In the Cockpit, the heavy rain and hard wind felled trees and created sinkholes.

It took a while, but eventually we made it back to Accompong, bloodied and bruised, almost unrecognizable after our ordeal. Losing that young girl devastated me; even though she had saved our lives, the tragedy of her sacrifice continues to weigh heavily on my heart. It may always linger. After pulling Zinzi to safety, I watched her try with all her heart to save Othella, but the collapsing sinkhole made it impossible to reach her. We stood in silence, unable to move, unable to accept that such a young girl, such a brave girl, was no longer with us. Those moments will remain with me for the rest of my life. We saved her once; she saved us in return. We tried to reach her, but couldn't. So, there's no guilt in losing Othella, just grief—another loss to mourn.

Othella left this earth with a defiance that I can only dream of. She was a hero.

Robbie was inconsolable. How could he not be? He and Othella had fallen in love, and it was new and promising— they were so young. But then he said something puzzling. "She tried hard to change, but the bad things wouldn't let her be."

I wanted to ask him why he thought that. What did he mean? The girl I knew was sweet, kind, and so smart. But Zinzi took my hand, sensing I had questions. She said, "Let it be. Let's just remember how she saved us."

So, I have. I hugged Zinzi hard then. Not only was I grateful for her and Othella, but also Katherine, Zinzi's mother, and Robbie—they saved Tully's life.

We all had someone to whom we owed a debt.

Tully and I arranged for Robbie to catch the next ship back to Chicago. We stayed a few more days at the Constant Spring Hotel to recover. Unsurprisingly, my father showed up and asked to join us for dinner. I declined. I had learned enough about him and his crimes at the Tynesdale Estate to last me a lifetime. A dinner with him felt pointless. I didn't feel the same about Maxi, though. I telegrammed her that Tully and I would be coming home soon, and I looked forward to her being there.

Katherine may never return from the Caribbean. It's been over a year, and she's still traveling, continuing to explore the history of ancient Africans through the dances and rituals of our descendants. She is in Haiti now, the longest stretch of her expedition. I can't wait for her to return, and to hear about everything she's seen and done—and to watch her dance again.

"I'm here, Vivian Jean," Tully shouts, coming into the parlor where I've taken a seat, to rest my swollen feet.

He kneels in front of me and takes my hands into his. "We received a telegram from Kingston," he announces. "It's from Zinzi, and the news is glorious." He reads it aloud:

We did it! The union is no longer just a dream but a reality for Jamaican workers. Love and be happy, Zinzi and Byron.

"That's wonderful. I'm so happy for her."

"And for Jamaica, too." Tully stands up and kisses me on the cheek. "Silly question, but are you hungry? I picked up some sandwiches on my way home from the ballpark."

"What kind?" I ask wistfully. He knows my cravings.

"Italian beef. We can eat them in here." He hurries off. "I'll be right back."

I sigh and settle back into the chair. Contentment brings a calmness I can barely describe. I don't count on life to be perfect. I've lived through enough sadness to know better. But life does have stretches of unmatched happiness, laughter, and achievement. What's important to me is that I keep my heart and mind ready to receive those blessings. There's nothing sadder than missing out on the good when it comes for you.

ACKNOWLEDGMENTS

Writing each book is a journey, and this isn't the first time I've expressed that very sentiment in my acknowledgments. Authors understand this, but we couldn't achieve what we do without a community of family and friends who support us through the brilliantly bright days, when the words are flowing, and those other days when we can't find a word that doesn't end in *ly*.

But before I go off on a tangent, I'd like to thank my publisher, Kensington Books, along with the editorial team, including Wendy McCurdy and Sarah Selim. Thank you. Thank you.

I also want to express my gratitude to my publicist, Michele Addo-Chajet, and the marketing and sales team, led by Alexandra Nicolajsen. Many others from Kensington's social media, graphics, and cover design departments have contributed to getting this novel on bookshelves across the United States and beyond. I appreciate all your hard work.

I would also like to thank the best team of author friends a gal could have—Vanessa Riley, Nancy Johnson, Nina Crespo, Veronica Forand, Pintip Dunn, Xio Axelrod, Kennedy Ryan, and Victoria Christopher Murray. A special shout-out to my writing buddy, the talented romance author Dylan Allen, and my beta reader, Nadine Monaco.

Oh yeah, let me not forget the women of the Tall Poppy Writers. Your support and enthusiasm are unparalleled!

Finally, a shout-out to the Joseph (you know who you are) and the Stovell families, including my son, Reggie, and granddaughter, Rhea!

AUTHOR'S NOTE

—◆—

With great admiration and respect, I have written a manuscript inspired by Katherine Dunham, the renowned choreographer and dancer, and her anthropological fieldwork.

In 1935, Katherine Dunham (June 22, 1909–May 21, 2006), a celebrated dancer, choreographer, anthropologist, and social activist, traveled on the first leg of her Caribbean expedition from Chicago to Jamaica to conduct anthropological fieldwork on ancient African dance and its legacy in the Caribbean. She spent several months in Accompong, a remote Maroon village deep in the mountains of Cockpit Country, before continuing to Haiti and other islands. Her Caribbean journey, financed by the Rosenwald Foundation, lasted two years. She wrote several books about her studies and other topics, with the pertinent nonfiction titles I read listed under resources.

Known as the Haitian hurricane of 1935, Hurricane Jérémie struck the eastern coast of Jamaica on October 21 as a tropical storm but reached hurricane force winds the next day. Dunham had left for Haiti before the hurricane's arrival. I reference the storm indirectly in this story because its impact in the Cockpit was different than from the lowland areas.

In my novel, Dunham has a small team that includes several fictional characters and three protagonists: Vivian Jean, Othella, and Zinzi. However, in the nonfiction world, Dunham traveled alone.

Her unique journey to Accompong provided much of the background, atmosphere, and historical context for the sections of my story where the action takes place in and around the Maroon village. However, I want to clarify that Miss Dunham undertook her expedition from 1935 to 1936 as a solo project, traveling throughout the Caribbean and spending most of her time in Haiti. Her anthropological fieldwork became the foundation for her inspiring dance, which integrated authentic African dance and culture into her choreography teachings. I had the honor of meeting Miss Dunham in person toward the end of her life when I was a dancer in Chicago.

Other historical figures mentioned in the novel include Augusta Savage (American sculptor, February 29, 1892–March 1962). According to some records, she made several trips to the Caribbean. Historical figures were also present in the manuscript, such as Anne Spencer, who grew up during the Harlem Renaissance and frequently traveled to Jamaica. Anne Spencer was an American poet, teacher, civil rights activist, and librarian who reportedly journeyed to the Caribbean.

The Greenbergers are fictional characters but are composites of symphony orchestra conductors like Bruno Walter, Otto Klemperer, and Erich Leinsdorf, who were exiled from Germany due to the Nazi regime's persecution of Jews.

Allan George St. Claver Coombs (August 1901–July 1969) was a Jamaican trade unionist. In my story, the character of Allan Coombs is inspired by the real person, but primarily fictionalized regarding his activities in 1935 Kingston. He was one of several labor movement leaders who influenced Zinzi's narrative. The Tynesdale Estate, a sugar plantation and rum factory, is fictional but also grounded in the industries of 1930s Jamaica, where workers faced challenges, making unions essential for their welfare and survival.

SOME HISTORICAL FIGURES AND FACTS THAT INSPIRED THIS FICTIONALIZED STORY

- In 1935, Dunham was awarded travel fellowships from the Julius Rosenwald and Guggenheim Foundations to conduct ethnographic fieldwork in Haiti, Jamaica, Martinique, and Trinidad, studying the dance forms of the Caribbean. One example of this was studying how dance manifests within Haitian Vodou.
- In May 1935, in Jamaica, workers loading bananas in St. Mary went on strike. They blocked roads to prevent strikebreakers from being brought in and cut power lines, which led to a riot. Armed police were sent to the town.
- That same month, port workers in Trelawny went on strike. There was rioting when a police gunshot killed one worker.
- Kingston banana loaders went on strike and organized a march; on the second day of the strike, police opened fire on the crowd, wounding a woman.
- In May 1936, Jamaica Workers and Tradesmen's Union, a trade union, launched.
- An article in the *Chicago Defender* mentions a party hosted by the Abbotts for the Count and Countess di Abbatino. The same article references Josephine Baker and her new husband. I included this item even though Miss Baker was never a countess and the article was a misattribution. She did become a French citizen, but not until her 1937 marriage.
- In late October of 1935, a hurricane struck the Caribbean, taking the lives of two thousand Haitians.

In Jamaica, there were deaths, but only three, according to news reports in the British papers. However, damages exceeded $2.5 million. The banana plantations in parts of Jamaica were destroyed. Citizens in 1935 could be forewarned about an approaching storm, though not as effectively as the early warning systems in place today. In countries like Jamaica, despite the thriving cruise liner business, predicting a storm days or hours in advance was not yet a reliable science.

PRINTED RESOURCES

Journey to Accompong by Katherine Dunham
British newspapers, including the *London Times* (coverage of labor issues and the banana industry versus sugar)
A Touch of Innocence by Katherine Dunham
Dances of Haiti by Katherine Dunham
Island Possessed by Katherine Dunham
The Colonial Caribbean in Transition by Bridget Brereton, and Kevin A. Yelvington.

DISCUSSION QUESTIONS FOR READERS AND BOOKCLUBS

1. Historical context: How does the novel depict the historical backdrop of 1935, especially concerning the themes of race, gender, and class? Was there anything that surprised you about the setting?
2. Character Development: The three female protagonists—Othella, Vivian Jean, and Zinzi—each have distinct backgrounds and motivations. Which character did you find most compelling, and why?
3. Character Development: As co-star of the novel, Katherine Dunham was drawn from articles, her own writings, and various other sources. What insights did you gain regarding her dedication to anthropology and African dance? What aspects of Katherine's story surprised you?
4. Identity and Transformation: How do the characters evolve throughout the story? What role does the expedition play in shaping their individual journeys?
5. Sisterhood Survival: The novel highlights the necessity for women to support one another during challenging times. How do their relationships develop, and what insights does the book offer regarding female solidarity?
6. Secrets and Truths: Many characters conceal parts of their past or identity. How do these secrets influence their actions and decisions? What do you believe the novel conveys about truth and deception?
7. Themes: The book explores themes of love—both romantic and platonic—and its connection to power. How do the dynamics of love and power manifest for each woman?

8. Katherine Dunham's Influence: This novel draws inspiration from the real-life choreographer Katherine Dunham. How does her presence, whether directly or indirectly, affect the experiences of the characters?

9. The Role of Nature: How does the ruggedness of Cockpit Country impact the story? Is it more than a location or backdrop? Does it serve as a metaphor for any of the characters?

10. Cultural Exploration: What have you discovered about Jamaican Maroon culture and the history of Caribbean dance through this novel?

11. Final Thoughts: Were you satisfied with the novel's conclusion? What do you believe happens to each of the women after the events of the story?

12. The Meaning of the Title: The title comes from Langston Hughes's poem "Union." In what ways do the poem's themes—oppression, rebellion, and power structures—show themselves in the novel?

13. The Silk Cotton Tree: What does the silk cotton tree symbolize for Vivian Jean? How does its symbolism evolve throughout the novel?